Discover the series you can't put down . . .

'A high level of realism . . . the action scenes come thick and fast. Like the father of the modern thriller, Frederick Forsyth, Mariani has a knack for embedding his plots in the fears and preoccupations of their time'

Shots Magazine

'The plot was thrilling . . . but what is all the more thrilling is the fantastic way Mariani moulds historical events into his story'

Guardian

'Hums with energy and pace . . . If you like your conspiracies twisty, your action bone-jarring, and your heroes impossibly dashing, then look no further. The Ben Hope series is exactly what you need'

Mark Dawson

'Slick, serpentine, sharp, and very, very entertaining. If you've got a pulse, you'll love Scott Mariani; if you haven't, then maybe you crossed Ben Hope'

Simon Toyne

'Hits thrilling, suspenseful notes . . . a rollickingly good way to spend some time in an easy chair'

USA Today

'Mariani constructs the thriller with skill and intelligence, staging some good action scenes, and Hope is an appealing protagonist'

Kirkus Reviews

'If you haven't read any Mariani before but love fast-paced action with a historical reference, maybe this one won't be your last'

LibraryThing

'A breathtaking ride through England and Europe'

Suspense Magazine

'This is my first Scott Mariani book . . . and I totally loved it. It goes on at a good pace, and for me Ben Hope was brilliant, the ultimate decent good guy that you are rooting for'

AlwaysReading.net

'Scott Mariani writes fantastic thrillers. His series of Ben Hope books shows no sign of slowing down'

Ben Peyton, actor (*Bridget Jones's Diary, Band of Brothers, Nine Lives*)

'A really excellent series of books, and would make a wonderful television series as well!'

Breakaway Reviews

'Scott Mariani seamlessly weaves the history and action together. His descriptive passages are highly visual, and no word is superfluous. The storyline flows from beginning to end; I couldn't put it down'

Off the Shelf Books

Scott Mariani is the author of the worldwide-acclaimed action-adventure thriller series featuring ex-SAS hero Ben Hope, which has sold millions of copies in Scott's native UK alone. His books have been described as 'James Bond meets Jason Bourne, with a historical twist'. The first Ben Hope book, *The Alchemist's Secret*, spent six straight weeks at number one on Amazon's Kindle chart, and all the others have been *Sunday Times* bestsellers, most recently with *The Templar Secret*. Scott was born in Scotland, studied in Oxford and now lives and writes in a remote setting in rural west Wales. You can find out more about Scott and his work on his official website: www.scottmariani.com

By the same author:

Ben Hope series

The Alchemist's Secret
The Mozart Conspiracy
The Doomsday Prophecy
The Heretic's Treasure
The Shadow Project
The Lost Relic
The Sacred Sword
The Armada Legacy
The Nemesis Program
The Forgotten Holocaust
The Martyr's Curse
The Cassandra Sanction
Star of Africa
The Devil's Kingdom
The Babylon Idol
The Bach Manuscript
The Moscow Cipher
The Rebel's Revenge
Valley of Death
House of War
The Pretender's Gold
The Demon Club
The Pandemic Plot
The Crusader's Cross
The Silver Serpent
Graveyard of Empires
The White Knight
The Tudor Deception
The Golden Library
The Templar Secret

To find out more visit **www.scottmariani.com**

SCOTT MARIANI

PASSENGER 13

THE BEN HOPE NOVELLAS:

PASSENGER 13 & BRING HIM BACK

Harper North

HarperNorth
Windmill Green
24 Mount Street
Manchester M2 3NX

A division of
HarperCollins*Publishers*
1 London Bridge Street
London SE1 9GF

www.harpercollins.co.uk

HarperCollins*Publishers*
Macken House,
39/40 Mayor Street Upper,
Dublin 1, D01 C9W8, Ireland

Passenger 13 first published in 2013
Bring Him Back first published in 2011
This edition first published by HarperCollins*Publishers* Ltd 2026

1 3 5 7 9 10 8 6 4 2

A catalogue record for this book is available from the British Library.

PB ISBN: 978-0-00-883008-3

Set in Minion pro by Amnet

Printed and bound in the UK using 100% Renewable
Electricity by CPI Group (UK) Ltd

For Genevieve, who made possible
the return of Ben Hope

FOREWORD

As I sit writing this note, the Ben Hope thriller novels are set for a resurgence after a hiatus spent writing historical fiction, in the shape of the four novels featuring Will Bowman, set during the period of the Third Crusade and the time of Richard the Lionheart.

When I made the decision to reinvent myself as a historical novelist, it seemed to me that my old character Ben Hope was ready – and happy – to hang up his spurs. We'd been together for a long time, with more than thirty books to his name. You'd think he had had enough of being shot at, pursued, blown up, and generally having a pretty hectic and wild existence. For my own part, I was happy to exchange car chases for cavalry charges, gunfights for sword battles and Ben Hope's venerable 9mm Browning pistol for an old English longbow.

But you should never say never . . . I hadn't yet finished writing the second of my new historical series when from somewhere deep inside me I began to feel the call. It was the voice of my old character shouting: 'I'm not done yet! I want back in! Retirement is *boring*!' And he and I are so close, after all these adventures together, that I couldn't ignore what he was telling me.

In the end the lure proved too much to resist, and so here we are. 2026 is set to be 'the year of Ben Hope', seeing not only his return in the thirty-first novel of the series, *The Jericho Road*, but also the re-release of two previous novels (*The Heretic's Treasure* and *The Shadow Project*) and this special edition of the Ben Hope novellas, *Passenger 13* and *Bring Him Back*, published together for the very first time.

When I first wrote both of these novellas, the Ben Hope series was still more or less in its infancy. Little did I know, back in those days, that it would grow to the extent it did (and in fact I still have no idea how many books there may eventually be!). As readers might notice, *Passenger 13* is somewhat unique in the series to date, for its lack of a historical mystery creating a present-day intrigue for our hero to solve. Instead, it's pretty much a straight-ahead contemporary thriller, revolving around the suspicious 'suicide' of an old military comrade and a conspiracy plot hatched by some very unpleasant and powerful villains. Chronologically it fits into a period of Ben Hope's life that predates the main novel series by a few years: we find him here as a younger man still attached to his Special Forces regiment, having not yet found his role as a rescuer of kidnap victims and instead getting drawn into an investigative role while officially on leave from the military. I can't quite remember offhand which novels I wrote before and after it: what I do remember very clearly is how much fun it was to take Ben into this James Bond-esque world of sleek yachts, warm blue shark-infested seas, tropical islands and white sandy palm beaches. I hope that sense of fun comes over in reading it.

It wasn't so long after writing *Passenger 13* that the idea came to me for something a little different, which would become the second Ben Hope novella, *Bring Him Back*. This story carries us a little further into Ben's chronological arc. Some time has gone by since the events of the first story and he has now quit the military, setting out on his own as a finder of missing people: in particular, missing children, a moral mission sparked by his own tragic personal past and the kidnap of his younger sister, Ruth. In *Bring Him Back* Ben is just starting out in his new independent career, taking on one of his first cases as a kidnap and ransom specialist. Needless to say, Ben's world being what it is, what starts as an apparently straightforward snatch soon turns out to be rather more complicated.

The psychic research background of this story wasn't quite the bizarre figment of my imagination that some might think. While the 'Indigo Project' is (I hope) an entirely fictitious creation, the real-life phenomenon of remote viewing has been well documented and intensively researched for many years. The Stargate Project really did exist, and Joseph McMoneagle and Pat Price really were alleged to have carried out the apparently inexplicable acts of psychic espionage briefly described in the story. Notable figures from this strange and fascinating world not named here include real-life former Stargate remote viewer Lyn Buchanan and Colonel John Alexander, formerly of the Advanced Systems Concepts Office, US Army Lab Command. Many of the people who pioneered this psychic research are still alive today, and readers interested in finding out more about them are encouraged to do a little research of their own. You can even find the CIA's own 'Firedocs' remote viewing manual online, containing previously classified information not made public until decades later.

I hope you enjoy reading this special two-novella edition. If you haven't already felt the lure of the wider Ben Hope series, then welcome aboard and happy reading!

Scott Mariani
Cardigan Bay, May 2026

SCOTT MARIANI

PASSENGER 13

Chapter 1

London
June, 2003

It was a sunny afternoon as the man walked into Selfridges via the Duke Street entrance and made his way through the bustling crowds to the restaurant and champagne bar overlooking the accessory hall.

If anyone had been paying close attention to him, they would have seen a man somewhere in his thirties or early forties, lean, neatly but unobtrusively dressed in a crisp dark suit. He had the bronzed complexion and jet-black hair of a Middle-Easterner; silk shirt, navy tie, gleaming patent leather shoes. The hand holding the calf-leather briefcase wore a large gold ring, but other than that there was nothing too ostentatious or especially noticeable about him.

It was 1.15 and the restaurant was filled with shoppers, tourists, people on lunch breaks. The man took a seat at the edge of the restaurant and slid his briefcase under the table by his feet. When the waiter came he was warm and friendly. From the lunch menu he ordered crispy baby squid with wild garlic mayonnaise, then for a main course a pan-fried fillet of Scottish salmon with kale and shrimps on the side. As he ate his lunch calmly, washing it down with a half bottle of good white wine, he watched the people come and go. A small group of Japanese tourists settled at a table to his left, surrounded by bulging shopping bags; to his right a young couple with their two small children, speaking French and scouring a London travel guide.

The man watched the little boy and girl. He smiled and went on eating. When he'd finished, he looked at his watch, picked up his case, and paid a visit to the bathroom. He was gone three minutes. When he returned, he settled his lunch bill in cash and then left.

And if anyone had been paying close attention to him, they would have seen that he'd left the gents' without his briefcase.

The man was on the corner of North Audley Street and Green Street when he took out the mobile phone and dialled in the number that sent an electronic signal to the remote detonator. The case was packed with an expertly prepared combination of RDX nitroamine high explosive and other substances that together were designed to produce a blast greater than a powerful car bomb.

The initial explosion engulfed the restaurant and champagne bar within one hundredth of a second. At its core, the temperature was high enough to vaporise human tissue on contact. Nothing at all would remain of the Japanese tourists, or the French couple, their little boy and girl, the bar staff or anyone else within a radius of thirty metres.

In the next three hundredths of a second the blast filled the ground floor of the department store, obliterating everything in its path. One hundred and sixty-eight shoppers were reduced to tatters of flesh and clothing; scores more were horribly maimed and burned.

The store's ground floor windows blew out onto Duke Street and Oxford Street. Passers-by were caught in a storm of flying glass. Vehicles skidded and swerved all over the road. Broadsided by the terrible shockwave, a passing bus mounted the opposite pavement and toppled over on its side, flattening fifteen pedestrians as they stood gaping in frozen horror at the smoke pouring from the shattered department store.

In the immediate aftermath of the blast came the moments of stunned, deathly silence.

Then the mayhem began. But before the first wild screams were heard among the devastation of Oxford Street, and long before the racing convoy of emergency services units came wailing in through the panic, the man in the dark suit was already heading fast towards Grosvenor Square and his two colleagues inside the waiting car.

Chapter 2

Brecon, Wales
Six weeks later, July 23

Whatever deal with God the jazz festival organisers had made to keep the rain off that year, he'd delivered in spades. The night was warm, the stars were bright, and over two thousand people were crowding the open-air gig.

Onstage, the band were delivering too: the bass and drums laid down a thundering groove as the alto saxophonist took up his instrument and blasted out a solo that scorched the air. The sax glittered red, blue, green under the lights. At the searing climax of the solo, the crowd roared its delight.

That was when Ben Hope started making his way towards the beer tent for another drink. Pretty damned impressive, he was thinking. Not quite up there with Coltrane, but pretty damned impressive.

The girl he was with didn't seem to share his enthusiasm. Ben didn't know much about her, except that her name was Ally, she was local, she was twenty-two, and she liked rum and Coke – a lot; was onto her fourth already.

But then, she knew even less about him. In his line of work, the less people knew the better.

In the beer tent, pressing to the front of the throng and speaking loudly to be heard, he ordered the drinks: the same sticky sweet shit for her, another whisky for himself. 'Not that one,' as the barman went for the blended cheap stuff. 'The malt. That's the one. Make it a double. No ice.' Reaching into the back pocket of his jeans for his wallet, Ben felt the muscles in his right side cramp up and he winced sharply. It took him a second to get his breath back – the kind of pain you know your face has gone pale.

'Been in the wars?' the barman asked cheerfully.

'You could say that,' Ben replied, laying a fiver on the bar and taking a gulp of his drink. The twelve-year-old scotch burned a warm river down deep inside him. The pain was passing already. It didn't hurt anything like the way it had when he'd taken his R&R leave three weeks ago. Considering the close-range impact of the AK-47 rifle bullet that had gouged through his side and severely cracked three of his ribs before going on to pass right through a wall, he didn't think his recovery was going too badly.

'Got a cigarette?' Ally yelled over the music when she'd finished her drink. She frowned at the one he handed her. 'What are these?'

'They're Greek,' Ben said, lighting it for her, then one for himself. Lying about what he did for a living often entailed lying about where his job took him, and it was second nature now. In fact the cigarettes were Jordanian, one of the last of the packs he'd bought a few days before his SAS squadron had been dropped in the Iraqi western desert to seize key airfields.

He hadn't had much chance to smoke them. A couple of weeks after securing the airfields as forward operating bases and pushing eastwards into the desert, supported by RAF Harriers and unmanned Predator reconnaissance spy planes as they clashed with retreating Iraqi forces, Ben's unit had received a report that two undercover SAS soldiers, posing as Arabs to investigate an Iraqi police captain in the Basra area suspected of passing information to Shia militiamen, had been hijacked and abducted by an armed gang. Just a few weeks earlier, six military police had been hacked to death in the same area.

Within hours of the report, an unofficial rescue mission had been greenlit deep within the corridors of Whitehall and two dozen troopers under Ben's command were kitted up and en route to Basra on a Hercules transport plane.

SAS intelligence sources were sound on the location of the hostages, not quite as sound on the force of men holding them. Assaulting the stronghold under cover of darkness, Ben's squad had quickly found themselves heavily outnumbered by battle-hardened militants determined not to give up their valuable hostages. In just a few minutes of furious fighting, the floor was littered with spent cartridge cases and dead men. Ben had been first through the door of the hostages' cell, taking out three of the guards before they could react.

The fourth guard, the one with the AK, had been hiding behind a doorway. Ben hadn't had time to react as the gunman had come leaping out with a wild scream and let rip with his rifle. The next thing Ben had known, he was waking up in the military hospital, pumped full of painkiller, his side heavily bandaged. It wasn't the first time a bullet had found him, it wasn't the worst, and it might not be the last. But at least the hostages had been extracted safely.

'Are we going soon?' Ally said. 'This music's giving me a headache. Or maybe it was that shitty cigarette.'

Ben shrugged. The next act up was a jazz-rock fusion guitar trio, and that wasn't so much his thing anyway. 'Fine,' he said, and they walked away from the crowd towards the car. The bright red V6 Alfa Romeo GT came courtesy of the regiment. Perks of his rank.

Beyond the festival enclosure, the enhanced police and security presence was as noticeable as at any other large-scale event in Britain that summer. Ever since the Selfridges bombing in June, the whole country had been in a state of red alert. And as Ben drove back through the outskirts of Brecon towards Ally's place, it was no surprise that the news programme that came on the radio headlined with the breaking story that, after a frenzied manhunt, Scotland Yard had finally detained a suspect.

'*. . . early reports suggest he may have been part of the same extremist Jihadist terror group responsible for the Lisbon Embassy bombing in February, in which seven people died.*'

Ben grunted. The antiterrorist boys had had their hands full the last few weeks. And the odds were it wasn't over yet. Every city in Britain was braced for another attack, security services stretched to breaking point. The tension everywhere was palpable.

'*In another breaking story,*' the presenter went on, '*Cayman Islands authorities fear that today's air crash off the island of Little Cayman may have claimed the lives of all twelve passengers and three crew members. It has emerged in the last few minutes that the aircraft's British pilot and owner of Cayman Islands Charter, Nick Chapman, is thought to have ditched into the sea in a deliberate act of suicide . . .*'

Ben hit the brakes. The Alfa Romeo slewed to a halt in the middle of the empty road.

'Hey! Watch it!' Ally yelped, nursing her shoulder where she'd jolted against her seatbelt.

'Shush.' Ben turned up the radio volume.

'. . . *a Home Office source has revealed that Chapman, a former member of the British armed forces, may have served with the SAS during the 1990s. Police and rescue divers continue to comb a large area of sea, but as yet no survivors have been found in what appears to be the worst air tragedy ever to hit the British territory . . .*'

Ben said nothing more as he drove Ally the rest of the way back to her place on the edge of Brecon.

'Don't you want to come in, then?' she smiled at the door.

'I have to get back,' Ben said.

'When will we see each other again?' she asked.

Ben hadn't even heard the question. 'Thanks, Ally. I had a lovely time,' he said, and drove away.

Chapter 3

The place Ben had rented during his leave was a little ivied stone cottage right on the River Usk, in wooded countryside a few miles outside the Welsh market town of Brecon. Low ceilings, exposed beams, thatched roof, old-fashioned leaded windows that peeked out through ivy and climbing roses. The stone fireplace was adorned with brass ornaments, and in a nod to tradition a pair of crossed cricket bats hung over the mantelpiece.

Ben didn't care too much for cricket, but he did care for the peace and quiet of the place, as far as you could get from the boiling white heat and madness of the desert war front line. He could have spent these few weeks at his house near Galway Bay on the western Irish coast, but they didn't hold annual international jazz festivals there and the gunman who'd almost managed to kill him had kindly done so at just the right time to allow him to catch some acts he'd long wanted to check out.

Jazz was the last thing on his mind that night as he burst inside the cottage and went straight over to flip on the TV. Scanning through the channels in search of a news programme he grabbed a fresh bottle of Laphroaig from the cardboard box that served as his temporary drinks cabinet, ripped off the cap and poured himself out a triple measure.

When he found a news programme he wasn't surprised to see that the Cayman Islands air crash was one of the headline items. He listened and watched intently: interviews with shocked island airport authorities; grim-faced mourners; aerial footage of Royal Cayman Island Police and Navy rescue craft pulling wreckage from the water. From the air it was clear that the inter-island shuttle aircraft must have come down on a bar of exposed coral reef in the middle of the sea while on a routine crossing from the tiny island of Little Cayman to Grand Cayman, its larger sister seventy-five miles south-west. The plane appeared to have detonated on impact. Judging by the charred state of the bodies so far recovered, nobody had stood a chance of escaping a horrible fiery death.

Ben gulped whisky and went on watching. The three-engined Britten-Norman Trislander being too small a plane to carry a 'black box' flight data or cockpit voice recorder, the primary witness on whose testimony the suicide theory hung was the air traffic controller reported to have been in radio contact with the pilot shortly before the crash, struggling to talk him out of bringing the plane down. In the aftermath of the crash, the controller was unavailable for comment.

Four of the dozen passengers aboard the CIC inter-island flight had been British: a holiday couple, their son, and a retired dentist. But the main focus was on the man the media were already branding 'kamikaze pilot' and 'suicide killer', Nick Chapman. His final words to the air traffic controller, captured on tape moments before the crash, were a distorted, muffled yell over the chaos of the screaming passengers and the roar of the propeller engines. *'I'm taking her down! I'm taking her down!'*

As the dramatic audio clip played, the TV screen flashed up a photo of the man who'd said those words and plunged fourteen people to their deaths along with him. A tanned, lean-faced man of forty-six, smiling warmly for the camera. His hair was greyer than Ben remembered it.

But there was no doubt about it. He was the same Nick Chapman that Ben had served with in 22 SAS, not so many years ago.

Chapter 4

Five days later, Ben was standing on the edge of the family burial plot in a little churchyard near Bath, where Nick Chapman – or what remains of him the Cayman Islands salvage teams had managed to retrieve from the sea and flown to the UK – was being laid to rest.

Other than the few reporters and photographers who'd tried to get in and been turned away at the gate, only a smattering of people had turned up to pay their last respects to the deceased. Ben looked around for Chapman's ex-wife, Joan, but there was no sign of her. The only face he recognised was that of Hilary, their daughter. Last time he'd seen her had been a few years earlier, when he'd been one of the twenty or so regimental guys invited to her engagement party. Then, she'd been the happy fiancée, bubbly and full of laughter. Now, even with her face half hidden behind oversized sunglasses and her straggly blond hair, she looked pinched and haggard and aged way beyond her twenty-four years.

It was warm under the sun. The minister read a few words. His manner was somewhat forbidding, somewhat disapproving, a distant echo of the days when suicides hadn't been allowed church burials. Ben quickly tuned out and stood there watching the coffin being lowered into the grave, lost in his own thoughts and memories of the man inside it. Nick Chapman had done a lot of brave and worthy things in his time. None of them would be remembered now. It was a miserable, deeply saddening end to what should have been an honourable life.

What saddened Ben most of all was the thought that, perhaps, the tragedy of July 23 had been inevitable. Of the troubled soldiers he'd known – and the extreme physical and psychological demands of the life of an SAS soldier took its toll on a few – Nick had been the one most ravaged by depression. After many years in the army, his problems had finally become too crippling a burden for him, and with drug and alcohol dependency mounting, the trauma of his divorce from Joan tearing him apart, he'd finally hit rock bottom. During an SAS operation in Serbia, Nick had barricaded himself into a room with a bottle of gin and threatened to blow his own brains out. Shortly after that incident, in October 1998, he'd been quietly dismissed from Her Majesty's Armed Forces.

Many months had passed during which Ben had heard nothing from his friend, and often feared the worst. Then, out of the blue, two years ago, a card in the mail: Nick was up on his feet, had qualified as a commercial pilot and had set up a successful little air charter business in the Caribbean. He'd found Paradise, he'd said. He'd sounded truly happy, freed from his demons, as if the dark days had finally been put behind him. Ben had fervently wished it would stay that way.

And now this.

Ben didn't want to judge Chapman for what he'd done. He was trying not to. Trying hard. He could scarcely bring himself to believe his friend had done this. And yet . . .

Sensing a presence next to him, Ben looked round and recognised the face of McNeill from B Squadron. He smiled sadly. 'Hello, Mac. I didn't expect to see anyone else here.'

'Almost didn't come,' McNeill said dourly. 'Now I'm here I feel like spitting on the grave.'

Ben said nothing.

Afterwards, he was walking slowly back towards his car when he heard footsteps running up behind him and a woman's voice calling his name. He stopped.

'You probably don't even remember me,' she said, catching up. Her face was flushed behind the dark glasses, her voice husky from weeping.

'Of course I remember you, Hilary. My deepest condolences.'

She hung her head. 'Thanks, Ben. Or should I say Major?'

Ben disliked using his title. 'Just Ben,' he said.

Hilary glanced quickly to one side, then the other. He could see something was alarming her. 'Can I talk to you?' she said abruptly.

He shrugged. 'Sure.'

'Not here. Can we go somewhere?' She moved towards his Alfa Romeo. Another glance over her shoulder, as if she thought there was someone else there behind the gravestones and the bushes.

'What about your car?' he said.

'Please, can we just go? I really need to talk to you.'

There was only one road through the village. Quarter of a mile beyond the last house, Ben saw a country pub up ahead on the right. 'Buy you a drink?' he said.

She nodded. 'I could use one.'

The gravelled car park was almost empty. It was quarter to twelve and the lunchtime clientele obviously hadn't turned up yet. Ben pulled up a chair for Hilary at one of the outside tables.

She shook her head. 'I'd rather not be outside.' The sunglasses hid much of her expression, but the tone of her voice was edgy.

'Whatever you want,' Ben said. He noticed the way she kept glancing back over her shoulder as he led her into the coolness of the building. She walked straight across to a corner alcove by the window. Laid her handbag on the table and sat with her back to the wall so that she could watch the car park and the road. Ben asked her what she wanted to drink. 'I don't care, as long as it's strong,' she replied.

He came back with a whisky for himself, a gin and tonic for her. She sipped it gratefully, then took off her shades. Her eyes were raw from crying. She kept glancing nervously at the window to her right. Her hands were curled into tight fists on the table. No wedding ring, Ben noticed.

'You came alone,' he said diplomatically.

'You're referring to Danny?' Hilary shook her head ruefully, staring into her drink. 'That was over a long time ago. I should never have married the arsehole.'

Which was pretty much what Nick had confided to Ben at the time, though he'd kept his mouth shut for fear of hurting his daughter's feelings.

'Your dad was a good man,' Ben said softly. He touched her hand, then withdrew his, not sure it was the right thing. 'I don't care what anyone says. Whatever he might have been going through . . .'

Hilary glanced sharply up at him. 'It's all lies, Ben.'

'What's all lies?'

'That dad killed himself. All lies.'

Ben looked at her. He could feel her pain. What could he say to her? That he'd been there himself once, after his mother's own suicide? That back then, in his teens, he'd have done anything to persuade himself that she hadn't ended her own life – believed almost anything rather than accept the truth?

'The cops said they found antidepressants at his house,' she said, shaking her head vehemently. 'Uh-uh. No way.'

'You know, maybe they did,' Ben ventured. 'It wouldn't have been the first time, Hilary. Maybe we just need to accept that.'

She shook her head harder, breathing noisily with emotion. Her face was so tight that the muscles of her jaws were bunched up under the skin. '*No*, Ben,' she insisted. 'You don't realise the hell he went through to get away from all that. And anyway, I just know. I *know*, all right? Don't you understand?'

'I understand that you're in a lot of pain,' he said gently. 'But we all need to try to reconcile ourselves with what's happened. It's not going to be easy, but I promise you that, in time, it will get better.'

'No, Ben, you *don't* understand. How could you?' Hilary paused, as if she was struggling with herself over whether to come out with whatever it was she was clearly desperate to say next. She leaned across the table, lowered her voice and came out with it. 'I have proof that dad didn't kill himself.'

Ben stared at her.

'I know. It sounds crazy. But you've got to believe me.'

Ben could see the absolute earnestness in her eyes. 'What kind of proof?' he asked.

With another furtive glance at the window, Hilary reached into her handbag and took out a mobile phone. 'This kind,' she said.

Chapter 5

Hilary thumbed the keys of the phone, held it to her ear for a moment and then passed it to Ben. 'Listen,' she hissed.

Not knowing what to say, he took the phone from her, put it to his own ear and heard the robotic voice of the Orange answering service. There was a pause; then the message began.

Ben's brows knitted at the sound of his old friend's voice, barely audible above a background of crackling and white noise and a roaring screech that was hard to identify. Nick sounded extremely agitated and frightened, clearly fighting to keep his voice calm.

'Darling, it's me, it's dad . . . Listen to me . . . Something's . . .'

For a few seconds, Nick's voice was lost in the noise. Ben thought he could hear other voices, a distorted, incomprehensible pandemonium of yelling and screaming. There was no question that something terrible was happening in the background.

'The plane . . .' Nick Chapman shouted over the chaos. 'It's . . .' He seemed to pause. When he spoke again, his voice sounded strained to breaking point with sadness. 'Hilary, I love you. Dad loves you. Remem—'

Whatever last words Nick had spoken after that, they were dissolved in a storm of fuzz and static. Then it was the voice of the answer-phone service in Ben's ear again: *'To listen to the message again, press one. To save it, press two . . .'*

Ben pressed one and closed his eyes as the message played over again. At the end, he pressed two to save it, then laid the phone on the table. His ribs were burning as if he'd been shot again.

Hilary was staring at him expectantly, her eyes moist with tears. She snatched up the phone with a trembling hand. 'What did that sound like to you? Like a man who wanted to die? A man about to kill himself? Tell me.'

Ben's mind swam. None of this made any sense. He remembered the audio recording of Nick's radio communication with the air traffic controller. *'I'm taking her down!'*

'Let me hear it again,' he said.

Her expression hardened. 'You don't believe it, do you?'

'I just want to hear it again.' He reached out his hand to take the phone from her fingers. 'Give it here. Please.'

She clasped it tightly to her chest. 'You still think he killed himself.' Her face was white with fury.

'Hilary, I didn't say that. I just don't understand what I'm hearing. Who else knows about this message?'

She shook her head. 'Nobody. I don't trust *anybody*.'

'Something like this, and you don't report it to the police?'

'The police!' she exploded. 'It was the fucking police who planted the drugs in his house. Don't you understand? Can't you see? Cayman Islands police. A British territory? They're all mixed up in it together.'

'Hilary, I know this is awful for you, but we need to take this one step at a time. To suggest that there's some kind of conspiracy going on—'

'Explain this, then!' she rasped at him, waving the phone in his face.

Ben couldn't explain it.

'I *know* something's going on,' she said. 'I'm being followed. Someone's been watching me. I think maybe they're tracking my car. That's why I wanted to come in yours.'

'I'm sorry, Hilary. This all sounds crazy to me. You're upset, you're emotional . . .'

'Next thing you'll be saying I'm on antidepressants, too, right?'

'I'm just trying to make sense of this whole thing. How can you be so sure someone's following you?'

'I'm an SAS soldier's daughter. I'm not stupid. I can tell stuff. And I think they're tracking my car.'

'Who?'

'Them.'

'What do they look like?'

'They don't look like anything. They're just . . . *there*.'

'What do they want?'

'They want me, Ben. They know I know the truth.'

Ben was at a loss for words.

Hilary was glowering at him with icy contempt. 'To think my dad spoke so highly of you. He respected you so much. I thought you might understand. Thought you'd be different. But I was wrong, wasn't I? Well you know what? I don't need you to believe me and I don't need your help.'

'Hilary—'

'Go fuck yourself!' She stood up.

'Hey, come on.' Ben reached out to take her arm and guide her gently back into her seat. The last thing he'd ever have done was use force on her, but she tore defensively away from him, lashing out and knocking over her drink. The gin and tonic spilled across the table. The glass rolled to the edge and shattered on the floor.

Ben said, 'Hilary, please. Where are you going?'

'Don't worry about me,' she spat. 'I'll get the fucking bus back.'

He opened his mouth to protest, but she was already storming away towards the door, clutching her phone in her hand. The barman glanced up in alarm from his newspaper as she ran past him and burst outside.

Ben went after her. From the pub doorway, he could see her running across the pub car park towards the empty road, heading in the direction of the village. He took a few strides after her, then stopped and gave up the idea. She was upset. It wasn't right to force himself on her like that. He turned back towards the pub, went inside and started heading back towards the table. 'Sorry about that,' he said to the barman. 'I'll pay for the glass.'

'No problem,' the barman said, and went off to grab a dustpan and brush.

It was at that moment that Ben heard the harsh rasp of the engine outside. A diesel van engine, approaching at speed.

Something wasn't right.

He moved towards the window and peered out to see a battered white Transit van approaching. It was the only vehicle in sight, and it was approaching Hilary at speed as she half-jogged, half-ran along the grassy verge in the direction of the village outskirts. She was too preoccupied to notice it coming.

Something was terribly wrong. But by the time Ben felt that crawling icy sensation grip his body, it was already far too late to do anything.

In the final yards before it reached her, the van didn't slow down. Didn't indicate left and pull out a few feet from the kerb, the way any normal driver would when passing a pedestrian on a stretch of country road.

Instead it slewed a foot to the left so that its wheels sprayed mud and grass into the air. And bore straight down on Hilary. There was no squeal of brakes, no warning blast of the horn.

She didn't notice it until the last instant. Ben caught a fleeting glimpse of her face as she turned – the look of shock, the mouth opening to cry out.

The crunching impact of four thousand pounds of fast-moving metal against a hundred and twenty pounds of frail living human flesh and bone was one of the most sickening sounds a person could hear, and Ben heard it distinctly from a hundred and fifty yards off. He yelled 'No!'

Hilary Chapman's body hurtled up the steep angle of the van's bonnet, cannoned off its windscreen and was tossed high in the air. She flew over the roof and landed with a crunch on the road.

Only then did the driver slam on the brakes.

Ben was already outside and sprinting towards the scene. He saw the van skid to a halt in a cloud of dust and smoking rubber. Saw the shattered body of the young woman he'd been talking to just moments earlier lying in a heap. Saw the driver's door swing open and a guy jump out. Nondescript, thirties, short brown hair, T-shirt and jeans.

The driver saw Ben running towards him, but he didn't do any of the things a normal guy would have done in the circumstances. He didn't panic. He didn't scream out in horror at what he'd done.

Instead he left his engine running and strode quickly over to the bloody body on the road. He dropped down in a crouch and reached a hand out to her neck. Feeling for a pulse.

Ben was seventy yards away and running as hard as he could. The pain in his right side screamed for him to slow down.

The driver had done feeling for a pulse. He unpeeled the fingers of her closed fist, took something from her hand and dropped it in his pocket.

Hilary's phone.

Ben ran harder. A roar of 'Hey! Stop!' exploded from his lungs.

The driver hurried back to the van. He climbed up into the cab. Slammed the door with a clang. Peered past the bloodied web of cracks that the impact had left on his windscreen, engaged gear and accelerated hard away, his wheels throwing up torn grass and mud.

Ben was just feet from the back door. 'Stop!' he yelled again, so loudly he tasted blood at the back of his throat. He made a flying leap to grab the rear door handle – and missed, sprawling to the ground with a cry of pain from the yank on his stitches. In less than a second he was back on his feet, but the van was already roaring off up the road. There was nothing more Ben could do.

Not even take its registration number.

Because it had no plates.

He ran over to Hilary. Kneeled down in the spreading pool of her blood and knew instantly that her killer needn't have bothered checking for a pulse. Her eyes were staring right into his. Seeing nothing. Her neck was broken and her entire ribcage was crumpled inwards.

Ben sank his head down to his chest and his vision blurred with the tears of grief and fury.

Chapter 6

A small crowd of people quickly gathered as villagers came running down the road and a couple of cars stopped. Someone gave Ben a tartan travel blanket, and he used it to cover Hilary's body. He stayed at her side until the police and ambulance came, when the paramedics took over and he returned to the empty pub.

Still numb, Ben gave his witness statement to one of the uniformed cops, watching out of the window as he watched the paramedic team load Hilary's broken body into the ambulance and take her away. There was no siren. No hurry.

Until the last minute, he'd been quite prepared to tell the cops the truth and give them an exact account of what had happened. Then he thought about the things Hilary had told him. *Don't trust the police.* Her voice echoed in his mind, along with the voice of his conscience that was tormenting him for having failed her so badly. He hadn't listened. Hadn't taken her seriously.

And now he was thinking: *what if she'd been right?*

'Your name?' the cop said.

The guy looked like an arsehole anyway. Ben didn't like his officious manner. 'Oscar Gillespie,' he replied. It was the first name that came into his head, an unholy mash-up of two of his favourite musicians.

But it seemed to do just fine. The cop wrote the name down on his form. Obviously not much of a jazz fan. 'Do you have any ID? Driving licence?'

Ben could see his parked Alfa from where he was sitting. 'I got the train. No ID on me.'

'Address?'

'No fixed abode.'

'Occupation?'

'None,' Ben said.

The cop looked at him, then asked, 'Your relationship to the deceased?'

'A friend of the family, on her mother's side,' Ben said. 'We'd come from her father's funeral.'

'The barman says you were arguing.'

'She was upset,' Ben said. 'Most people would be, if their father had just committed suicide. I was trying to calm her down. She became emotional and ran out into the road. I didn't see anything until I heard the impact. By the time I got to her, the van driver had already left the scene. I suppose the guy panicked when he saw what he'd done. Maybe he thought there were no witnesses.'

The cop spent a while noting it all down. 'You didn't get the registration of the van?'

'No,' Ben said. 'I didn't get the registration.'

The cop gave him a speech about needing to be contacted if there were any further questions or the possibility of attending an ID parade. Ben said yes to everything, and gave him a false mobile number to call. Then, once the police had left him alone, he bought another drink from the sullen, shocked-looking barman and sat with it a while, replaying the scene in his mind. He'd witnessed a lot of bad things in the last few years, but he knew this one was going to stay with him a long time.

Two options: one, the whole thing had been a terrible accident. A woman who believed she was being followed had just happened to be run down by a van with no registration plates, whose driver had just happened to be the kind of guy who would drive off and steal her phone into the bargain – the phone on which she'd just happened to have received an apparently crucially important message.

The second option couldn't possibly make any less sense than that. Ben boiled it down: Hilary had been right about being followed, but it hadn't been her car they'd been tracking. The target had been her phone, and the man sent to kill her had also been under orders to retrieve it. Even ordinary civilians had some inkling that the technology required to triangulate mobile phone signals was a big deal. High-level stuff. The same was true of having people killed when they knew too much – or when someone thought they did.

Ben thought about the message Nick Chapman had left for his daughter. Whatever the hell it meant, somebody out there had been prepared to kill to obtain it.

He finished his drink. Laid the empty glass on the table. He looked at his watch, checked the date.

Eleven days and twenty-one hours still to go before he was due to return to the SAS Regimental Headquarters at Credenhill, Herefordshire, and catch his transport back out to Iraq.

Eleven days and twenty-one hours that he owed to Nick and Hilary Chapman.

Chapter 7

The twenty-one hours had already elapsed by the time Ben stepped off the plane at Owen Roberts International Airport on the island of Grand Cayman. A tiny speck on the map, the largest of the trio of islands lost in the vast expanse of ocean between Cuba to the north, Jamaica to the east and the Mexican coast some four hundred miles to the west. Tax haven to some of the world's most rampant capitalists, centre of pilgrimage for seekers of sunshine and laid-back Caribbean cool, Mecca for thousands whose perfect vacation was to stick on diving gear and come face to face with a brightly coloured fish. So this was Nick Chapman's Paradise, all seventy-six square miles of it.

Ben made his way through passport control among a throng of tourists. He was glad it was low season. Stepping outside with his only luggage, a green military haversack, over his shoulder, he breathed in the warm, palm-scented breeze from the Caribbean Sea. Owen Roberts' runway virtually overhung the beach; beyond the single terminal, which looked more like a tropical country clubhouse than an international airport, the glittering ocean was the purest and clearest crystalline blue.

At the nearby Andy's car hire, Ben shelled out three hundred Cayman Islands dollars for a week's rental on a silver Jeep Wrangler and headed into the islands' capital,

George Town, looking for a hotel. The one he chose, painted white like virtually every other building in the capital, was just a hundred yards from the waterfront. His room overlooking the sea was small and utilitarian, and suited him perfectly. He took a shower, changed into a loose-fitting white shirt over jeans and stood on his balcony a while, watching the waves roll in and smoking one of his Jordanian cigarettes while pondering his first move.

Behind him on the bed was the postcard that Nick Chapman had sent him after moving to the island. It was creased and tatty now after spending two years folded up inside the paper jungle of Ben's wallet. He walked over and picked it up, scanned the handwriting for the thousandth time and wondered what the hell had happened to his friend.

Only a few drops remained in Ben's whisky flask. 'Need to do better than that,' he muttered to himself, surveying the bottles inside the mini-bar. He slipped on his shoes and went downstairs. The hotel lounge was large and airy, done out in a phoney kind of post-Colonial Officers' Mess style with large fronded plants everywhere and whirring fans on the ceiling. As he was getting his flask filled up with the best scotch available at the bar, Ben ordered a beer and perched on a bar stool to sip it. He'd never really seen the point of beer, other than as a way to cool down on a hot day. If he wanted to get drunk, he wanted to do it in the fastest and most efficient way possible.

It looked as if the group of men in the corner of the hotel lounge were set on doing it the slow, sloppy way, and they'd obviously been at it most of the afternoon. Listening in on their conversation, Ben quickly realised they were the stragglers left over from what must have been a fair army of media invading the place in the aftermath of the suicide plane crash.

'Hey, guys,' he said, carrying his drink over to their table and pulling up a chair. 'Who are you with?' The opening shop-talk line of roving reporters the world over. Within minutes, the journalists were enjoying a round of fresh beers on their new best buddy. It wasn't hard to get them talking. 'Who're *you* with?' asked the oldest of the group, after introducing himself as Ray Doyle of the Miami Herald.

'I'm on my own,' Ben said, which seemed to be a good enough reply. Not that anyone cared. The consensus was that, a week after the event, the crash flight story had completely burned itself out and there was nothing left to hang around for. All that remained was the bitter rancour that a lot of people obviously felt for Nick Chapman. Frank Lopez of the Prensa Latina News Agency out of Havana shook his head in disgust at the mention of his name. 'How anyone let a screw-up like that behind the controls of a fucking aircraft is beyond me.'

Doyle gulped his beer and nodded in agreement. 'Total wacko,' he grated. 'The daughter too. Dope head, what I heard. The moment daddy decides to check out taking a bunch of innocent lives with him, she goes and throws herself under the nearest goddamn car. I mean, that is one fucked-up family.' Doyle and a couple of the others laughed uproariously at the idea.

Ben's fist clenched around his beer glass and he glanced downwards to hide the spark of anger in his eyes. After a pause he asked, as casually as possible, 'Anyone get the name of the air traffic guy who talked to Chapman on the radio?'

Doyle looked blank. Lopez clicked his fingers, trying to remember. The one called Tibbets got there first. 'Drummond,' he said. 'The guy's name is Bob Drummond.'

‘That’s it,’ Lopez said. ‘But forget it, amigo. He won’t talk to you. Nobody wants to talk about nothing any more. It’s yesterday’s news.’

‘That’s the kind I like best,’ Ben said, and they all found that very amusing too.

Chapter 8

Long before the reporters finally staggered away from the hotel bar to start packing their bags for home, Ben was at the wheel of the Wrangler, blasting the two miles south-east back out of George Town towards Owen Roberts International airport, with the top down and the warm tropical breeze in his hair. He passed rows of stately white beachside homes. Yacht clubs and marinas. A colourful-looking bar and grill restaurant with a signpost on its terrace proclaiming 'RELAX! YOU ARE ON CAYMAN TIME'.

He left the Jeep in the main airport car park and headed for the air traffic control building a little way from the terminal: a squat white tower topped by a dark glass hexagonal observation centre bristling with antennas and dishes. A couple of security guards were hanging around the entrance – one white, portly, middle-aged, the other black with some seriously impressive dreadlocks that looked incongruous with his uniform. They were sharing a joke over a cigarette and leaning against the wire fence with their backs to Ben, so that he slipped through unnoticed. He pushed through a set of glass doors and found himself in a busy reception area where a harried-looking guy of about seventy was manning the desk and talking on two phones at once.

Ben walked up to the desk and asked him if Bob Drummond was working there today. The old guy gave him an exasperated look and pointed down the corridor to Ben's right. 'You'll have to talk to Maud in personnel. It's the third door. Yeah, Barry? Did you fax through those reports yet? Then where the hell are they?'

Ben left him to his apoplexy and wandered down the corridor. At the third door he paused, knocked and went inside a tiny office dominated by a broad desk and an even broader heavyset woman packed tightly into a swivel chair and wearing a name tag that said 'Maud Biggs'. The smile he flashed at her met with a leaden stare.

'Hi, I was wondering if Bob Drummond is working here today?' he asked. Maud shook her head without a flicker of expression. Ben clicked his tongue. 'That's a pity. I'm an old friend of Bob's and he said that anytime I was on the island I should drop in and see him. But I lost his home address. You couldn't help me out with that, could you?'

Maud's face remained immobile, but at the mention of anything to do with clerical files her eyes darted involuntarily towards the filing cabinet to her left. Reflex action, like a dog salivating at the mention of food. Lagging by about half a second, her conscious mind kicked in and she shook her head severely. 'We don't give out details of employees to anyone.'

'All right, I'll level with you,' Ben said, beckoning her close. 'My name's Jerome Ryerson. I'm with the Lotto,' he added with a conspiratorial grin, and flashed his tatty old British Armed Forces ID card at her, too fast for her narrow-set eyes to focus on it, and keeping his thumb over the emblem. 'I'm here to tell Bob that he just won twelve million dollars,' he went on, and Maud's eyes opened wide. 'The only address we have for him is this one and I urgently need him to sign his claim form. I don't think he'd want to miss out, do you?'

Maud was still gazing at him in heavy-browed stupefaction when another woman appeared in the office doorway. 'Maud, can you help me? The damn thing's frozen up again. Do I need to enter that reference code *before* the sixteen-digit number, or *after* it?'

Maud levered herself out of her chair and waddled to the rescue, shooting a bewildered look at Ben and muttering at him to wait there. While the two women were hunched over the computer in the office across the corridor, Ben went straight over to the filing cabinet, glided open the drawer labelled 'PERSONNEL A – M' and flicked through the index cards to D for Drummond. Finding the one he wanted, he managed to stuff it under his shirt just in time before Maud came waddling back into the room.

'What was that about twelve million dollars?' she said, frowning.

Ben waved his mobile phone at her. 'Sorry, there's been a mistake. Head office just called. Looks like we do have the address after all. Thanks for your time.'

He waited until he was safely back in the Jeep before he examined Drummond's file. The photo showed a beefy-looking guy in his late thirties, cropped brown hair, bad skin, droopy moustache. Ben scanned quickly through his resumé. Drummond had joined the Cayman Air Authority Navigation Services Regulation Unit back in '94 as a general assistant before gaining promotion four years later to the Approach Control team at Owen Roberts. His home address was on Shamrock Road, in the district of Bodden Town, a few miles to the east.

The road skirted the south side of the island and took Ben into a suburban residential neighbourhood where he quickly found Drummond's nondescript little townhouse just off the street. There was a Ford Taurus parked in the drive, behind a blue van with 'Bodden Town Cleaning Services' emblazoned on the side.

Ben pulled up by the kerb and walked over to the house. The front door was ajar, and he heard a woman's voice from inside. He knocked and pushed the door open a couple more inches to see a tiny grey-haired woman with a severe expression screeching orders at a pair of guys in overalls the same blue as the van. She stopped in mid-command and turned to glare at Ben.

'Mrs Drummond?' he asked.

'You gotta be kidding me – Mrs Drummond,' she snorted. 'Who're you?'

'I was looking for Bob.'

'Get in line. You find him, you tell that worthless piece of shit he owes me three months' back-rent. And he needn't try coming back to get his stuff. I've cleaned the place out.'

'When did you last see him?'

'Five, six days ago. I was coming over here to see him about the money when I saw him take off with these two guys in a car.'

'Friends of his?' Ben said.

'I never saw them before, but I live across the other side of the island. You one of them debt collectors? Or a cop?'

'Just a friend,' Ben said.

Her look softened a little. 'Listen, son. Don't waste your time on that jackass. Bob Drummond's a gambler and a low-life. He ain't no-one's friend.'

Chapter 9

It was already late afternoon, and the sun was beginning its long, slow dive towards the shimmering blue ocean horizon, by the time Ben arrived at the Cayman Islands Charter complex on the far side of the island, an area called West End, near Seven Mile Beach.

Seeing his friend's place of business brought back the sadness as he parked up in the near-empty car park and walked towards the buildings, following a sign that said VISITOR RECEPTION.

The CIC offices were housed in a long, low, glass-fronted modern building. The little stretch of lawn in front was golf-course perfect. Two palm trees flanked the entrance, waving gently in the breeze.

Behind the office buildings, next to the check-in and boarding areas for charter and inter-island shuttle passengers, stood a cluster of aircraft hangars – not the type that Ben was used to, the massive brutish military hangars capable of swallowing a Hercules troop transport. CIC ran a more modest kind of fleet. A white Britten-Norman Trislander sat parked on the concrete, identical to the one Nick Chapman had been piloting the day of the crash, with CAYMAN ISLAND CHARTER in bold black script across its fuselage. A slightly odd-looking design of aircraft, Ben observed, with the lumpy third engine protruding from the tail-fin housing and overhanging the rear of the fuselage like a scorpion's tail. Renowned for its practicality as a short-range civilian utility aircraft: quiet, manoeuvrable, economical to run.

But not much fun to die in. Ben ran his eye along its fifty-foot length and tried not to imagine what it must have felt like to be trapped inside it as it plummeted towards the sea.

Parked a few yards behind the Trislander, sitting low off the concrete on its clumsy-looking fixed undercarriage, was an aeroplane that Ben doubted very much had ever been used for CIC operations. He'd seen photographs of the old wartime Sea Otter, but never a real example before. The single-engined flying boat had been manufactured by Supermarine, the makers of the legendary Spitfire fighter, and had been the last biplane ever commissioned by the Royal Air Force. Fewer than three hundred had ever been built. The thing was a relic from a bygone era, still sporting the mounting brackets for its three Vickers machine guns and payload of four 250-pound bombs – and yet it looked completely pristine, repainted in gleaming bright golden yellow. Ben stood admiring it for a moment or two, then turned and walked into the main office building.

The reception area was as deserted as the visitors' car park. Ben guessed that business couldn't have been exactly thriving in the last week or so. To the left of the reception desk was a door that said STAFF ONLY. He figured that staff only areas were much better places to learn valuable details than public areas. He pushed it open and found himself in a large, neatly ordered office. There was nobody here either, but he could sense a familiar presence nonetheless.

The instant he walked in, three things told him this had been Nick Chapman's office. The first was the neatness. Ben hadn't met an ex-soldier yet whose daily habits hadn't been permanently imbued by the discipline of military life. Especially SAS life. The second was the framed photograph of Hilary Chapman sitting on the empty desk surrounded by papers, files, tubs full of pens.

The third was the print that hung on the wall above the empty desk chair. Ben even knew the name of the artist: M.C. Escher, famous for the mind-bending optical illusions that he'd designed into his artwork back in the mid-twentieth century. Nick had always been into that kind of stuff, sticking postcards up by his bunk wherever they'd happened to be stationed that wasn't in the middle of some desert or jungle: a flight of stairs that climbed in an infinite loop without ever getting anywhere; paradoxical structures and impossible realities that seemed to defy logic and tricked the eye into seeing what couldn't be.

The picture hanging on the wall had been one of Nick's favourites. It showed a symmetrical circular mosaic-like web of interlocked patterns. If you looked at them one way, what you saw were legions of heavenly white winged angels on a dark background. Cock your head a little to the side, narrow your eyes, change your perspective, and the angels suddenly melted away and the background leapt into focus to become a horde of sinister, bat-like black demons against a field of white. Nick had used to say it helped him remember the line between good and evil. Ben had always remembered that.

Another door swung open at the far end of the office and a woman walked in. She was maybe thirty-six, thirty-seven. Tall and straight, tanned, dark-haired, wearing it in a loose ponytail. She was halfway to the desk and reaching out to pick up a file from a stack when she suddenly registered

Ben's presence in the room and froze, looking at him with wide eyes. 'Who are you?'

'I was looking for the manager,' Ben said.

'I'm Mrs Martínez, Mr Chapman's personal assistant. I'm acting manager in his . . . his absence.' Her voice was strong but the tightness in her throat threatened to overwhelm it at the mention of his name. She covered her emotion, cleared her throat and added firmly, 'And you can't come in here. Maybe you didn't see the sign that says "staff only"?'

'There's nobody in reception.'

She rolled her eyes and tutted. 'Jennifer. That damn temp's always on a coffee break. I'll buzz Rachel. She'll take your booking.'

'I'm not interested in making a booking.'

'Right. You want flying lessons? Then you need to see Phil in the blue building behind the hangar area.'

Ben shook his head. 'I didn't come here for lessons either.'

She cocked her head to one side and put her hands on her hips. 'Then may I ask what it is you do want?'

'I have some questions about your late employer, Nick Chapman. I won't take up much of your time.'

The PA let out a sigh. 'I thought you media people were all gone now. Haven't you had enough?'

Ben was already tired of playing games. He came straight out with the truth, as simple as he could make it. 'I'm not a reporter. My name's Ben Hope. I was a friend of Nick's and I've come here to find out what really happened to him.'

Mrs Martínez flinched noticeably at his words. She narrowed her eyes, looking hard at him, seeming to scrutinise every detail of his face. After a long beat she replied slowly and carefully, 'If you'd been watching the news, you'd know what happened.'

'I don't always believe the news,' Ben said.

'Listen, everyone here is very upset. We really don't want to be pestered right now. The press have been flocking around here like goddamned vultures every day.'

'Just a couple of questions and I'll be gone.'

'Please,' she said. 'Nobody here wants to answer any questions. Just go away. Leave me alone, okay?' She considered a moment, then added, 'I mean, leave us all alone.' Before she could stop it, tears had welled up in her eyes and were rolling down her face. She wiped them away.

'I didn't mean to upset you,' Ben said. 'I'm very sorry.' There was a stack of headed compliment slips on a little stand on the desk next to a computer terminal. He grabbed one and picked up a pen that was lying nearby. 'This is my number,' he said, writing. 'Call me if you change your mind.'

Back out in the reception area was a young blonde in a short skirt whom Ben took to be Jennifer, the temp. She was pretty, with blue eyes and an elfin quality about her. She threw Ben a glance, smiled coyly and busied herself arranging some flowers in a vase as he headed for the exit. He didn't make a big deal of noticing it, but he was aware of the way she watched him through the glass all the way back to his Jeep, the elfin look gone, replaced with an inscrutable expression that Ben couldn't quite fathom.

Chapter 10

Ben headed back down south towards George Town, on the road running parallel to Seven Mile Beach with the sweep of white sands and the spectacular view across the West Bay to his right. Watching the sun sink closer towards the sea and bathe the whole island in a shimmering copper haze, he could understand what had brought his old friend to this idyllic place.

A couple of miles from the Cayman Islands Charter office, a black SUV was parked in a lay-by off a long empty straight. Ben sped past, then saw in his mirror that the black car was indicating to pull out behind him.

Its driver wasn't hanging about. By the time the vehicle was filling his rear-view mirror, Ben had started paying more attention to it. A Chevy Blazer four-wheel-drive, big and bulky, dark-tinted windows, bull bars and extra driving lamps on the front. It was sticking too close to his tail. He eased off on the gas, letting the Jeep slow to just over fifty, expecting the Blazer to pass him.

It didn't. Instead it matched his speed, still sticking much too close. Ben slowed the Jeep down to a crawl. The Blazer slowed down too. Ben hit the gas and roared the Jeep up to seventy. The Blazer followed suit, making no attempt to hide the fact that it was deliberately tailing him.

Ben remembered what Drummond's landlady had said about her tenant taking off with some men in a big black car. *Interesting*, he thought, hit the brakes and slewed hard over to the dusty verge.

It probably wasn't what a detective would have done. But then, Ben didn't pretend to be a detective.

He climbed out of the Jeep. The Blazer had stopped twenty yards behind, just sitting there. Ben walked up the verge towards it. The vehicle's black bonnet was filmed over with dust. Behind the tinted windscreen he could see two men in the front seats. Their eyes were hidden behind dark glasses, but they were fixed right on him.

'Can I help you?' Ben said, in a tone that wasn't friendly, wasn't hostile.

The men kept staring at him. Neither moved until he was just a few feet from the front of the Blazer – then the driver slammed it into drive, pulled aggressively back out into the road and went speeding off in a cloud of dust.

Ben watched it go, then started walking back towards the Jeep.

Definitely interesting.

Ben drove back through the falling dusk to the hotel, showered, opened up his holdall and changed into a fresh black T-shirt and black jeans. He never had been too imaginative when it came to his wardrobe. He slipped his wallet into the back pocket of his jeans, then wandered down to the bar and ordered a steak with a green salad and a glass of red wine. He took his meal outside onto the patio and sat watching the colours of the sunset, listened to the breakers crashing in against the rocks.

All his life, he'd loved the sea. The sound relaxed him, helped him think. Taking the folded postcard from his wallet, he spent a while staring at Nick Chapman's address near Rum Point. It was time to make another visit, one that Ben's instincts told him was best kept nocturnal. He took his time over a second glass of wine. By now the ocean was dark, just the distant white crests of the waves visible under the moon.

It was sometime after ten when he went up to his room, grabbed his leather jacket and headed out into the night, twirling the Jeep keys thoughtfully around his finger. The warmth of the day was cooling fast in the ocean breeze, and he shrugged on the jacket, wincing a little at the pull on his stitches.

Ben was still a few yards from the Jeep when the group of men appeared out of the shadows and quickly converged on him.

Chapter 11

There were four of them, all over six feet, all built on a fairly grand scale – somewhere between eleven and twelve hundred pounds of tattooed muscle and lard ambling up towards him. And judging by the lethal assortment of hardware they'd brought along to play with, it wasn't to ask the time.

The four stopped, forming a semi-circle cutting Ben off from his Jeep. Nobody spoke. The only sound was the rhythmic meaty thwack as one of them slapped the thick of his aluminium baseball bat against his palm. One of his companions was casually swinging a bolo knife. Maybe fourteen inches of black leaf-shaped blade, just this side of a machete, and Ben guessed every one of those inches was shaving sharp. With a rattling *chink-chink*, another of the men unravelled a length of heavy steel chain from his fist.

The biggest of the men, standing around six-five in denim and biker boots, seemed to be the leader. In the hierarchy of moronic bruisers, size was always the dominant factor. The survival knife stuck crossways in his belt was some cheap mail-order job with a sawback blade and knuckleduster hilt. His head was shaved and gleaming under the moonlight. A line of tattooed teardrops ran down his cheek from his right eye, disappearing into the thick black beard that hung halfway down his chest, fashioned into twin spikes, rigid with hairspray. Going for the demonic look, Ben guessed.

'You guys look like you're auditioning for a part,' he said. 'Or did you escape from a freak show somewhere?'

The black beard opened in a grin, showing a glint of a gold tooth. 'We're the reception committee, motherfucker,' he said in a voice that was about half an octave lower than was human.

'I get it,' Ben said. 'You're what they call the frighteners.' He smiled. 'Here to intimidate me.'

'Smart guy.'

'I catch on fast. So when does the frightening part begin? I have to be somewhere.'

The baseball bat kept on slap-slapping. The bearded guy fingered the hilt of his survival knife. 'How do you feel about wiping someone else's ass, little man?'

'Excuse me?' Ben said, genuinely intrigued.

'See, most folks would find the idea of wiping someone else's ass is pretty fuckin' repellent, no?'

The guy waited for Ben to comment. When he realised Ben wasn't going to, he went on in his bass rumble. 'Say you had to wipe asses for a livin', like if you was carin' for old folks or somethin'. Sure, to start with, every time you had to wipe an ass you'd feel like pukin' afterwards. Or maybe even while you was doin' it. But after a while, you'd get used to that shit. Then wipin' some old fucker's ass wouldn't seem like nuthin'. You could wipe a hundred asses before breakfast. Now, see the point I'm makin' . . .'

Ben had been waiting for the point.

'The point I'm makin' is that in my line of work, it ain't wipin' asses. It's spillin' blood. You get me? And I've been doin' this shit so long I can't even remember a time when spatterin' some fucker's blood all over the sidewalk made me feel one way or the other. This is what I do. You hear what I'm sayin', motherfucker? Talking about you. You're gonna get fucked up permanent, right here, right now.'

Ben's hand went slowly to his jeans pocket. He took out his cigarettes and lighter. Clanged open his Zippo and lit up. Through a cloud of smoke he said, 'Well, Beard, that was a pretty good speech. You certainly have a gift for metaphor. Out of curiosity, did you have to look up the word "repellent"?'

Beard's cocky grin twisted into a scowl and he slipped his fingers inside the knuckleduster hilt of his knife. The slap-slapping behind him stopped.

'Listen to this asshole,' muttered the one with the chain.

'I don't get to hear speeches like that very often,' Ben said. 'In my line of work we don't generally have time for them.'

'Your line of work,' Beard repeated, just a little uncertainly. The grin returned, but there was a touch of nervousness to it now.

'I appreciate you guys have to make a living too,' Ben said. 'But this is one occupational hazard you don't want to have to deal with. So I think you ought to turn around and head back to the bar you just came from, call your boss and tell him he shouldn't send you on jobs where you're so badly out of your depth.'

Two seconds of silence. Then the survival knife was out of Beard's belt and swinging through the air.

Here we go, Ben thought. The downward slash. Hallmark of the truly amateurish knife fighter, the guy who's learned all he knows from third-rate movies, has got lucky once or twice while dealing with people even more clueless than him, and is confirmed in his vision of himself as a formidable urban warrior. It would have been much too easy to twist the knife out of Beard's hand, break three of his fingers in the loop of the hilt and then embed the thick blade right in the top of his skull.

Ben didn't do that. Instead he twisted it out of Beard's hand, broke three fingers in the loop of the hilt, used Beard's ears as handles to drive his face down into his rising knee and then sent the blade whirling with a meaty *thunk* deep into the right thigh of the guy who was coming up flailing the chain.

With a scream that drowned out Beard's, the man let go of the chain and clapped his hands in a gibbering panic to where the knuckleduster hilt was protruding from his leg. The chain's momentum carried it hissing through the air a couple of feet, until it connected with the face of his associate with the bolo knife.

Hard. Ben heard the crack of bone over the thwack of the impact. The bolo dropped to the ground as its owner keeled over like a felled tree, clutching at his shattered nose and cheekbone, either too shocked to make a sound or choked by the broken bits of teeth in his throat.

The fight had lasted about three seconds so far. Ben stepped over the writhing, groaning Beard towards the last of the attackers who was still standing. The guy swung his baseball bat a couple of times, but his heart wasn't in it. 'Fuck,' he muttered in a hollow voice, then turned and ran like hell, still clutching the bat. Ben watched him go. He was a much better sprinter than he was a fighter.

Taking a draw on his cigarette, Ben walked over to Bolo and stamped on his face, twice. A few feet away, his friend Mr Chain was making a high-pitched agonised keening as he tried to yank the knife blade out of his thigh. It had missed the femoral artery by an inch or two but there was still a lot of blood spilling across the concrete. Ben decided he'd had enough of the guy's noise, and shut him up with a kick to the head that sent him slumping over sideways and bounced his skull off the ground.

Beard was trying groggily to get up, raising his body off the concrete with his left hand, the broken fingers of his right tucked tight between his legs. Ben's boot swiped his left arm out from under him and rolled him over on his back. Beard stared up at him in terror. His nose was split open and bleeding almost as profusely as Chain's leg.

Ben crouched down next to him and flicked cigarette ash on the guy's face. 'Just you and me now, Beard,' he said. 'I reckon as you're the leader of the gang, that qualifies you as its spokesman too. So speak. Who sent you?'

'I . . . I don't . . .' Beard gasped.

'You're not really going to give me the "I don't know" routine, are you?'

'Listen, mister . . . I swear . . .'

'Fine,' Ben said. He dug the Zippo back out of his jeans pocket. Flipped open the lid and thumbed the wheel. The spark ignited the fuel inside to produce the warm flickering orange flame and that smell Ben loved.

The flame from Beard's beard as its rigid spikes went up like a magnesium flare was considerably brighter, and the stink of burning hair and skin far less pleasant.

Beard shrieked in terror. None too gently, Ben used the man's denim jacket to beat the fire out.

'Didn't your mother warn you about using too much hairspray?' Ben said. 'That stuff's flammable.'

‘You crazy sonofabitch!’ Beard screamed.

‘I think I asked you a question,’ Ben said. ‘Not going to ask you a second time.’

Beard’s eyes bulged in his scorched, blackened face. ‘I don’t fucking know! This guy offered us ten grand cash. Gave us your picture. It’s in my pocket.’ He pointed wildly with his good hand.

Ben yanked the photo out. It had been taken from inside a car, and showed him walking towards it. His Jeep was in the background, parked on the side of the stretch of road alongside Seven Mile Beach. Easy enough to figure out who his photographer had been: one of the two men in the black Chevy Blazer.

‘Some guy hired you? That’s all you know? A guy in a bar?’

Beard nodded desperately.

Ben showed him the lighter again. ‘Sure? You still have a bit left on that side. How about I even you up?’

‘No! Yes! I swear!’

Ben nodded. He supposed that a man with a burning beard would always tell the truth. It sounded a little like a Chinese proverb.

‘Get yourself another job, mate,’ he said, and walked to the Jeep.

Chapter 12

Cayman Kai was a cove on the wooded north side of the island, close to Rum Point beach. Nick Chapman's home had been a simple, elegant white bungalow with a broad veranda, surrounded by trees and privately situated at the side of a narrow coastal inlet with its own boat dock.

The place was all in darkness. As Ben got out of the car, he could hear music and laughter wafting across on the breeze from the nearby restaurant on Rum Point. He glanced around him: nobody was about, and the nearest neighbours were a good distance away beyond the whispering trees. He tried the front door, then the back. Finding them both locked, he turned his attention to the window catches: exactly the flimsy low-security kind of affair he'd have expected to find on an island with one of the lowest crime rates on the planet. In moments, he was inside.

The window he'd come through was that of the master bedroom. Ben stood perfectly immobile and utterly silent for a long time in the shadows, listening to the sounds of the house, hearing no sign of movement from anywhere. He reached into his pocket for the mini-Maglite he'd bought earlier in George Town, and cast the strong, thin beam of light around the room.

A mosquito net shrouded the double bed. A vase of dying flowers stood on the bedside table. On one white wall hung a large framed Escher print, the one with the never-ending staircase. On the opposite wall hung a picture of Nick and his team standing grinning next to a Cayman Air Charter Trislander on a grassy airfield. The aircraft had a pearly white new paint job and everyone looked ready to burst with excitement. This must have been CIC's inaugural launch. Nick himself looked tanned and fit and immensely proud.

Below that one was a photo portrait of Hilary, aged about fifteen, together with another from her graduation day.

Ben felt strange, and a little ashamed, to be breaking into the home of his dead friend. He left the bedroom and moved on through the house, treading quietly and cautiously, darting the torch beam as he went.

The police didn't seem to have turned the place over too roughly looking for clues. Everything was more or less tidy, down to the perfectly squared rugs on the tiled floors and the ordered arrangement of cushions on the living room sofa. Most of the walls were covered with photos of the bright golden-yellow Sea Otter and other aircraft, as well as a collection of spectacular aerial shots of the island that showed the depth of Nick's passion for the place.

Satisfied that he was completely alone, Ben spent some time in Nick's study, holding the shaft of the mini-Maglite between his teeth to sift through the papers in the drawers of the large antique desk, in the hope that he might find something the cops had missed.

He'd no real idea what he was looking for, but searching made him nervous. There was a lingering anxiety at the back of his mind that no amount of rational denial could completely erase: the fear of uncovering some evidence that Nick had been in the kind of trouble from which only suicide offered a refuge – irredeemable debts, maybe – or signs that the depression had returned.

What if – *just what if* – Nick really had ended his own life? The thought made Ben's mind swim. Then what had happened to Hilary? Was her death some bizarre coincidence? Like the fact that someone on this island obviously didn't like Ben going around asking questions? And if Nick hadn't killed himself, then what was the alternative? For all the hours Ben had spent going over and over it in his mind, he could think of nothing.

There was nothing in Nick's desk, either. No demands from the bank, no nasty letters threatening litigation, no doctor's prescriptions or empty pill bottles, no telltale Prozac capsule rolling loose in the bottom of a drawer. All Ben found among Nick's business documents were routine bits of paperwork and correspondence that gave the impression that CIC wasn't just solvent, it was booming. Inside a Manila file were some preliminary architect sketches for a major extension to the office buildings at West End, and a letter giving an estimated completion date in eight months' time. Ben studied the sketches and shook his head. *Did people suffering from chronic depression make plans like this?*

The bottom drawer contained Nick's private papers. Ben went through them guiltily. No sign of a Last Will and Testament. A cheery letter from Hilary, dated six months ago, with a few snaps of her on holiday somewhere with a girlfriend. An assortment of receipts and product guarantees. A handwritten list of forty or so names, headed 'party guests'.

A man contemplating suicide, planning a big get-together?

Ben put everything back as he'd found it and started going through the address book by the phone. Again, he could find nothing out of the ordinary. Nothing, except for the somewhat cryptic phone number at the back of the book. It had no name next to it, only a capital letter T that had been heavily circled as though it had some special significance.

Ben used his own phone to dial the number, and got straight through to an answering service. He switched off before the message prompt.

That was when he heard the click of a key turning in the front door lock, followed by the padding of tentative footsteps in the hallway outside the study. The beam of a torch swept by, shining under the crack in the door.

Ben turned off his Maglite. He crouched behind the desk, completely still and silent in the darkness.

The footsteps stopped right outside the study. Someone reached out and nudged the door half open. Torchlight shone inside the room.

And from the source of the brilliant white beam, there was the unmistakable metallic *click-clunk* of a well-oiled revolver mechanism being cocked, ready to fire.

Chapter 13

The footsteps moved closer inside the room. The torch beam swept from side to side. Ben tucked himself in tightly behind the desk, but he knew that he had zero chance of remaining hidden for long.

The torch beam flashed across the desk. Ben saw his own shadow appear on the floor. He had a split second to react before the intruder did.

Nobody, not even a trained SAS soldier, really wants to launch themselves, unarmed and blind, at someone holding a cocked and loaded revolver. But under the circumstances, Ben didn't have a lot of choice. Surprise was his only advantage, and he used it. With a roar he burst out from behind the desk, shining his own torch straight back at the intruder's face. And hurled himself at the guy in a flying leap.

There was no deafening gunshot while he was in the air. Ben's shoulder connected with what felt like the intruder's midriff, driving him violently backwards against the wall. The intruder let out a grunt of pain and shock. The torch beam slashed upwards to point at the ceiling, then fell towards the floor. There was the distinct thump of a chunky revolver landing on the rug.

Pinning the wildly struggling intruder down hard with a knee to the throat, Ben reached for the switch of the side lamp.

And with a shock, recognised the face staring up at him as that of Mrs Martínez, Nick's PA.

He instantly relaxed the pressure on her neck before she blacked out. She was wheezing and clutching her throat as he hauled her to her feet and set her down in a chair. 'I wasn't expecting to meet you again so soon, Mrs Martínez,' he said.

'How did you get in here?' she gasped, rubbing her neck.

Ben stooped to pick up the fallen revolver. It was a Smith & Wesson Model 28, the 'Highway Patrolman' version of their large-framed .357 hand cannon. Four-inch barrel, blue steel. Enough firepower to stop a Freightliner truck. The US Highway Patrol had used them to stop runaway vehicles by blasting holes in the engine blocks.

'That's a lot of handgun for a nice lady like you to be carrying around,' Ben said. He eased the hammer down. Pushed the knurled catch behind the recoil shield and flipped out the cylinder to see the six bright brass cartridges stamped FEDERAL .357 MAGNUM. He tipped the rounds out into his palm, dropped them in his pocket and laid the unloaded pistol on the desk. He could see her eyeing it. 'Did I hurt you?' he asked.

'I'm fine.' Her throat and jaw were turning a fine red, but it would fade in an hour or two. He wasn't so sure the pain in his side would ease as fast. His little altercation with Beard's boys earlier hadn't done his healing wound too many favours, and leaping up from behind the desk just now had added an unpleasantly sharp new dimension to the discomfort that had him worrying about busted stitches.

'You want to know why I broke into Nick's house, Mrs Martínez, and I'll level with you,' Ben said. 'I'm here because people aren't answering my questions and I get the feeling my presence on this island is less than welcome in some quarters. I don't think Nick would have minded me coming to check out his place. Now, you level with me. I'm wondering why someone with a key to the front door would come armed with a flashlight and a Magnum.'

'What questions?' she said.

'Ones that would help me understand the truth of what really happened out there that day.'

She hesitated. 'I'll answer your questions if you'll let me go over to that bookcase.' She pointed across the other side of the study.

'What's that? The old "hidden weapon in the bookcase" trick?'

'Please. I'm not that stupid.'

'What's in the bookcase?'

'You'll understand.'

'Slowly,' he said.

Avoiding his eye, she crossed the room, stopped at the bookcase and gazed along the rows of titles. Most of Nick's collection seemed to be aviation-related. She plucked at the spine of a big, thick leather ring-bound book, slid it out and held it tight against her chest.

'Now set it down on that table and step away from it,' Ben said.

She did as he said. Ben approached the table and flipped open the leather cover. It was a photo album, nothing more.

'I need to see something,' she said. 'It's important.'

'Be my guest,' Ben said.

Mrs Martínez flipped through a few pages of the album. She stopped, pressed a finger to one of the pages, stooped a little to peer at it more closely, then flipped another page and did the same again. She looked up at Ben, studying his face with the same careful scrutiny he'd noticed that afternoon at the CIC offices. 'Okay,' she said. 'Now I know for sure.'

'Know what?'

'What I came here tonight to find out. I thought I recognised you when you walked into the office today. But I needed to be sure that you were the same Ben Hope Nick used to talk about.' She spun the album round on the table so he could see the picture. It was a shot taken at Hilary Chapman's engagement party. Ben was in the background, holding a glass.

'And here,' she said, flipping back a page to another shot of some of the men of A Squadron, looking hot and exhausted in filthy fatigues, sitting around a clearing in some tropical hellhole that could have been either of the SAS's jungle training grounds in Belize or Borneo. There was Ben in the middle, his face partially blacked, in the process of field-stripping an AR-15 rifle. Technically speaking, Nick shouldn't have even had such potentially compromising photos in his possession, though sneaking the occasional memento home wasn't uncommon practice.

'You haven't changed a lot,' she said.

'Thanks. So now you know who I am, Mrs Martínez, will you talk to me?'

'Call me Tamara,' she said. 'And yes, if Nick trusted you as a friend, then that's good enough for me.'

Ben saw the connection right away. 'Tamara, as in the large capital T in Nick's address book, next to a mobile number?'

She nodded. 'You've been straight with me, now it's my turn. Nick and I were having an affair for the last eighteen months. That's to say, *I* was having an affair with him. I was the one that was married with two kids. It was our secret, obviously. A very well-kept one, until now. I even had a secret phone he used to call me on.' She paused a long time, then added softly, 'I loved him so much.'

Now Ben understood the depth of pain in her eyes. She hadn't just lost a work colleague.

'Why the gun, Tamara?'

'It's my husband's. I don't normally . . .'

'Walk about the island packing a pistol?'

She shook her head. 'No, this is one of the safest places in the world. But I'm scared. I'm scared to death.' The tears in her eyes caught the light. She opened her mouth to speak, then closed it. But the words building up in her throat were too strong to be hemmed in and after a few moments' hesitation she blurted it out.

'Nick didn't kill himself,' she said.

Chapter 14

'I don't think we should hang around here too long,' Ben said after a beat.

Tamara sniffed, wiped a tear. 'We can go back to my place. It's okay – there's nobody there right now but me and the maid. You follow me.'

After tidying up behind them and making sure nobody was lurking around outside, they left the villa by the front door. Tamara had parked her Mazda people carrier among the shadows of the trees. Ben watched her climb in and her car lights come on, then got into the Wrangler and followed. They drove eastwards across the island for a few miles, to an area called Omega Bay Estates. The Mazda led the way into what was obviously a prestigious and highly expensive gated community, and pulled up outside a sprawling house set far back from the road.

'Where's your husband?' Ben asked as she led him inside. The tears had dried up now.

'Dwight? Away on some legal conference. He'll be gone another ten days. Even if he was here,' she added with a grimace, 'he'd be off sailing around the bay on that damn boat of his. And the twins are staying with my mom in Miami.'

Where Nick's place was unassumingly tasteful and comfortable, the Martínez residence purposefully screamed 'rich lawyer' as loudly as it could and shoved its opulence right in your face. Ben got the impression that wasn't down to Tamara's influence. He paused to look at a photo of Dwight Martínez on a sideboard, posing with his motor yacht in the background, a sleek white vessel with the name *Santa Clara* on her bows.

Dwight might have been a fine figure of a man in his youth, but Ben doubted it. He was almost perfectly spherical in shape, all three hundred pounds of him, with thin sandy hair that looked glued on and a smile that was more like a sneer. Ben glanced covertly back at Tamara and muttered 'Jesus' under his breath.

'Let's get a drink,' she said, and led him towards the kitchen. In the passage was a reproduction antique display cabinet filled with shotguns – a showy brace of Purdeys, a couple of skeet guns and a short-barrelled Remington semi-auto that looked as if it was kept for home defence. 'Dwight's quite the sportsman,' Ben commented as he followed Tamara into the enormous kitchen.

'Don't get me started. Pity any poor creature that crawls or flies when he and his law cronies get together. You want a beer?'

'I'd sooner have a scotch,' he said.

'Sounds good to me.' Tamara opened a cupboard, fetched out a bottle of Bowmore and two glasses. Ben walked over to the long breakfast bar and pulled out a stool. 'Mind if I smoke?'

She shook her head as she poured out the drinks. 'Go ahead. There's an ashtray on the side.'

'Want one?'

'Uh-uh. I quit months ago.'

Ben lit up. Clanged the Zippo shut and blew out smoke. Tamara joined him at the breakfast bar, setting the bottle down between them on the marble top. Handed him his glass and took a long, deep gulp of her own, as if she really needed it. 'This has been a tough time for me,' she said in the controlled voice of someone battling their emotions.

Ben didn't reply. Looking at her he could see a strong-willed woman bravely trying to hold it together, trapped in a nowhere marriage and unable to grieve openly for the man she'd loved. He knew there were times she must veer close to the edge. He understood it. He'd been there in the past, and would certainly find himself there again in the future. Some things didn't go away.

'Nick said you didn't have any family,' she said. 'Is that still how it is for you?'

'That's still how it is,' Ben said.

'I think he told me you're from Ireland? You don't sound it.'

'I wasn't born there,' he said. 'But I love Ireland. My mother was from Galway. I have a home there.' He pictured it in his mind: a large rambling old house close to the rocky shore where he loved to spend time alone whenever he could, sometimes sitting for hours gazing out to sea. He often missed it.

'You talk about your mother in the past tense,' Tamara said.

'She died a long time ago.'

When Tamara understood he wasn't going to elaborate, she asked, 'Do you have any other family?'

He shook his head. 'It's just me and Winnie. She was my parents' housekeeper. She moved with me to Ireland after they died and now she just looks after the place for me when

I'm not around. A mad old bat, and it drives her crazy trying to keep me in line,' he added with a smile, which quickly dropped from his face. 'She's the only family I have left now.'

Tamara sensed there was something paining him, something he kept bottled up deep inside and didn't want to talk about. 'You want a top-up?' she asked him.

He nodded, and slid his half-empty glass across for her to refill.

'Why are you here on Grand Cayman, Ben?' she said. 'You don't believe this bullshit about suicide either, do you?'

'Let's start from the beginning,' he said. 'Tell me what you know.'

'I know Ni—' she started, then broke off. 'I knew Nick. He told me all about his history – the divorce, the breakdown, his depression, how he'd left the army under a cloud. He didn't try to hide anything from me. But that was years ago. He wasn't depressed any more. He was one of the most contented people I've ever known. Did you see that yellow plane outside the office?'

'The Sea Otter.'

'Nick rescued it from a scrapyard and restored it himself. His pride and joy. He was like a boy with it – any excuse, he was in the air. He had a passion for it that was so infectious, he even got me learning to fly. Nick loved planes, he loved this island, and the new life he'd created here . . .' Tamara paused a moment, swallowed and added in a choked voice, 'And he loved me. That's why this Cifuentes stuff made no sense to me, no sense at all.'

'Cifuentes?'

'Dr Carlos Maria Cifuentes. This psychiatrist in Miami who was allegedly treating Nick for severe bipolar disorder and prescribing antidepressants for about the last nine months. At least that's what the police report said.' Tamara shook her head vehemently. 'But there's no way Nick would have touched that stuff, let alone go all the way to Miami for it. He swore he'd never go near antidepressant meds again, after all the horrendous side effects he'd had in the past. He wouldn't even take painkillers for a headache. And most of all, if he'd been suffering, I *know* he wouldn't have kept it from me. He'd have reached out to me for help.' Tamara was working hard to stay composed, but it was a struggle for her and she was knocking back the whisky as she talked.

'So I called the clinic. Guess what. They'd never heard of a Dr Carlos Maria Cifuentes. The whole thing was fabricated to make people believe that Nick would have *done* that. Of all the reporters that came swarming over this whole island picking over the bones, wouldn't you think at least one would have checked it out and seen what was going on? No. Of course not. The bastards.'

Tamara's voice had risen to a breathless pitch of anger. She stopped suddenly, breathing hard, and collected herself. 'You know, even if Nick had wanted to die, he'd never have done it in a way that could harm someone else. Mark and Cindy, the co-pilot and flight attendant – they were two of our best friends. And they'd just gotten engaged. And all those poor people – and the *children* . . .' She closed her eyes.

Ben told her about his investigations that day: his visit to Bob Drummond's place; Drummond's unexplained and somewhat sudden disappearance; the mysterious black Chevy Blazer; the men outside his hotel.

'Who were they?' Tamara said, frowning.

'Just heavies for hire, local Cayman boys. They didn't even know who they were working for. But the two in the car – they might have been a different matter.'

Tamara shook her head in bewilderment. 'So what the hell is going on?'

Both their glasses were empty. Ben reached for the bottle and filled them again. 'Before, I didn't know what to think. Now, I think there's only one possible scenario that makes any sense.' He looked at her. 'You're right. Nick didn't take that plane down. Someone else did. Maybe some kind of sabotage. Right now, I'd go with a bomb. Whatever it was, Nick was forced to crash-land in the sea. Maybe he hit the reef accidentally – I don't know. Whether everyone else was killed right away, I don't know either. But what I do know is that Nick was alive long enough *after* the crash to call his daughter, to leave her a message to say goodbye. I'm sure he'd have called you, too, if he'd had time. He obviously didn't. As to what happened next . . . well, that's what I intend to find out.'

Tamara said nothing, just stared into her drink.

Ben went on. 'Whoever's behind this whole thing must have known that Nick called Hilary. That could mean they were tapping her phone, but I don't think that's likely. What I think is more likely is that someone retrieved Nick's phone from the wreck and was able to trace his call to her. They didn't know how much he'd been able to tell her about what had happened. So they couldn't take any chances. She had to be silenced, and all trace of the message had to disappear.' He paused to take a gulp of whisky. 'And it could have been avoided, if I hadn't acted like a jerk. I didn't listen to her. I let her run out into the road and they mowed her down like a daisy.'

'Hold on. You mean—?'

'You hadn't heard?'

'I've been avoiding the TV, the radio, the newspapers, everything,' Tamara breathed. She closed her eyes and rested her head in her hands. 'Oh my God. Oh Christ. I can't bear this.'

'And now the moment I land on Grand Cayman and start poking around, someone's not happy about it,' Ben said. 'And they're going to get a lot more unhappy about it, because I haven't even started yet.'

She looked at him. 'What are you going to do?'

'I'm going to find the people responsible and kill them all,' he said.

Tamara's face had turned pale. 'Give me one of those cigarettes.'

'I thought you'd quit.'

'I just started again.' Tamara cupped her hand lightly over Ben's as he lit the cigarette for her. She coughed. 'These are strong.'

'They're Jordanian,' he said. 'Let's talk about Dwight. He seems to make a lot of money.'

'A gross amount. He made partner last year.'

'Can you be absolutely sure you and Nick kept your relationship secret from everyone?' Ben asked.

'Are you saying that *Dwight*—?'

'Jealous husbands have been known to do rash things. It takes money and connections to make murder look like an accident and cover your tracks halfway around the world.'

'Dwight wouldn't give a shit if I walked out tomorrow. And I was going to. I still am going to. The guy might be an asshole. And believe me, he *is* an asshole of the first order. But he's not a killer. He wouldn't have the guts.'

'It was just an idea,' Ben said. 'We're going to need more of them if we want to figure this out. Someone out there, someone powerful, wanted Nick out of the way. Why?'

Tamara stared into the middle distance as she smoked. Her brow flickered as a thought seemed to come to her. Her eyes hardened and she nodded slowly to herself. 'Brigman,' she said. 'Shit. *Brigman*. Why I didn't think of it before . . .'

'Okay, who's Brigman?'

She turned her gaze on him. 'Julius T. Brigman. He's a Texan who settled here about twenty years ago. Owns half the luxury real estate on Grand Cayman, and just about all the yacht charter business. Last October, he decided he wanted to break into air charter as well, and made Nick an offer to buy him out.'

'I'm guessing that Nick turned him down.'

'Sure he did. In no uncertain terms. But Brigman's not the kind who gives up so easily. He kept coming back. The offer went up and up. Nick kept on refusing. Then one evening in November, when Nick was alone at his place, Brigman turned up with two of his gorillas, and laid down a final offer. Nick told him to take a hike. It got a little ugly. Brigman became abusive, and in the end Nick grabbed him by the scruff of the neck and kicked his ass out into the street. Told the gorillas he'd break their arms if they ever came snooping round his house again.'

Ben had to smile.

'Nick joked about it for months afterwards,' Tamara said. She stubbed her cigarette out angrily. 'Damn, how could I have forgotten?'

'Julius T. Brigman,' Ben said thoughtfully.

'*There's* someone with the dough to make anything happen,' Tamara said. 'Anything he wants. He's a billionaire, Ben. Number one big shot on the island. And he's a ruthless sonofabitch who'd stop at nothing to make a buck.'

'I imagine everyone would know where such a big shot lives?' Ben said.

'Cobalt Coast. Up on the North Side. I haven't been there myself but I knew a woman who worked as one of Brigman's gardeners for a while. Said the place was a real palace.'

'Then it looks as if it's time to pay Mr Brigman a social call,' Ben said. He drained his whisky and stood up.

'Right now?'

'I'm impetuous that way,' Ben said. 'Before I go, one small favour.'

'Name it,' Tamara said.

'I don't think Dwight will mind if I borrow his Smith & Wesson?'

Chapter 15

Tamara's friend's description of the Brigman residence had been, if anything, understated. Lit up like a space station in the night and throwing a golden glow beyond its high walls and across its own secluded little Cobalt Coast bay, the towering mansion made the average Columbian drug baron's pad look like a slum shack. Ben rolled the Jeep to a halt under a stand of palms a hundred yards up the coast road, killed his lights and engine, and watched and listened.

It was after midnight, but it sounded as if the party going on within the walls of Julius T. Brigman's luxury fortress was just getting into its stride. The music was live Dixieland jazz. As Ben sat watching the huge house, a white Lamborghini came growling up the road, slowed on the approach to the gates and drove into the floodlit courtyard; a guy in a tux climbed out and escorted a sequined blonde towards the entrance, where a pair of square-shouldered goons in dark suits lumbered up to check invites and wave them inside. Why did rich people always seem to think that bodybuilders made good guard dogs?

Ben reached inside the Jeep's glove box and took out the Highway Patrolman. He flipped out the cylinder, then cradling the revolver in his left hand he dug the six .357 Magnum cartridges from his pocket and slipped them one by one into the clean, oiled chambers. He snicked the cylinder shut, stepped out of the Jeep and slipped the revolver into the waistband of his jeans, so that it sat snugly behind his right hip and was covered by the hem of his shirt. He bleeped the Jeep's locks and started strolling up the road towards the house. As he approached the gate, a swoopy bright orange Panther De Ville glided by and drove inside ahead of him. It parked outside the house and another glammed-up party couple stepped out.

Watching the security goons do their job, Ben wondered if they were the same two gorillas Brigman had taken with him for backup when he'd paid Nick his visit back in November. A slightly superior subspecies of thug, compared to the cut-price specimens who'd been sent to confront Ben outside the hotel. Considering the guy's obvious wealth, Ben found it a little insulting.

The gorillas went through their paces one more time as Ben approached the entrance. They could have been twins. Identical outfits, identical buzz-cuts; and they obviously both spent the same number of hours working out in the gym. They looked like they'd been practising their scowls in the mirror together. Maybe they injected each other's backsides with steroids, too.

'Whoa,' said one, blocking Ben's way with his palm. 'Invite. Let's have it.'

'I don't need an invitation,' Ben said.

The second security guy grinned evilly and folded his arms across his chest. He could barely touch his hands together in front of him. 'Yeah? How you figure that?'

'Because there's nobody to stop me from walking right in this door. Unless they want their teeth shoved down their throats.'

Ben didn't have time to hang around waiting for a reaction. He'd taken two steps towards the entrance before the first gorilla made a lunge for him. The musclebound arm was so slow-moving that Ben could have lit a cigarette in the time it took to reach him. He trapped the guy's porky wrist. Twisted it up and round, hard and fast, into a modified Aikido lock that he knew from personal experience felt like having your arm sheared off at the shoulder with a blunt blade.

The gorilla let out a shrill wail. Ben twisted the arm a little harder, then sent the guy cannoning into his associate and the two of them went crashing to the ground.

'Lay off the 'roids, boys. Pretty soon you won't be able to move at all.' Ben stepped past the floundering bodies and into the entrance. In moments, he was mingling with the party crowd and heading towards an archway that led through to the inner courtyard. On a podium to one side, the Dixieland jazz ensemble was crowing happily away while couples danced. Waitresses dressed like Hugh Hefner playmates circulated, serving champagne from silver trays.

Ben walked into the middle of the courtyard, gaining a few odd glances from people noticing his informal attire. He collared the first fat fuck in a tux who dared to stare at him, and said loudly, 'I'm looking for Julius Brigman.'

The music faltered. The animated buzz of conversation dropped down several notches and the crowd edged away.

'I'm Brigman,' said a Texan drawl behind him. 'Who the hell are you?'

Ben turned to see a short man pushing his way towards him through the crowd. Brigman was about sixty-five, in a tailored smoking jacket that managed to contain his bulk elegantly. He had white slicked-back hair and a closely trimmed white beard, and there was a five-inch stump of a Havana clenched between his teeth. The effect was Old Southern Aristocracy. A latter-day Robert E. Lee.

'Someone who'd like to have a word in private,' Ben said, letting go of the other man, who quickly moved away, straightening his collar and muttering indignantly, 'That guy's nuts.'

Brigman's eyes bulged. He puffed cigar smoke in Ben's face. 'You've got one hell of a nerve, walking into my home and demanding to talk to me. You know who I am, son?'

'Maybe you'd rather have this conversation in front of all these people?' Ben said.

Brigman stared a moment longer, then he plucked the Havana from his mouth, rolled it between his fingers and smiled. 'Okay, you bought yourself exactly one minute. Come with me.'

The muttering crowd parted to let them through as Brigman led him down a corridor of archways and into the cool, plant-filled interior of his palace. 'In here,' he said, opening a door onto a plush salon.

There was a gasp from inside as a couple who'd strayed from the party straightened themselves up suddenly on a divan and looked round.

'Clarissa, honey, this gentleman and I have some business to discuss,' Brigman said.

Clarissa hitched up the strap of her dress and led her red-faced beau away by the hand, her high heels clicking on the marble. On her way out of the room she flicked a look at Ben and gave him a coy little smile.

Brigman shut the door behind her and turned to Ben. 'I don't believe I had the pleasure of being introduced to you, sir.'

'It doesn't matter who I am,' Ben said. 'What matters is what happened to my friend Nick Chapman.'

Brigman's cigar had gone out. He made a show of relighting it, puffed a great pall of smoke and said, 'Now, are we talking about the same Nick Chapman who didn't have the guts to face life, or the decency to check out alone someplace with a quart of Jack and a sixgun?'

Ben slipped his hand up to his right hip and drew the Highway Patrolman out from his waistband. 'Like this one?'

Brigman's eyes flicked to the revolver, but he didn't seem unduly disturbed by its presence. 'That supposed to scare me?'

'I have a problem,' Ben said. 'Because I don't believe my friend crashed his own aircraft. I think someone else is responsible for his death, and the deaths of all those people.'

'And you've come here looking for someone to pin it on,' Brigman said.

'You could make it easy for yourself,' Ben said. 'Tell me how you did it.'

'Should I call my attorney or the boys downstairs? I just have to click my fingers and they'll bust your head sure and good.'

'If you're talking about Abbot and Costello on the gate, I think you'll find they've already seen enough of me,' Ben said. 'As for the rest of the boys, you might want to call the hospital.'

Brigman stared at him, confused. 'What rest of them? I don't know what the hell you're talking about, son. None of my people are in hospital. Now, I need to attend to my guests, so if you don't mind . . .'

'That armchair looks comfortable,' Ben said, motioning with the gun. 'What is that, Louis XV?'

'Louis XVI,' Brigman said suspiciously.

'Why don't you take a seat on your nice little velvet throne there and tell me all about how you tried to snap up CIC last year?' Ben said. 'And then about how you decided that if you couldn't have it, you were going to screw it for good and then start setting up your own? What's the matter, Brigman, it's not enough to rule the waves, you wanted to rule the sky as well?'

Brigman stared incredulously for a moment, then burst out laughing. 'Oh boy,' he said, wiping tears from his face. 'So that's what this is all about. You have some balls, I'll give you that. Especially for an Englishman. You know, my great-great granddaddy was with the Continental Army under Washington in 1781, when we kicked your Brit asses at Yorktown.'

'Half Irish,' Ben said. 'Mine was with the 69th New York Infantry when we helped Lincoln whip the South a few years after.'

Brigman chuckled. 'All right. You know what, I like your style, son. You want to know about the offer I made Chapman? Sure, last year I'd've torched half the island to get hold of a hot tomato like CIC. But if you were a little better informed, my friend, you'd know things have kind of changed for me since then. I ain't buying any more, I'm selling. This place is the last piece of property I own on Grand Cayman, and it'll be sold in a week. I'm going back to Dallas and you' – motioning with the cigar – 'you just gatecrashed my farewell party.'

Ben said nothing.

Brigman smiled. 'You want to verify that with my attorney? Go ahead. He's right outside. Better yet, go talk to Doc

Rotella. He's the one who diagnosed me, right around Christmas time. Lucky if I see another.'

'Right,' Ben said.

'Oh, so you need proof? Step this way.' Brigman heaved himself up out of the Louis XVI chair and led Ben across the room to a gleaming door set into the walnut panelling. 'That look like a goddamn multi-gym to you?' he said, pushing the door open and waving his arm at the machine that took up a large chunk of the room next door.

Ben stared at the machine, all readouts and dials and tubes. Beside it was a chrome-framed hospital bed with crisp white sheets and a satin pillow, encircled by a rail with a curtain drawn to one side. Clustered around like a circle of wagons, six medical gurneys were loaded with surgical equipment and a huge array of drugs and medicines. The room looked like a private clinic.

'Hemodialysis,' Brigman said. 'Twice a day, an evil bitch of a nurse hooks me up to that infernal device and it sucks the shit out of this old carcass of mine. Not that it does me much damn good, after a lifetime pickling my kidneys in scotch and bourbon,' he added with a grunt.

Ben was lost for words. He suddenly felt like an idiot. A rash, dangerous, violent idiot who'd come storming into a dying man's home with a loaded weapon and a head full of wild ideas.

'Precious little point in stopping now,' Brigman said. He took another puff on his cigar, then plucked it out of his mouth and surveyed it tenderly. 'You're looking at a runaway train, son.' He grinned at Ben. 'Whatever life's left to me, I have every intention of enjoying it to the full. If I never make another dime again, I still have about two hundred fifty thousand bucks an hour to live on until I finally drop dead, and that's plenty good enough for me. You think I'd be interested in corporate takeovers right now, Mr . . .?'

'Hope,' Ben said. 'The name's Ben Hope.'

'Believe me, Mr Hope, I might have done a few things in my time I ain't too proud of. A guy who comes up from nothing, the way I did, doesn't make his billion without breaking a few arms. Hell, I can admit that now – what are they gonna do to me? But I ain't gonna be your whipping boy for whatever you think happened to your friend Chapman. I'd suggest you go look elsewhere. Anything I can do to help, you be sure to let me know.'

'I made a mistake,' Ben said. 'I apologise to you, Mr Brigman.'

Brigman slapped him on the shoulder. 'No hard feelings, son. I'm a tough old turkey and life's getting a mite short to hold a grudge. Maybe put that gun away, huh? Then how about you come outside with me and have a drink before you go.'

Chapter 16

It was after four in the morning by the time Ben got back to his hotel. The strong black instant coffee he made in his room was pretty bad, but it masked the stale taste of bourbon on his lips. It would take a good deal more to wash away the sting of guilt and defeat.

He stood on his balcony and watched the sunrise, then stripped off his clothes and stepped into the shower. Under the cool water he carefully peeled the dressing off his aching ribs and checked his wound. It was livid and inflamed, and there were spots of blood on the dressing that there shouldn't have been.

So much for R&R, he thought to himself. Something had got torn in there, but the stitches seemed to have held. He patted himself dry, dabbed antiseptic cream on the wound and put on a fresh dressing that he covered with a clean black shirt.

By eight-thirty, the sun was already hot and he was back in the car, cutting northwards up the Seven Mile Beach road towards CIC. He walked into Nick's old office without knocking and found Tamara sitting alone at the desk.

'You're up early,' she said.

'I'm up late. And you can forget about Julius T. Brigman.' He sat on the edge of the desk and told her what he'd found out.

Tamara leaned back in her chair and pursed her lips. 'It seemed to make such sense. Who sent those guys to beat you up?'

'Someone else,' Ben said.

'Where do we go from here?'

'Somewhere else,' Ben said.

'Will a cup of coffee make you more communicative?'

Ben shook his head. Gently so as not to yank his stitches any more, he reached into his back pocket for his whisky flask.

Tamara wrinkled her nose. 'Isn't it a little early in the morning for that?'

'Hair of the dog that bit me,' Ben said.

'You'll wind up like Brigman.'

He ignored her, unscrewed the little chrome cap and knocked back a slug.

'I was awake all night thinking,' she said. 'Maybe the Brigman connection *was* too obvious. I had another idea. What if there was some fault with the aircraft and the manufacturers tried to cover it up to save themselves a bunch of lawsuits? Someone with a history of depression would be an easy target to pin it on.'

Ben screwed the cap back on his flask and shook his head. 'They'd pin it on CIC maintenance personnel, neglectful servicing. And I don't think they'd be running around murdering their scapegoat's relatives. A lot easier just to call their insurers.'

'Then what?'

'Something else,' he said. He slid off the edge of the desk and started pacing up and down the office.

'Does it really help you to pace like a caged tiger?' Tamara asked him irritably.

A caged tiger was exactly what Ben felt like, but Tamara was right – pacing wasn't going to help. He stopped, looking around him for inspiration. His gaze locked on to the Escher print on the wall over the desk.

The angels, then the demons. It was impossible to see them both at the same time. When you focused away from one, the other came into view, creating a whole paradigm shift, an altered reality.

Sometimes it wasn't what was there – it was how you looked at it. You just needed to look with different eyes.

'We're approaching this thing from the wrong angle,' Ben murmured after a long pause.

'Tell me what you mean,' Tamara said. 'And don't say "another angle".'

'You have the passenger list on file?' he asked.

She tapped the screen in front of her.

'Let me take a look,' he said. 'And maybe I will have that coffee after all.'

Ben spent the next half hour studying the computer with such intensity that, watching over his shoulder, Tamara thought he might melt the screen. With the CIC files in one window and running web searches in another, he systematically checked each of the twelve passengers' names against local and international news reports, as well as whatever else he could dredge up from the internet.

He started with the four British nationals on the crash flight. Their profiles quickly came together. Colin and Sandra Hartnoll and their son Jamie had been on holiday from their home in Leeds: Colin Hartnoll had taught geography at a sixth-form college, Sandra had been a legal secretary, and Jamie had been taking a year off before University. The fourth

Brit was Gordon Love, a retired private dentist who'd emigrated to Little Cayman some years earlier and had been travelling to London to visit his daughter, Helen, and her husband, Clive.

Then there were the De Groots, a family of four from Amsterdam. According to online news sources Ruud De Groot was an ophthalmologist; his wife Ursula was a stay-at-home mother taking care of little Jan, 8, and Carice, 11.

Ben could see nothing here at all. He moved on to the next on his list. Monica Steinhart, 28, originally from Long Island, had been a freelance diving instructor based on Little Cayman. On July 23 she'd been travelling across to Grand Cayman to take a class of novices out to Stingray City off the north point.

The last three passengers to meet their deaths that day had been tourists from Tampa, Florida: Jim Duggan, 22, a postgrad college student and his sister Fay, 19, together with her twenty-year-old boyfriend Terry Bassini, who worked in his father's motorcycle customising business.

As far as Ben could see, all twelve had been just ordinary people, pursuing their ordinary lives. Whether it had been work or pleasure that had brought them together on board the doomed aircraft that day, there was nothing whatsoever to suggest anything more than just a horrible coincidence for all concerned.

'What do these figures here mean?' he asked Tamara, pointing at the six-digit numbers next to each name or group of names.

'Booking references,' she replied. 'Nick always believed in keeping the system simple and easy. When a customer makes a booking, we issue them with a number. All they have to do is show up, quoting it when they give their name, for the flight steward to check against the records. That way there's no hassle with issuing printed tickets. We also take a phone number and an address on the island, for security reasons. It all goes down together on our records.'

'Okay,' Ben murmured, and went on searching the screen.

'What are you looking for exactly?' she asked him.

'I don't know. But there's something we're missing here. I'm sure of it.' He reached for his coffee. It was cold but he took a slurp anyway. 'Tell me about the co-pilot, Brady.'

'Mark? What's to tell? He joined CIC just a few months after it started up. Before that, he was with a charter outfit in Nassau. He often rode co-pilot with Nick, sometimes the other way round.'

'What else?'

Tamara sighed. 'I think I told you already that he and Cindy – that's Cindy Masterton, the flight attendant – were going to be married in the Fall. Nick was going to be their best man. What are you shooting at?'

'Ghosts and shadows, so far.' Ben said. 'How many Trislanders does CIC have left? Two?'

'Just one flying. The other's grounded. Business is that bad.'

'Who are the crew?'

'Jack Burgess is the chief pilot, his co is Mort Clegg. Jo Sundermann is the flight attendant. They've all been with the company since the beginning. So have the flying school instructors, most of the office staff, even the nice old man who tends the grounds. CIC's like a little family, Ben. Nothing sinister or corrupt going on. No secrets.' She paused. 'Well, just the secret that you already know about.'

There was a soft knock at the door, and a man Ben hadn't seen before stepped nervously into the office. Mid-thirties or thereabouts, thin and weedy, balding with thick glasses and protruding front teeth. He had three ballpoint pens in the breast pocket of his shirt and was clutching a sheaf of papers to his chest.

Tamara said, 'Ben, this is Grant Singer, the company accountant. Grant, Ben was a good friend of Nick's.'

Singer gave Ben a handshake like a damp facecloth. 'I didn't mean to interrupt,' he said hesitantly. 'But I was just going through the bank records for the last month and there's a discrepancy here that I need to run by you.'

Tamara hesitated, then said, 'All right, I have a minute.' The accountant spread his sheaf of papers across the far side of the desk and began going through them with her.

Ben got up from the desk, walked aimlessly around the office, thought about a cigarette. His mind was swirling with thoughts and questions, and he was only half-aware of what Singer was saying in his insistent, whining voice.

'I don't see anything,' Tamara said.

'There on the statement printout,' Singer whined. 'The payment reference number. Now look on our own records. How come it's not there?'

'Ask Wendy. She does all the data entry.'

'I already did. She's no idea what happened here. Without that information, we can't refund the customer if he was booked on one of the cancelled flights.'

'It's only a few dollars, Grant,' Tamara said. 'Can't we deal with this some other time? I'm kind of in the middle of something here. Tell you what, you leave the papers with me and I'll go through them afterwards.'

'Only a few dollars,' the accountant muttered under his breath as he left the office. 'Sorry about that,' Tamara said when he'd gone. 'Grant's a valued member of the team but he gets a little anal sometimes. What's up?' she added, noticing Ben's expression of puzzlement.

'Can I have a look at those?' he asked, walking around the desk to examine the accounts paperwork.

'Why?'

'Just a feeling.'

'I shouldn't let you see confidential business documents,' Tamara said. 'But hey, you've already seen everything else, so why not?'

Ben was already studying the anomalous figures that Singer had underlined in ballpoint. The payment in question had been made on July 21, two days before the crash: the sum of eighty-eight Cayman Islands Dollars, paid by credit card by a Mr L. Moss. As Singer had pointed out, there was no mention of an L. Moss on CIC's own records. No payment, no payment reference, no phone, no address.

'What flight did this Moss book on?' Ben asked.

Tamara shrugged. 'Well, that's the whole point. There's no way we can tell that right now.'

'The information's lost?'

'It's not lost,' she said irritably. 'I'm sure it's just mislaid. Things are a little screwy at the moment, as you can imagine.'

'Does CIC often mislay booking data?'

'Of course not. Grant would have a heart attack.'

Ben was silent for a minute, then asked, 'When did flights start running again after the crash?'

'Jack and Mort went out again for the first time the day before yesterday,' Tamara said. 'They're out right now, as we speak. But we're still only firing on one cylinder. We've had to make a load of refunds, hundreds of customers either pissed off about losing their flights or scared to get on one of our planes. It's pretty dire.'

'But this L. Moss hasn't come forward for his refund?'

'There'd be a record of it if he had.'

'Then maybe Moss was on one of the flights before the crash?'

'Could have been anytime between the twenty-first and the twenty-third,' she said, nodding. 'Or else it could have been in the last couple of days.'

'Then even if his name and booking details somehow got accidentally wiped off the computer records, the flight steward would still have had a record of him boarding the plane.'

'Theoretically. Why are you asking all this?'

'Can you check?' Ben asked.

'I can try.' Tamara glanced at her watch. 'Jack and Mort will have landed on Little Cayman around now. I don't think they've got more than a couple of passengers. Let me see if I can call the flight attendant direct on her cell.' She put the desk phone on speaker and hit a speed dial button. 'Hi, Jo, got a moment? Need to confirm a boarding reference to see if we need to refund this person or not, but I can't find any record of it at this end. Customer's name is Moss, Mr L. Moss. If he did fly, it was sometime before we shut down, or sometime since we started up again.'

'L. Moss?' a woman's voice said over the speaker. 'Nope. Don't think so. Wouldn't be any of mine.'

'You sure you don't remember him?'

'Pretty sure. You know me.'

‘Okay, thanks, Jo.’ Tamara ended the call. ‘You know, he could still turn up,’ she said to Ben. ‘He might call anytime, yelling for his money back along with all the others.’

‘I can think of one reason why he wouldn’t do that,’ Ben said.

‘What reason?’

‘We could be looking at the crash flight’s thirteenth passenger.’

Chapter 17

Tamara stared at him. 'Moss couldn't have been on board,' she protested. 'They recovered all the bodies . . . except for Fay Duggan and the little Dutch boy.'

'In an ocean full of sharks and barracuda, that doesn't necessarily mean it wasn't there,' Ben said.

Tamara blanched and sat down heavily in the desk chair. 'But . . .' she began, then fell silent and bit her lip in agitation. 'The security video,' she said suddenly. 'That would tell us right away. Everyone boarding an inter-island flight gets filmed on surveillance camera at either end. Nick hated the idea, but the authorities insisted on it after 9/11. Not that anyone ever checks the footage.'

'Can we view it on here?' Ben said, pointing at the computer.

Tamara nodded. 'I can narrow it right down to the date and time.' While she was clicking keys, Ben got up and went over to the coffee machine for a fresh cup.

'Christ,' she said after a few moments.

He turned. 'Found it?'

'Hold on.' She clicked more keys. '*Shit*. I don't believe this.'

'What?'

'It's not here,' she said. 'It's not giving me anything.'

Ben stepped up behind her chair. 'Try the previous day.'

Tamara keyed in the date July 22 and hit Enter. Almost instantly, the video footage appeared onscreen: a high-resolution digital image of a line of passengers waiting to board. Most of them were wearing shorts and T-shirts, floppy hats, dark glasses, cameras on straps. A little girl was skipping up and down dragging a teddy by the leg.

Tamara stopped the playback. 'Let me try again,' she muttered, typing July 23 back in and stabbing the Enter key.

Nothing. Blackness.

She turned to Ben. 'It's been deleted,' she gasped.

'Who else has had access to the system?'

'Nobody.'

'Are you sure?'

Ben walked away from the desk, thinking furiously. In his mind's eye, he played back his memory of the pretty blonde who'd been arranging flowers in the CIC lobby the day before. He remembered the curious way she'd watched him leave.

Shortly after that, the black Chevy Blazer had seemed to pick up his trail. Almost as if it had been waiting for him. The same black car that might, just might, have picked Bob Drummond up from his place several days before and magicked him away somewhere.

'What about Jennifer?' Ben said.

Tamara looked taken aback. 'Jennifer Pritchard? The temp?'

'Where is she now?' he asked.

'She called in sick first thing this morning.'

'How long has she worked here?'

'Only since July 22. She came through an agency.'

'The day before the crash. CIC had been advertising a vacancy?'

Tamara nodded. 'Like I said, business had been picking up like crazy. She came with all the right paperwork, Ben. References, qualifications, the works. We knew all about her.'

Ben shook his head. 'You don't know anything about her. If you don't believe me, call her at home, right now.'

'Now? To say what?'

'I'll talk to her,' he said. 'Just make the call. Go ahead.'

Tamara got the number from the files and picked up the phone. She dialled. Waited a moment, then looked at Ben. 'There's no dial tone.'

'That's because the number doesn't exist,' Ben said. 'Call the agency. They'll tell you they never had a Jennifer Pritchard on their records.'

'This is insane,' Tamara said.

She checked. Ben had been right.

'You're never going to see her again,' he said. 'She was planted here to delete information from your system. Now she's gone.'

'But then why was she still here until yesterday?'

'Because of how suspicious it would've looked if she'd upped and vanished right afterwards,' Ben said. 'And because it takes a few days for a news story this big to die down to nothing. They might have been worried about somebody like me turning up asking questions. They needed someone to listen at doors, to call in the troops to check out anyone who might still be snooping around.'

'Who's *they?*'

'That's simple enough,' Ben said. 'The same people who don't want it known that the crash flight had a thirteenth passenger,' Ben said. 'Namely a Mr L. Moss.'

Tamara gaped at him. She shuddered. 'Oh, my God. What do we do?'

'First thing, you need to get off this island. It's dangerous for you here. Go and get your kids from your mother's place in Miami and take them on a holiday somewhere. Don't tell anyone where you're going. Okay?'

She hesitated, then nodded sullenly. 'Okay.'

'Call me when you get there. Don't use your regular phone, use the secret one you used for calling Nick.'

'What about you?' Tamara said, looking at him with big eyes.

'I need to borrow a couple more things from Dwight,' Ben said.

Chapter 18

The lawyer's fifty-foot motor yacht, the *Santa Clara*, was moored at Harbour House Marina a few miles from George Town, off North Sound Bay. Tamara had been quite happy to let Ben have the keys to her husband's pride and joy, and after returning to his hotel to grab a couple of hours' sleep and a shower, Ben made his way to Harbour House, strolled out along the jetty where scores of gleaming boats and yachts rocked gently on the swell, and climbed on board.

In the handsome wheelhouse, he quickly familiarised himself with the controls and set the GPS navigation system on a course for Little Cayman. The twin 500-horsepower engines fired up with a throaty burble. He slipped the moorings, the stern and bow thrusters pushed the boat away from its dock, and they were off.

Ben crossed the calm blue waters of North Sound at a steady fifteen knots cruising speed. His course took him through the main channel between the northern tip of the island and the jagged outcrop of Fisherman's Rock, after which he was in open sea. Once Grand Cayman had disappeared entirely over the southern horizon, Ben was able to let the motor yacht more or less steer herself. Now and then he sighted another vessel, mostly smaller boats, apart from the cruise liner that passed by, huge even at more than a mile off.

He'd had two main reasons for wanting to cross over to Little Cayman by sea rather than by air. The first was the advantage of being able to land wherever he wanted on the shores of the smaller island, free from the snooping eyes of anyone who might be watching his movements. The second was that the other items he'd borrowed from Dwight Martínez couldn't be so easily carried on board a public shuttle flight. The Highway Patrolman revolver was inside Ben's green canvas bag on the bunk in the main cabin, next to the semi-auto Remington home defence shotgun from the lawyer's gun cabinet. Dwight was turning out to be a handy supplier.

As to Ben's reasons for wanting to visit Little Cayman in the first place: he figured that just because the enigmatic Mr Moss had been conveniently deleted from CIC's computer files, it didn't mean that all trace of him could be erased from existence. If the guy had boarded the flight on Little Cayman, there'd be a trail, however obscure, leading back from there. All Ben had to do was find it.

For a long time, the *Santa Clara* burbled on alone across the empty sea. Only the slightest breeze ruffled Ben's hair as he stood at the deck rail, smoking a cigarette and gazing out across an endless expanse of the most vivid blue water he'd ever seen, so clear that shoals of colourful fish were visible now and then beyond the ripples from the *Santa Clara*'s hull: thousands of them, moving in one coordinated mass just a few feet below the surface.

Then a dark shape flitted up from the depths and the shoal of fish he was watching scattered in panic.

Tiger shark, all twelve or thirteen feet of him. Ben recognised the wedge-shaped head and dorsal stripes all too well from an uneventful but memorable encounter during joint underwater combat training with New Zealand SAS near Auckland a couple of years earlier. As he watched, the shark's fin split the water momentarily, disappeared below the surface; and with a flick of his tail he was gone.

Just a reminder not to trail one's fingers and toes in the lovely refreshing water.

After a few hours, the shores of Little Cayman came into view. As the *Santa Clara* motored towards a tranquil little cove, Ben reflected on how tiny the island seemed, a cockleshell surrounded by endless ocean. Little Cayman's highest point was just forty feet above sea level, but the strong likelihood of the entire place being swept clean away in the event of a Tsunami obviously hadn't been enough to dissuade the 175 or so permanent inhabitants that Ben's guidebook told him lived and worked there.

One of those was Maurice – or Maur*eece*, as the all-smiling, dreadlocked owner of the car hire place near the bay pronounced it. Maurice's speciality was banged-up old nails, and for thirty dollars he offered Ben a day's rental on a Toyota four-wheel-drive that looked as though it might have done service in the Iraqi desert at some stage of its very long life. No paperwork, and Maurice didn't take any notice of the object, wrapped in a blanket, that Ben had brought with him from the moored yacht and loaded into the back of the Toyota. Ben was liking the guy already.

'Visiting someone on the island?' Maurice asked with a beaming smile, pocketing Ben's cash.

'Old pal of mine lives here,' Ben said. 'We lost touch a while back, but I thought I'd drop by.'

'I know most folks on this island. What's his name?'

The list of what that L initial could stand for had been growing in Ben's head: Lionel, Louis, Lucien, Luther, Luke, Lloyd . . . 'We called him "Mossy" in the army. Mossy Moss,' he said, playing it safe.

Maurice reflected for a moment. 'Name don't ring no bells. You sure he lives here? Lot of people come and go.'

'Maybe he moved away,' Ben said. 'No worries. All I want to do is chill out for a while.'

'You sure come to the right place for that. Nearest thing to Paradise on earth.'

'That's good to hear,' Ben muttered to himself as he drove away in a cloud of dust.

On an island no more than ten miles long by one mile wide, it was only a short drive to the first of the hotels on Ben's list. There were just three on the island, which made his process of elimination a good bit easier.

His routine was the same in all of them: 'Hi, I'm looking for a friend of mine, Mr Moss. I think he might have checked out, and wondered if he'd maybe left a forwarding address?'

Three attempts, three blanks, and the day was wearing on. No Mr L. Moss appeared on any of the hotel registers. Once his list was exhausted, Ben climbed back in the beaten-up Toyota and decided to pay a visit to the Little Cayman airport. Maybe he'd find someone there with a memory to jog.

Or maybe that was just a desperate long shot.

At the end of a dusty road flanked by grass-roofed huts, open-air bars and beachside villas, Ben reached the island's only airfield. Now he could see what had made Nick's mini-squadron of Trislanders so perfect for their purpose. Few other commercial aircraft could have made use of the short runway, which was no more than a strip of patchy grass, burned into yellow stubble by the sun.

The airport complex looked more like an old-fashioned filling station. A prefabricated building served as a check-in lounge and waiting room. An adjoining lean-to housed an ancient fire engine that probably hadn't been driven in years. But what could have been a cheerful, laid-back environment was still clouded by the gloomy memory of the CIC air crash. A desultory queue of just seven passengers hung about in the check-in area waiting for the next shuttle flight. Which, the dour woman at the check-in desk informed Ben, was due in twenty minutes' time.

He was beginning to realise he had a lot to learn about the detective business. What had started out feeling like a rich source of potential information was already crumbling away to nothing, and one look at the woman's dull face told him there wasn't much point in probing her with discreet questions. Forget playing the reporter card.

Behind the check-in counter was a small office scattered with the usual computer terminals and screens. He wondered if Jennifer Pritchard, or whatever her real name was, had been able to hack into the Little Cayman end of the computer system and make the footage from the day of the crash disappear from here too.

She probably had.

But it was still worth checking out. Heading casually into the men's toilets, Ben closed himself in a cubicle. After a moment's pause for the sake of realism, he worked the flush. While the pipes were groaning and gushing, he quickly stepped up on the toilet lid, reached up to the grimy window overhead and undid the window catch, so that it would be easy to slip through from outside. That part would have to wait until after dark.

There was the whole rest of the day to kill first. Just half a mile from the airport Ben found a little bar called Claude's, parked the Toyota under some trees and wandered into the lazy atmosphere of the bar-room, where a few drinkers were sitting round playing cards and sweating in the heat. The radio was playing Stevie Ray Vaughan's cover version of 'Voodoo Chile'. The most active guys in the place were the two workmen who were busy mounting a large mirror on the wall behind the bar.

The barman was a chunky, fleshy white guy of around fifty, in a flowery shirt open halfway to the waist. He turned away from surveying the workmen and greeted Ben with a surly nod. 'I'm Claude. What can I get you?'

'Whisky.'

'Whisky it is. You want the regular or the expensive?'

'That one,' Ben said, spotting the half-full bottle of eighteen-year-old special cask strength Islay malt on the counter.

'The hard stuff,' Claude said, reaching for the bottle.

'Make it a double,' Ben said. He perched on a stool and laid a twenty dollar note on the bar. When Claude set the glass down in front of him, he drained it down in one gulp. Feeling better already, he lit a cigarette. The ashtray on the bar read 'Quint's shark fishing'.

'I'll have another double,' he said to Claude.

Claude looked at him, raised an eyebrow and picked up the bottle again. 'Go easy with this stuff,' he said as he poured it out. 'This ain't your normal whisky.'

'Helps me think,' Ben said.

'It goes to people's heads. Makes 'em crazy if they can't handle it.'

'First time I've heard of a barman telling people not to drink.'

Claude pulled a face. 'Yeah, well, the last time I had a customer start knocking down too much of this stuff, I ended up with three hundred bucks damage.' He pointed angrily at the new mirror that the workmen had almost finished mounting to the wall.

'I'll have to try not to smash anything,' Ben said, turning to his drink.

'Fucking prick,' Claude muttered.

Ben looked sharply up at him – then realised Claude was still complaining about his troublesome customer. He obviously hadn't got over it yet. 'Comes in here bawling everyone out, acting the big shot. Treats Raoul like shit. Then starts flashing cash in here like there's no tomorrow. No tomorrow. I like that one. That's funny.'

'You think so?' Ben said, thinking about carrying his drink over to one of the empty tables.

Claude grinned. 'Sure. Cause for him there really *was* no tomorrow. Raoul took him to the plane. You know, the plane that crashed?'

Now Ben was giving it his attention. 'Yeah, I get the part about the plane. But I don't get who Raoul is.'

'Cab driver. My brother in law. Anyway, this prick hires him to drive him to the airfield. On the way, tells him to stop here so he can tank himself up even more than he is already. Raoul says, he's not a fucking chauffeur. Guy throws a wad of dough at him. So Raoul waits for him in the car. Guy starts knocking back that same whisky you're drinking.

Pretty soon he's out of control with it. Carrying on about how he's flying to London or someplace and how he's gonna kick ass.' Claude made a dismissive gesture. 'Like I was interested. I just wanted this loudmouth sonofabitch out of my place, and I told him so. Now he's *really* pissed off. Me and Dave had to sling his ass out of the door, but not before he'd managed to throw his glass through my damn mirror.'

Claude turned and motioned towards its replacement above the bar. 'I liked that old mirror. Hung there more than fifteen years, and some asshole who can't hold his liquor goes and smashes it.' He pointed at Ben's glass. 'So all I'm saying is, mister, go easy on that stuff. You're still thirsty after this one, I'll pour you a beer. How's that?'

'I'll pass on the beer,' Ben said. 'Where can I find Raoul?'

Claude looked at him. 'What for?'

'I need a taxi ride,' Ben said.

Chapter 19

'Where to, mon?' Raoul drawled over his shoulder with a Jamaican lilt as Ben climbed in the back of the taxicab outside Claude's thirty minutes later. The Peugeot 504 made Ben's rental Toyota look showroom-new. Reggae thumped over the speakers and the tang of cannabis smoke was imbued into the worn-out fabric of the seats.

'How about a little scenic tour?' Ben said.

'Sure,' Raoul said, lurching away from Claude's. 'You wanna go right round the island? It ain't a big place.'

'Just as far as it takes for you to answer a few questions,' Ben said, tossing a thin wad of cash over the backrest of the front passenger seat. Raoul thumbed the money expertly with one hand as he drove, and flashed Ben a dazzling smile in the rear-view mirror. 'What you wanna know?'

'Tell me about the guy who smashed up Claude's place.'

'You a cop?' Raoul looked worried for a second, probably thinking about the pot he'd got stashed away in the glove compartment or somewhere. Ben knew that the Cayman laws on ganja-smoking were pretty Draconian.

'A cop's the last thing I am,' Ben told him. 'Relax. Talk to me about this guy you drove to the airport the day the plane went down.'

'A real rat's ass,' Raoul declared , launching enthusiastically into his story. 'He was already totally canned when I went to pick him up. By the time we got to Claude's, the guy'da picked a fight with Mike Tyson.'

'Why's that?'

'Because of what was on the radio,' Raoul said simply.

'He didn't like your music?' Ben said.

'No, mon. He didn't like the *news*.'

'The news?'

Raoul nodded. 'The news about London. You know, the terrorist thing? Bombs and shit? They were talking about the sisterfucker that did it. This guy, he suddenly goes crazy. Starts yelling at me: "Turn that crap off! Turn it off right now or you can kiss my ass for your money!" So I turned it off. Like I'm gonna lose my fare over what goes on in fuckin' London, right?'

'Claude says he got you to drop him off at the bar and wait for him. What happened next?'

'Drunk fuck. After they threw him out, he gets back in the taxi. I take him to meet the plane, like he wanted.'

'You saw him get on the plane?'

Raoul shrugged. 'Sure. He got on the motherfucking plane and it flew away. Then it crashed.' He shrugged again. 'Feel sorry for the rest of those folks. Not for Mister A-hole.'

'You wouldn't happen to know Mr A-hole's name?' Ben said.

Raoul waved towards the glove box. 'Guess it must be in my book,' he said.

'Another ten bucks in it for you if you let me see it,' Ben said.

'No problemo.' Raoul flipped open the glove box, battered about inside, yanked out a tattered and much-thumbed notepad and passed it back over his shoulder for Ben to examine. Raoul had his own special book-keeping system. Ben turned back a few pages, tracing his finger down the date entries scrawled in the grubby left-hand margin until he'd worked his way back to July 23.

And there it was: there in Raoul's chicken-scratch capitals, the name he was looking for.

'Moss,' Ben read out loud. Beside it was the name 'Palm Tree Lodge'.

'That's the guy,' Raoul said.

'This address. That's where you picked him up from?'

'Uh-huh. So what now, mon?'

Ben had a feeling he wouldn't be returning to the airfield that day. 'Scenic tour's over,' he said. 'Take me back to my car. Then you can show me the way to Palm Tree Lodge.'

Chapter 20

Palm Tree Lodge was one of a row of little white wooden houses scattered along a deserted stretch of beach. As Raoul's taxi disappeared into the distance, Ben climbed out of the Toyota and trudged across the soft white sand. Palms rustled overhead, shading him from the late afternoon sun as he walked up to the house. He climbed the three sandy steps to the veranda, knocked on the front door and waited for a response. There was none. After a couple more knocks, he crossed the shady veranda to the nearest window, and peered through.

The place looked empty. Chairs had been stacked up in a corner, as if cleaners had gone through the place. Ben headed back down the steps to the sand.

The next house along the beach was just about visible through the trees. As Ben approached he saw a dusty Renault Scenic parked outside, and a couple of kids' bicycles propped against the rail of the veranda. He could smell charcoal smoke and grilling sausages. Rounding the side of the property he caught sight of a twenty-something guy in colourful shorts, flip-flops and a Whitesnake T-shirt, tending to a spitting, flaming barbeque. In the background, two young children were diligently helping their mother set the picnic table.

The couple smiled amicably as Ben approached. He apologised for interrupting them, and asked if they knew whether the place next door was vacant – if it was, he told them, he'd be interested in renting it.

'Can't help you there,' the guy said, flipping a sausage away from the flames. 'We only got here this morning. But we got the number of the agency that rents them out. Babe, can you get the card from inside?'

Armed with the number, Ben thanked them and continued up the beach. He took out his phone as he walked. It was after six, but he hoped there might still be someone in the property agency office. Just as the answer-phone was about to kick in, someone picked up. 'Is that Sunshine Villas?' Ben said. 'I was interested in renting one of your properties. Palm Tree Lodge. Can you tell me if it's vacant?'

'Sorry, sir,' came the reply. 'That isn't one of ours. I believe it's let privately.'

'Would you know who I could contact about the place?'

'Afraid not, sir. But if it's a beach property you're interested in, we do have a whole selection of—'

Ben cut them off and put the phone back in his pocket. He walked on, following the curve of the beach. From beyond a thick stand of palms up ahead he could hear the offbeat sound of Afro-Cuban jazz drifting towards him on the breeze. As he passed by the palms he caught sight of a little open-air beach bar at the foot of a wooden jetty, shaded under a stripy awning. He headed across the white sand towards it.

Feeling thirsty and maybe influenced by the catchy Cuban rhythms, Ben ordered a daiquiri at the bar. The owner-manager, a cheerful black guy in a Fedora hat, was a pretty useful cocktail maker. White rum, lime juice, not too heavy on the sugar. Ben took his time over his drink, deep in thought. The breeze from the sea was freshening as late afternoon turned into early evening.

'Nice little place you have here,' he said when he went to get a refill.

'Pays my bills, you know?'

Ben pointed at the white wooden house in the distance. 'You wouldn't happen to know the guy who lives in Palm Tree Lodge over there, would you? Mr Moss?'

'Oh, you must mean Larry,' the barman laughed over the rattle of the cocktail shaker.

'Yeah, Larry,' Ben said, like he'd already known.

'You know him?'

'Sure, we grew up together in Ireland,' Ben said.

'Shit, I never would've taken Larry for an Irish guy. Sounded real English to me. You here on vacation, mister?'

Ben nodded. 'Thought I'd drop in on my old friend. But he's not at home.'

'That figures. Haven't seen him for a week or so. Must have gone, I reckon. Shame. He was one of my best customers the coupla months he was here. Always running out of booze, always needed ol' Cuban George to sell him a bottle. He was here just 'bout every day.'

'Did Larry mention anything about a trip to London?'

'Don't think he said nuthin' about that. We talked about sport mostly. Sometimes he didn't talk at all. But I sure do miss him.'

'Pity when you lose a good customer.'

'Oh, there'll be another,' Cuban George said, waving in the direction of Palm Tree Lodge. 'They come and go, you know? Sometimes one guy on his own. Sometimes two at a time. Mostly they keep themselves to themselves.' He raised an eyebrow meaningfully. 'Me, I don't ask. I got an open mind. Questions get a guy into a whole lot of trouble.'

'You got that right,' Ben said. 'So the place is empty right now?'

'I ain't seen nobody there for a couple of days. After Larry left, there was a few guys hanging around there. Coupla cars. Then nothing since.'

The place must have been totally cleaned out, Ben thought. 'Do you remember what day Larry left?' he asked.

'Wouldn't normally, but it was the day that plane went down, man. That's a day nobody round here's gonna forget in a hurry.' Cuban George shook his head mournfully, then suddenly frowned as a thought came to him. 'Say, you don't s'pose Larry was on that plane, do you?'

'I'm sure Larry's just fine,' Ben said. 'Do you know who owns the place? I'm looking to rent something myself. It'd suit me down to the ground.'

'No idea, man. Like I say, I never ask questions.'

As the sun went down, Ben sipped down his second daiquiri and went over what he knew so far. There couldn't be much doubt that Larry Moss had been the enigmatic thirteenth passenger on board the fatal CIC flight that day. It seemed that he'd been on his way to London: possibly intending to take a direct flight there from Owen Roberts on Grand Cayman, maybe via Havana, Mexico City or Miami. It didn't matter. What mattered was that someone hadn't wanted him to get there. And didn't want anyone else to know he'd ever boarded the plane.

That was where the facts ran out and the questions resumed: the whos and whys that, right now, were pretty unanswerable. Ben didn't like dead ends.

'Say hi to Larry for me if you see him,' Cuban George called as Ben walked away across the sand.

'I'll be sure to do that,' Ben muttered in reply. As he retraced his steps back down the beach, the glorious reds and golds of the sunset dipped over the sea and silhouetted the palm trees against the sky like something out of a picture postcard. The empty lodge was half-hidden in shadows by the time he got back there. Ben climbed the steps onto the porch, glanced left, glanced right, then kicked the door in with a *crump* of splintering wood.

The inside was pretty basic, almost Spartan: the walls bare, white-tiled floors throughout. The kitchen had a tiny table and a couple of plain wooden chairs. Microwave, two-ring stove, empty fridge, empty cupboards, bare work-tops. The two basic bedrooms were the same, showing no sign of recent habitation. There was fresh linen in the storage drawers under the beds, waiting for the next visitor to arrive – maybe weeks in the future, maybe longer. In the small living room, dust covers had been stretched over the single armchair and the sofa. The TV was unplugged from the wall. The bookshelf was empty, like the coffee table. No books, no magazines, no papers, no sign of Larry Moss to be seen anywhere.

First he'd never been on the plane. Now he'd never been here either.

Ben had the distinct feeling that Little Cayman's stock of potential leads had just dried up on him. Where to next?

If Moss had had a boat or access to one, he'd have used it to get off the island instead of jumping on a CIC Trislander. Which meant that in order to get here in the first place, he must have travelled via Grand Cayman: where lay Ben's only chance of picking up the trail again.

How exactly he intended to do that, and what he was even looking for, were things he could figure out on the seventy-five-mile journey back across the sea.

Chapter 21

Nightfall brought a rise in the wind, and the sea was choppy as Ben piloted the *Santa Clara* at a steady pace back towards Grand Cayman, lost in thought, only vaguely aware of the boat's motion under his feet.

Reckoning by the motor yacht's GPS, he'd crossed just over fifteen miles of sea from when he saw the lights reflected on the window next to him, and turned to see that there was another vessel tracking along the same course, about half a mile away across the black water. He stepped away from the wheel and walked out on deck, but it was too dark to see what kind of vessel it was. What was certain was that she was coming up fast in his wake, her navigation lights and spotlamps growing larger and brighter with every passing minute.

Returning to the wheelhouse, Ben steered a couple of points to starboard and opened up the throttle by a few revs. He glanced back at the *Santa Clara*'s foaming, curving wake, white against the dark waves as she peeled gently off her course. The spotlamps of the vessel behind were dazzling now as they drew closer. Behind their strong glare he could just about make out the boat's silhouette: a large motor launch, taller and wider than the *Santa Clara*. Maybe a seventy-footer, maybe bigger. And whoever was on board, it was clear from the way the launch was following his course that they were definitely interested in catching up with him.

Being followed at night by an unidentified pursuer wasn't something that made Ben feel easy. In some parts of the world, commercial and private shipping was still widely preyed upon by pirates – but he was pretty damned sure that the Cayman Islands weren't one of them. Who, then? Coastguard? Police? He didn't think so.

Ben gunned the throttle harder; the *Santa Clara*'s engine note climbed a notch in pitch as her propellers dug her stern deeper into the water, lifted her bows and sent her skipping across the waves.

The big launch kept cleaving through the water after him – Ben could see the bow wave breaking white against the dark hull as the vessel came relentlessly closer and closer. He accelerated to near full throttle and felt the *Santa Clara* respond, bouncing over the sea at a bracing twenty-five knots. Any other time, the sensation of speed would have been exhilarating, but the knowledge that he was being chased by a much larger, more powerful and certainly more numerously manned craft blunted his excitement somewhat. He considered his options: they were few. In open waters, there was nowhere to run to except straight ahead, in the hope that he could outrun his pursuers.

And that hope was already fading fast. The launch was in his wake now, just fifty yards behind and still overhauling him. The blaze of the spotlamps was casting deep shadows across the yacht's deck, so close he almost thought he could feel the white-hot halogen bulbs searing his back. He felt naked and hopelessly exposed in their glare.

Full throttle. The rev counter needle touched the red and kept climbing. The engine note was becoming a shrill howl and he knew he couldn't keep this up for long without risking damage.

He glanced back again. The launch was getting dangerously close, so close he could hear the heavy diesel rumble over the tortured note of the *Santa Clara*'s own engine and the crash of the waves on her sides.

Closer still – and for a couple of horrified moments Ben thought the launch's pilot meant to ram his stern, crushing the yacht's hull like an eggshell, running her down and sinking her – but then the launch veered hard to port and started cutting up alongside him, just a few feet of white water between the two vessels.

Ben was completely off course by now, but the only thing on his mind was evasion. He steered hard away from the launch, bracing himself against the wheelhouse bulkhead as the motor yacht tilted sharply into the turn and the starboard rail was engulfed in foaming water.

But it was going to take more than the *Santa Clara*'s agility to shake the launch off. It veered right after him, quickly drawing level again. Through the white spray Ben thought he could make out the figures of men on deck.

A dull report, and something flew across the water. Ben instantly knew what it was – a grappling iron, fired from a hand-held projectile launcher. The black four-clawed hook smashed into the side of the *Santa Clara*'s wheelhouse, sending splinters of glass flying. It bounced back and its curved claws raked the deck. Ben twisted the wheel as far as it would go to starboard, trying to widen the gap between himself and the launch in the hope that the grappling iron would fall back into the sea. The *Santa Clara* began to peel off at a sheer angle – then gave a violent judder as her course was checked.

Ben threw a glance out of the shattered wheelhouse window and saw that one of the hook's claws had gained a grip around his port rail, the steel cable anchoring it to the launch's deck shrieking taut.

Ripping down the fire axe that was fixed to the wheelhouse bulkhead, Ben left the boat to steer itself and raced out across the slippery, heaving deck. The wind tore at his hair and salt spray soaked him instantly. He swung the axe down hard on the end of the steel cable as it sawed against the *Santa Clara*'s side. And again. In two blows he'd severed half the strands of the cable.

But just as he was about to deliver a third, another grappling hook was fired from the deck of the launch. Ben didn't register until a fraction of a second too late that it was flying right at him. Before he could get out of the way, the heavy impact caught him on the arm and shoulder and sent him sprawling on his back, knocking the axe from his hand. The grappling hook burst through the remaining wheelhouse windows and entangled itself around the smashed framework.

By the time Ben had staggered back to his feet, the launch was reeling the *Santa Clara* in with its powerful winches. He ignored the pain in his side and the blood he could taste on his lips from the fall.

He was about to be boarded.

Chapter 22

The vessels touched with a thump as the winches drew them together. The launch pilot closed down his throttle, dragging the *Santa Clara* to a halt. Ben ran to the wheelhouse and activated the port bow thruster in an attempt to combat the pull of the winches. The narrowing gap of water between the hulls churned furiously, but he knew the little yacht was hopelessly outpowered. At any moment, the engines were going to stall or burn out.

Ben shut everything down. The *Santa Clara*'s bows settled in the water and she began to rock in the heavy swell, helplessly tethered to the launch's dark hull.

But Ben wasn't going to let himself be boarded just like that. Snatching a stubby Maglite torch and a roll of black waterproof repair tape from the equipment rack, he flew down the companionway from the wheelhouse and darted into the main cabin. He could hear and feel the grinding of the launch's side against the yacht's, and the yells of the launch crew as they prepared to leap across the gap between the two boats and take him by force.

He picked the Remington shotgun up from where he'd left it on his bunk earlier. Working feverishly fast, he tore off a two-foot length of tape and used it to attach the Maglite to the forend of the weapon, so that it pointed along and under the barrel. He twisted the head of the torch until its beam was focused tight and narrow. Rather cruder than a laser sight, but extremely effective for night work. At close range, whatever the light beam shone on could be blown apart quarter of a second later with a blast of 00-buckshot.

Ben worked the shotgun's bolt, feeding the first of the eight cartridges from the tube magazine into the breech. He slung the shotgun over his shoulder on its sling. Grabbed the Highway Patrolman revolver from his bag and stuffed it into the back of his jeans. Raced back up the companionway and burst out of the wheelhouse.

The lights of the launch were even more blinding at close range. Through the white glare he could see the shapes of men running across its deck.

And something else. The unmistakable glint of gunmetal under the spotlights, marking the contours of a weapon that Ben had seen so many countless times that even in near-total darkness it was as familiar to him as his own face in the mirror. His unexpected guests were carrying MP5-Ks. The K designation stood for Kurtz, German for short. The stubby compact 9mm machine carbines were the kind of weapon favoured by professional assault teams.

So much for the coastguard.

One of the boarding team leaped across. Then another. Ben felt the thud as they landed on the *Santa Clara*'s deck and scattered. One crouched behind the tender while another raced up the port side-deck, the two of them quickly joined by another three MP5-toting crew from the launch.

Ben ducked down around the side of the wheelhouse as he heard footsteps thudding towards him. He counted: one – two – three – *go*. Straightened up and twisted round to point the shotgun, turning on the bright white Maglite beam and shining it right in the guy's face.

Shoot or be shot. Ben dropped his aim a foot and squeezed the trigger without hesitation. His hearing disappeared in a wall of noise. The recoil of the heavy twelve-gauge load slammed the butt of the Remington hard against his right shoulder, sending a jet of pain through his side.

But it was worse for the other guy. The boarder took the blast in the chest and was lifted clean off his feet by the impact. His weapon flew out of his grip and splashed into the sea.

Before his man was even down, Ben was swivelling the Remington up and across. Another stabbing knife of pain through his ribs as he fired straight into the blinding glare of a spotlamp. Glass showered the deck of the launch. The spotlamp went dark. He was about to fire at another when he spotted a fleeting shape moving low along the deck beyond the wheelhouse. He chased the figure with the torch beam. The shotgun boomed and kicked – but in anticipation of the pain from the recoil he'd jerked the shot a little to the left, missing his mark and blowing a serrated bite out of the *Santa Clara*'s side.

The percussive rattle of fully automatic gunfire sounded from the deck of the launch. Ben threw himself backwards as bullets punched into fibreglass all around him. He rolled behind the cover of the buckled wheelhouse, wedged the Remington tightly against its corner and blasted off four rounds as fast as his finger could move, the shotgun's heavy boom drowning out the chatter of the MP5. There was a yell of pain from the launch and the splash of a body hitting the water.

Eight shots gone. Ben pressed himself tightly against the wheelhouse and started reloading the shotgun with spare cartridges from the ammo holder attached to the stock. He'd slid three rounds into the magazine when he heard the frantic commotion from the water. An instant later, a terrible bubbling wailing scream pierced the air.

The man who'd gone overboard let out another animal howl of terror as he tried frantically to reach the *Santa Clara*'s side and haul himself out of the water. His body jerked as something hit him hard under the surface. He opened his mouth to scream again, but before the sound could burst from his lungs, a powerful unseen force dragged him under.

For an instant the water boiled and turned red. The man's bloody head and shoulders erupted from the surface, propelled violently from below. A glimpse of white teeth and an expressionless black eye; then the tiger shark dragged him back down into the churning bloody foam and tore him apart like a terrier shaking a rat.

Ben hadn't been distracted for more than a second or two, but it was long enough for him to be taken by surprise as a dark shape flew down from the wheelhouse roof. It was the man he'd missed moments before, now leaping at him, knife in hand. With no time to finish loading the shotgun, Ben swung the weapon like a club and felt the whack of solid beechwood on human skull. The guy slumped senseless against the side of the wheelhouse. Ben kicked the fallen knife away.

'Major Hope?' said a voice from the shadows.

Ben whipped round, clutching the shotgun – but the pain in his side slowed his reaction time just a fraction of a second too long. There was a curious popping sound, and something hit him with a startling impact high up in the shoulder. His fingers lost their grip on the Remington and an uncontrollable wave of muscle tremors swiped his legs out from under him and sent him crashing to the deck. The sensation was like nothing he'd ever known before, filling his whole body with a terrible tingling agony. He struggled desperately to get up, but his limbs were gripped by spasms and wouldn't respond to the commands from his brain.

Through a haze Ben saw a tall, thin man walk across the deck towards him. He was holding a taser gun in his hand, the curly wires connected to the dart that was embedded in Ben's shoulder. With his other hand the man reached inside his jacket and flashed an ID card.

'Jack Brewster, MI6.' The voice seemed to echo from some indeterminate place a million miles away. 'I'm sorry you're being so uncooperative, Major.' Another man appeared at Brewster's side, holding a syringe.

Ben felt a sharp prick in his upper arm as the needle lanced deep into his flesh. He muttered something incomprehensible, then closed his eyes and went limp on the deck.

Chapter 23

Ben awoke with a gasp. His arm shot out to grab the fallen shotgun that his senses told him was just a couple of feet away across the deck.

But something was wrong. It wasn't the solid timbers of the *Santa Clara* under him, but the soft, dry fabric of a car seat. Shaking his head to clear his blurry vision, he looked up and dimly recognised the figure of Jack Brewster turning round to speak to him from the front passenger seat.

Only then did Ben register the presence of the other two men in the vehicle: the guy wedged up against him in the back, and the driver speeding the car along a dark road.

'Sorry about the tranquilliser,' Brewster said. 'Couldn't have you taking down any more of my men. The effects will wear off by the time we get you to the plane.'

'Where are you taking . . .' Ben managed to mumble before the drowsiness sucked him back under again. The next time he regained consciousness, he was being hauled out of the back of the car. Two men steadied him by the arms as they walked him across tarmac to a building. He felt himself being shoved through a door and made to sit at a bare table. The two men left the room and locked the door behind them.

It was inside that tiny, stark room that Ben's senses slowly returned over the next thirty minutes or so. By the time he heard the door being unlocked and the two men came back to collect him, he was fully alert and on his feet.

'I don't suppose it would do me any good to ask where we're going?' he said as they led him down a corridor.

No reply. One of the men pushed open a door and Ben found himself looking out across a stretch of taxiway at a sleek white Gulfstream jet.

'I forgot my passport,' Ben said, stepping out into the night air.

'Move,' said the other man.

The jet's passenger cabin was quite empty, and looked more like a long, narrow luxury conference room than the interior of an aircraft. The moment Ben was on board, his escorts disappeared. A smiling hostess offered him soft drinks, which he turned down, and motioned him towards one of the very few seats, which he grudgingly sat in. He'd given up asking where they were going.

Minutes later, the jet began its taxi towards the main runway. Ben felt the rush as the aircraft soared upwards, and watched the lights of Grand Cayman grow tiny in the porthole by his seat.

Once the plane had levelled off to cruising altitude, a curtain swished aside and Ben's old friend Jack Brewster appeared. 'You might like to follow me,' he said with a lopsided smirk. 'Someone wants to talk to you.'

Ben wondered whether he could grab Brewster by his belt and collar and pitch him head-first through a window without being sucked out himself as the jet depressurised.

Maybe later on. Right now, he was more interested in knowing what this was all about.

On the other side of the curtain sat a man at a table. He was older than Brewster, early fifties, with a hawk-like face and swept-back dark hair, receding and greying at the temples. On the table at his elbow was a closed file. Calm and smiling, he stood up as Brewster showed Ben inside the screened-off compartment.

'Leave us, Jack,' the man said to Brewster, who disappeared back through the curtain. 'You're a very capable man, Major Hope,' he said when they were alone. 'It's reassuring to know that you're on our side. Egerton Sinclair, MI6.' He offered his hand. Ben just looked at it.

Sinclair withdrew the hand, sighed and sat down at the table. 'I don't like to talk business on an empty stomach. One of the disadvantages of my profession is that I very often have to eat at the most unsociable hours, and therefore alone. Would you care to dine with me?'

Ben took the seat opposite him. 'I'm not hungry. Being hijacked in the middle of the night does funny things to my appetite.'

'If you're sure. You won't object if I carry on?'

'You won't object if I smoke,' Ben said, taking out his cigarettes. 'And get me a whisky. Single malt.'

The hostess reappeared with a trolley, and placed a selection of covered dishes on the table. 'Excellent,' Sinclair said, helping himself to chicken casserole and some sautéed potatoes. 'Some scotch for our guest,' he instructed the hostess, who departed without a word and returned a few moments later with a matching Waterford decanter and glass.

Sinclair smacked his lips after a gulp of wine. 'Excellent,' he repeated. 'Now, before we go any further, Major Hope, I must apologise for the very regrettable incident outside your hotel on Grand Cayman. An unfortunate slip that would have been entirely avoided if my subordinates had been properly informed as to who you were. In the event, rather more unfortunate for the men who were hired to go after you.' Sinclair grinned. 'I'm also sorry we had to be somewhat forceful with you this evening.'

'You have a piece of chicken between your teeth,' Ben said.

Sinclair's grin dropped and he wiped at his teeth with his napkin.

'Let's talk about Larry Moss,' Ben said. 'I imagine you know who he is. Or was.'

'Indeed I do, Major. Indeed I do.'

'Then perhaps you'd care to enlighten me,' Ben said. 'That *is* the reason I'm here, isn't it?'

Sinclair chewed thoughtfully on a mouthful of chicken, washed it down with another gulp of wine, then looked earnestly at Ben. 'The information I'm about to reveal to you is strictly classified.'

'I wouldn't have it any other way,' Ben said.

Sinclair opened the file next to him, slipped out a photograph and laid it down in front of Ben. It showed a nondescript-looking man in his early fifties or so. Chubby-faced, with thinning fair hair and the sallow complexion of someone who'd spent a few too many years living out of a suitcase, raided a few too many hotel mini-bars.

'Larry Moss was one of our agents,' Sinclair said. 'One of the top operatives within a special counter-terror unit whose official name needn't concern us at the minute. His work took him all over the world, under a variety of guises.'

'A spook,' Ben said.

'To put it bluntly,' Sinclair said. 'And Moss was one of our most valuable agents, until while posing as a photographer in Pakistan, ostensibly there to infiltrate a suspected terrorist network, the damn fool fell head over heels in love with a certain young lady by the name of Salima. He thought she was a nurse. Needless to say, she wasn't.' Sinclair reached inside his file again and flipped another glossy 6X4 print under Ben's nose. The Asian woman in the photo was thirty or thirty-two, black-haired and strikingly beautiful.

'Nice, isn't she?' Sinclair said. 'And extremely dangerous. Salima Chopra, born in Kashmir, later to become part of a fundamental Jihadist group called Al-Badr. Needless to say, whatever attentions she paid our man Moss were rather less genuine than he foolishly believed. She and her associates were onto him from the start.' Sinclair shook his head sadly. 'It's the age-old story. God knows what he thought she saw in him, but there you are. Male vanity, perhaps. But I won't bore you with the details. The facts are clear: after scoring a triumph with 9/11, the enemy were determined to press forward to expand their operations all over the world, hitting us randomly wherever we'd least expect it. For that they needed specialised expertise, and Larry Moss certainly had that. In his military days he'd spent eight years with 321 EOD.'

Ben nodded. 321 Explosive Ordnance Disposal had long been the most prestigious bomb disposal squadron of the British Army, and its most highly decorated unit.

'To be able to turn a man like Moss, with his vast knowledge of explosives and demolition, would represent a major coup for a terror group like Al-Badr,' Sinclair said. He sighed. 'And I'm afraid that's precisely what happened. How and when the switch took place, we don't quite know. But it did.

Moss vanished from our radar, to reappear some months later, apparently a fully fledged convert to the enemy cause. We believe it was thanks to information he divulged to Al-Badr that another of our key agents was taken in Islamabad, and found a week later in a basement, battered to death and half-eaten by rats. Did you want some ice with that scotch?'

'Keep talking,' Ben said.

'Moss was a significant danger to us. This was a man who could take a whiz round your local hardware superstore and fill up a shopping trolley in five minutes with enough assorted goodies to knock you up an improvised car bomb capable of taking down an embassy building.'

Ben could believe it. SAS trained its men to do much the same thing.

'Three weeks ago,' Sinclair went on, 'an Intelligence tip-off led to the acquisition of one of Salima Chopra's associates in Lahore. During interrogation he revealed the location of their safehouse, which was subsequently assaulted by a US Special Forces team. We captured the lot – Salima included. But no Moss. He'd vanished again. All we were able to extract from the lovely lady and her colleagues was that there was a new terror strike in the offing. Moss's own idea, apparently. An attack that would make the Selfridges bombing in June, the handiwork of one of Al-Badr's sister groups, look like a mere opening gambit.'

Sinclair paused for effect. His jaw tightened grimly. 'This would have been it, the attack everyone has been anticipating for almost two years. The next 9/11. We had every reason to believe that Larry Moss intended to detonate an explosive device in an airliner over London.'

Chapter 24

Ben had finished his cigarette. He stubbed the butt out on the rim of Sinclair's empty plate and said nothing. He could see where this was leading, and every muscle in his body was tense. His ribs hurt.

'The Cayman Islands offered Moss the perfect environment to tuck himself away and construct the bomb,' Sinclair said. 'A device concealable enough to fit in a case, yet powerful enough to rip a sizeable aircraft in two. If he'd managed to pull it off, Moss would have been the first white suicide bomber in history. However, his willingness to die for his cause might have had less to do with religious fanaticism, and more to do with the fact that he was a sick man. He'd been treated for cancer eighteen months earlier. We can surmise that, given his raging alcoholism, it may have come back with a vengeance. But whatever his motivation, we can't escape the fact that if he hadn't slipped up at almost the last minute, we'd never have even known it was him, or seen this coming.'

'The credit card payment to Cayman Islands Charter,' Ben said through clenched teeth.

'Exactly. Moss had likely been operating on cash given to him by his associates. When the money ran out at just the wrong moment, he used his own credit card to book his flight off Little Cayman.'

'So Moss couldn't be allowed to reach Owen Roberts Airport. Is that what you're going to tell me next?'

Sinclair looked shocked. 'Good Lord, if you're suggesting that we had something to do with—'

'It had crossed my mind.'

Sinclair's face darkened. 'Absolutely never, on *any* account, would we have sanctioned such a thing,' he said emphatically. 'We were in position to arrest Moss immediately on landing at Owen Roberts. But he must have been drinking, or he must have made some terrible mistake. We only know that, somehow, the bomb detonated on board the CIC Trislander.'

Ben swallowed the last of the whisky in his glass and poured some more. His heart was beating hard and he could feel that the colour had drained from his face. He made an effort to control the tremor of rage in his voice. 'One of your dogs slips its leash. You're scared he's going to do something terrible. After all, you should know what he's capable of. I can understand that.' He paused. 'What I can't understand is how you people could justify pinning the blame on a former British soldier who risked his neck and almost lost his mind defending his country.'

Sinclair sighed. 'Of course. And believe me, I feel terrible about it.'

'You look as if you do,' Ben said. 'Sitting there with sauce on your chin and a bellyful of nice Cabernet Sauvignon.'

'What choice did we have?' Sinclair protested. 'The public couldn't be allowed to find out that one of our own agents had gone rogue, and that it was only sheer luck that he didn't succeed in bringing down an airliner over London. Imagine the bloody riot there'd have been. We had a matter of hours, *minutes*, to come up with a plausible, watertight cover story.

It was tragically unfortunate that Chapman happened to be the pilot on that flight, but his past record and history of severe depression provided us with an opportunity we simply couldn't afford to miss. The man was already dead. There was no bringing him back.'

'So you decided to destroy his reputation forever,' Ben said. 'You had antidepressants planted in his home. You faked the air traffic control radio recording and paid off Bob Drummond's gambling debts to make him keep his mouth shut and disappear, and then you concocted a phoney shrink to verify the suicide theory.'

'Disinformation is a key part of the department's work.'

'I can think of another word to describe it.'

'In this business, we're sometimes forced to make unpleasant decisions,' Sinclair said.

'I've heard that line before.'

'It doesn't mean we don't bitterly regret the collateral damage those decisions sometimes cause. The harm to a man's good name. The appalling psychological effect on his family. We were extremely distressed when we heard that Chapman's daughter had walked out in front of a car. Believe me, we do not take these matters lightly.'

Ben didn't say anything for a long time. 'So what now?' he asked eventually.

Sinclair spread his hands. 'Well, naturally, if you were a normal everyday member of the public, we would never have taken you into our confidence like this.'

'No, you'd probably have left me for the sharks,' Ben said.

Sinclair ignored the comment. 'Given who you are, and the fact that as one of Her Majesty's armed forces you're bound by a raft of non-disclosure agreements . . .'

'I keep my mouth shut about this.'

Sinclair nodded. 'We'll make it worth your while, I can assure you. You'll be well looked after.'

'I can hardly wait,' Ben said.

'We know we can trust you, Major.' Sinclair looked at his watch. 'My, how the time has flown. We'll be arriving in London in a few more hours. I'd suggest you get some rest.'

Chapter 25

Thin drizzle was slanting out of a leaden early afternoon sky as Ben stepped out onto the tarmac at Heathrow's private jet terminal. 'God, this is bloody awful,' Sinclair muttered at his side, putting up an umbrella.

Entering a country unofficially wasn't a new experience for Ben. He'd done it all over the world – but even so, the speed with which they breezed through the cursory check-in made him raise an eyebrow. No questions were asked, no passports were needed. A pair of serious-faced men in dark suits joined them, one speaking frequently on a radio, the other remaining silent and sticking very close to Ben. Ben didn't let it bother him.

When they were through, Jack Brewster handed Ben the leather jacket and green army bag they'd recovered from the *Santa Clara*, gave him a wry smile and walked away, motioning for the two dark-suited men to follow and leaving him alone with Sinclair.

'Now,' Sinclair said with a twinkle. 'I have a surprise for you.' He led Ben across an empty VIP lounge, punched a security code to open a door marked STRICTLY NO UNAUTHORISED ENTRY, and up a short corridor to a set of fire doors. 'Here we are,' Sinclair said with a flourish, pushing through the panic bar and swinging the doors open onto a covered forecourt at the rear of the building.

The row of parked cars outside made Ben raise his eyebrows a second time:

A Porsche 911 Turbo; an Aston Martin DB7; a Ferrari Maranello; a Bentley Arnage; a TVR Tuscan S, all lined up like something out of a millionaire's fantasy.

'Your choice, Major,' Sinclair said, beaming. 'If you decide you don't like the one you picked, you can swap it for another. Just say the word.'

'That one,' Ben said, and pointed out the tomato-red Ferrari.

'That would have been my choice too.' Sinclair rattled a set of keys and tossed them through the air to Ben. 'Didn't I tell you we'd look after you? And here's a little something extra,' he added, holding up a credit card. 'Now these we don't give out to just anybody. Special expense account. Everything on the house, so to speak. Our little way of expressing our appreciation. I hope you'll use it to enjoy the remainder of your convalescence.'

'You bet I will.' Ben snatched the card from him, climbed into the cockpit of the Ferrari and fired it up. The engine thundered like a twenty-one gun salute. Sinclair grinned a toothy grin, leaned down at the window and was about to say something – but his words were drowned out and he jumped back as smoke poured from the spinning tyres and the Ferrari took off.

Jack Brewster's goons opened up a gate. Ben roared through and stepped on the gas. Slashing through the traffic, the Ferrari covered the fifteen miles into central London in a ridiculously short time. The V12 was just getting nicely warmed up as Ben screeched to a halt outside the Ritz in Piccadilly, walked up to the desk and asked for a suite. 'The biggest you have.'

Minutes later, Sinclair's expense account was down £3,800 and Ben's sole, decidedly non-designer, piece of luggage was being taken up to the split-level grandeur of the Royal Suite. Ben's next act was to call up room service and have the kitchen run him up an extremely sumptuous, very late lunch, at an exorbitant premium he was more than happy to pay. The bottle of wine he ordered to go with it cost more than a full tank of fuel for his Ferrari. While he was on the phone he arranged for a hotel lackey to run across the street to Davidoff of St James's, the cigar merchants, to fetch him a box of Cohiba Esplendidos. He'd been in town less than an hour, and already Sinclair's expense account was taking a hell of a battering.

After eating his mid-afternoon lunch at the head of the table in his own private dining room overlooking Green Park – antique crystal, finest porcelain and silverware – Ben retreated to a master bedroom that would have made Marie Antoinette blush, flopped on the giant bed and lit up a cigar. When he'd smoked it to the stub he napped for almost three hours, then showered and changed into the last clean clothes that were stuffed in the bottom of his canvas bag.

By now it was after seven-thirty, and the drizzle had cleared into a fresh, pleasant evening. Ben called back down to room service and ordered a limo for the evening. 'The biggest and most expensive one you can get me,' he specified. When the sixteen-seater glittering white stretch monstrosity arrived, complete with mirror ceiling, giant TV and fully stocked bar, Ben had the chauffeur drive him a decadently short distance down St James's Street to a noisy bar where a single measure of ordinary whisky cost over six pounds.

Several hours passed before he finally emerged, now accompanied by two cackling, high-heeled young women whose names he was fairly sure were Linzi and Bev. He had the waiting chauffeur ferry them back along St James's Street to the Ritz, where he escorted his noisy companions into the hotel bar, fired up another Cohiba Esplendido and ordered three bottles of the most expensive champagne they had, at £500 a throw.

Sometime after dawn the following morning, a dishevelled, puffy-eyed Linzi and Bev came teetering uncertainly out of the lift and exited the revolving doors of the Ritz lobby under the disapproving gaze of the front desk attendant. Three hours later, after a lavish breakfast, Ben checked out, climbed into the Ferrari and blasted out of London.

He headed north-west on the M40 towards his old stamping-ground, Oxford. Leaving the motorway, he skirted the city and took the familiar A40 west. Cheltenham; Gloucester; Ross-on-Wye; over the Welsh border towards Abergavenny: the road grew emptier and the countryside greener the closer he got to his destination. He stopped off in Brecon to buy some provisions at the local Co-op with his own money, as well as a hefty piece of roasting beef from Mr Evans the butcher.

He was back at the cottage by midday. The grass in the front garden was an inch longer than he'd last seen it, but nothing else had changed by the banks of the burbling River Usk: the events of the wider world didn't make much of an impact out here.

Shifting down a couple of gears after his time in London, Ben spent most of the afternoon strolling by the river and exploring the surrounding countryside. Beyond the fence at the rear of the cottage, a broad meadow filled with wild flowers led to a stretch of woodland, untouched for centuries and thick with ancient gnarly sycamores, beech and laurel. Ben wandered in there a while, sometimes straying off the public footpath that wound for half a mile through the trees, crouching now and again among the ferns to examine the tracks of foxes and badgers on the moist, leafy forest floor. Twice he met a fellow walker on the footpath, smiled and wished them a good afternoon.

Back at the cottage, a light meal; then he settled in a comfortable armchair by the living room window with a glass or two of Laphroaig and the book he'd been slowly working his way through before leaving for the Caymans, Aristotle's *The Nicomachean Ethics*. Just after eleven o'clock, he laid the book down, rubbed his eyes and climbed the stairs to his bedroom for an early night. Seven minutes later, his bedroom light went out and the cottage fell into pitch darkness.

Not long afterwards, they came for him.

Chapter 26

The team leader waited until the cottage windows had been dark long enough for the target to fall asleep. He carried out a final, silently efficient check of his machine carbine and then muttered the command into his throat mike that his two colleagues hidden among the trees had been waiting to hear.

Without the least sound, not the crack of a twig, the three-man team stalked out into the long grass of the meadow and converged on the cottage, virtually invisible in their black assault vests and ski-masks. The infra-red night vision goggles they wore were the latest military issue. They were professionals at what they did, were thoroughly familiar with the nature of the target and would take no chances – but the observation of his behaviour since re-entering the country showed that he was entirely off his guard. The three men had been watching him earlier that day from leafy cover as he wandered unsuspecting through the woods, and they might have picked him off if it hadn't been for the proximity of the public footpath and the risk of being seen.

Now, under cover of night, was the time.

The team reached the fence at the rear of the cottage and silently climbed over into the garden. Without a word they split up: the team leader skirted around the stone wall to the front entrance; the second man crept towards the back door, and the third leaped, cat-like, up the grassy bank at the side of the house, where the corner of the thatched roof dipped low enough to jump across to. He landed lightly on the thatch, signalled to his colleagues and made his way stealthily towards the point their careful planning had told them was directly above the target's bedroom.

The back door snicked open with the barest sound and a black-clad figure stepped inside the hallway. The assassin paused a moment, listening keenly for any sound. The cottage was utterly silent. Through his goggles, its pitch-dark interior was lit up green and as clear as day.

He sniffed the air, caught the scent of tobacco smoke and whisky, and smiled to himself. They'd all seen the way the target had been knocking back the booze that evening. He'd be fast asleep now, dead to the world.

The assassin padded across the hallway towards the stairs. Raised the toe of his combat boot to the bottom tread, gently testing it with his weight in case it creaked. But the staircase was solid oak, soundly built, and didn't make a squeak. He climbed the next step, then the next. Halfway up the staircase, he could see the bedroom door through the turned oak banister rails. He silently pushed off the safety catch of his weapon with a gloved finger. Climbed another step.

And crashed downwards feet-first through the staircase, letting out a grunt of shock and surprise as it gave way under him with a crackling rending of wood. He dropped his weapon and lashed out with both hands to save himself, but there was nothing he could do to avoid falling straight down into the space below. He landed heavily on his back, whacking his head against something solid. He was in an under-stairs cupboard.

The door was bolted from the outside.

And the cupboard was filled with coils of barbed wire.

*

At the sounds of confusion and panic in his radio earpiece, the second assassin reacted instantly without trying to guess what had happened to his team member. That could wait until later. Slashing through the last layer of thatch with his combat dagger he kicked his way through to the inside. His boots connected with the thick bedroom ceiling beam. He leaped quickly down to the floor, and before the huddled shape of the man under the bedclothes ten feet away had had any chance to awaken or make a move, he'd emptied half a magazine of 9mm copper-jacketed bullets into it, filling the bedroom with the muffled chatter of the machine carbine and the tinkle of spent shell cases on the bare floorboards. The bullets ripped through the thin sheets. Blood spattered green in the night-vision goggles.

The sleeper hadn't stood a chance. *Maybe if the silly bastard had laid off the whisky*, the killer thought as he stepped quickly through the drifting gunsmoke and whisked away the bedcovers to put a final three-shot burst through Ben Hope's brain.

In the half-second that it took him to register the large, bleeding lump of raw beef and the cushions arranged under the sheets to look like the shape of a man, the wardrobe door had burst open behind him. The assassin whirled around – straight into the chopping double-handed swing of the cricket bat. It caught him across the temple with a resounding crunch of well-seasoned willow against bone, and he hit the floor in a coma.

Ben tossed the bat away and snatched up the fallen MP5. With a hard stamp of his heel he crushed the assassin's windpipe. Then he was across the room, through the bedroom door and out on the dark landing. He flew down the stairs, avoiding the gaping hole where he'd half-sawn through the oak treads earlier that day.

The man trapped inside the under-stairs cupboard was struggling furiously and crying out in panic. Ben unbolted the door and shone the tactical light beam of the MP5 in the guy's face. He was helplessly enmeshed in the barbed wire, thrashing to get free, the black combat clothing lacerated and bloody. Ben flipped the select-fire switch on his weapon to single shots. Put two in the man's chest and a third between his eyes. The thrashing stopped instantly.

Ben turned away.

If he'd done so a fraction of a second later, he'd have been dead. A line of bullet holes punched through the cupboard door right next to him. Ben felt the sting of splinters and a jarring bullet strike that knocked the machine carbine out of his hand and sent it spinning to the floor.

No time to go after it. Gunfire ripped a line of holes in the wall after him as he dived across the hallway and crashed through into the living room. The third shooter had come in via the front door and now gave chase, flame bursting from the muzzle of his gun. He had the advantage of being able to see almost perfectly in the near-total darkness, but Ben was more familiar with the terrain. Darting into the kitchen he kicked over the sturdy table. Antique pine, knotty and age-hardened and more than two inches thick: Ben hurled himself behind it and felt the high-speed hammering impacts churning up the tabletop as the shooter released another flurry of full-auto fire.

Then, suddenly, the room fell silent – the gunman's weapon had shot itself empty. Ben didn't intend to give him time to drop his spent magazine and slam in another from his belt pouch. He leaped out from behind the pockmarked table, reached down to his belt and drew out the slim carving knife he'd taken upstairs earlier that day and hidden in the wardrobe. When you knew you were expecting these kinds of visitors, you wanted to be as prepared as possible. His right hand was tingling violently from where the bullet had impacted against his weapon's trigger guard, but he could flex his fingers and he knew he hadn't been hurt.

That could change at any moment, though.

The shooter slung the empty gun behind him and ripped his combat dagger from his leg sheath. The two of them squared up to one other. All Ben could see was a moving patch of deeper black against the darkness of the room.

The black shape suddenly rushed towards him. Ben sensed, rather than saw, the blade come slashing towards his throat, and dodged it at the last instant. The killer advanced two steps, waving his blade this way and that. Ben retreated.

But now Ben had manoeuvred himself into exactly the position he wanted – right beside the double light switch on the wall. He flipped both switches on together.

The sudden glare of light made the assassin's night-vision goggles wash out and rendered him temporarily blind. Ben darted in, aiming the knife at the gap between the ski-mask and the bullet-proof, stab-proof vest he knew the guy would be wearing under his clothes. The assassin managed to tear off his goggles just in time to evade Ben's thrust and counter with one of his own. The blades clashed. A brief furious exchange of strikes and blocks, and they backed off. Blood dripped from the assassin's forearm, but not a lot of blood.

The two men circled one another under the glare of the lights, each trying to anticipate the other's next move. In a knife fight, cold steel against soft skin and flesh, there was no margin for error. Even a non-lethal cut to a major body part could produce enough of a sudden shock response to incapacitate you for a few critical moments. Then it was all over very quickly.

Ben readied himself. The assassin's blade came flashing towards him.

Chapter 27

Knightsbridge, London

The pulsating buzz of the phone on the bedside table dragged Egerton Sinclair up from the depths of a dream that was instantly forgotten as he sat up in bed, fumbling for the lamp. He cursed at the time on the bedside clock.

Sinclair carried three mobiles, and he kept them all close by at all times, whether he was at home in Surrey with his wife or here at the luxury apartment he used when he'd been working late or wanted to entertain a lady friend. Only one person in the world could be calling on the phone that was ringing at this moment. And if it was ringing, that meant there'd been complications. His heart began to beat strongly as he answered the call.

'We got him,' said the familiar voice on the other end. 'It's done.'

The wave of relief Sinclair felt quickly gave way to irritation. 'Then proceed according to plan. What are you calling me for at three in the bloody morning?'

A pause. Then: 'Ah, we have a problem.'

Sinclair kicked his legs out from under the sheet and perched on the edge of the bed, waiting for more.

'Hope wasn't working alone,' the voice said.

That didn't make any sense. 'So deal with it,' Sinclair told him. 'Fast.'

'Can't deal with it. I need to meet you.'

Sinclair trusted his associate, based on a catalogue of jobs that had always gone without a hitch in the past, however sensitive or complex. The man's edgy tone told him that something was definitely amiss – and it wasn't the kind of matter they could chat about over the phone, no matter how secure the line. Sinclair cupped his forehead in his hand and screwed his eyes shut. 'Are Ellis and Nash with you?' he asked.

'Ellis and Nash are down,' the associate replied.

Sinclair sprang up from the bed. 'Roger that. The usual rendezvous point. Can you make it there in thirty minutes?'

'Copy.'

Sinclair threw on his clothes and rushed out of the apartment. Three floors below in the private car park, he climbed into his Jaguar Sovereign and took off with a nervous screech of tyres.

Twenty-seven minutes later, Sinclair rolled the Jag to a halt under the arches of a crumbling Victorian bridge in a seedy district mainly frequented by crack dealers, well away from the eye of security cameras that haunted most of London. It was nearly quarter to four in the morning and he felt sick with fatigue and tension as he stepped out of the car and approached the black Audi A8 that was parked a few yards away under the gloom of the arch. His right hand was in his coat pocket, clutching the compact CZ 9mm pistol.

He hardly even sensed the movement behind him before he was being slammed into the rough brickwork of the archway and felt the muzzle of a gun pressing into the base of his neck. A hand dived inside his coat pocket and tore the CZ from his grip.

'Hope!'

'I'd crack your skull with this,' Ben said, grinding the muzzle of the MP5 harder into Sinclair's neck, 'but it'd mean having to drag you to the car myself. Get walking.' He grabbed the MI6 agent by the collar and shoved him roughly towards the assassins' Audi.

'Where are we going?'

'Somewhere nice and peaceful where we can have another of our little chats.' Ben opened the car boot and motioned at the occupant already inside.

'I think you two know each other.'

Sinclair stared at the trussed, gagged, struggling hit team leader. The man's ski mask was crusted with blood from where Ben had smashed his nose before kicking the knife out of his hand. Some hired assassins were too valuable to have combat daggers stuck in them.

'I told him I'd let him live if he delivered you to me,' Ben said. 'He was pretty quick to agree. You can argue about it on the way. In, please.'

'You've got to be joking,' Sinclair blustered. 'I'm not—' But before he could finish, Ben had bundled him into the boot with the other one and slammed the lid down on them.

The Audi felt heavy at the back as Ben took off with his cargo.

Chapter 28

In the dead of night it didn't take much over forty minutes to cut north-eastwards across the city to the wilds of Epping Forest. Ben steered off the main road onto a rough earth track that wound deep into the woods, and bumped and lurched over ruts for another mile and a half before he eventually stopped the car and killed the engine and lights. He climbed out into the moonlight that streamed down through the dark branches, and popped open the Audi's boot. Sinclair peered out, looking ashen and more than just a little jostled about.

Ben jerked his thumb. 'End of the line.' He kept the CZ pointed at the agent's head as he scrambled out, then shoved him roughly against the side of the car.

'You know you have no chance of getting away with this, don't you?' the MI6 agent muttered, his eyes glued to the pistol in Ben's hand.

'Maybe,' Ben said. 'Getting away with things is your department, after all.' Keeping the gun trained on Sinclair, he reached into the car boot. The trussed-up team leader was grunting and straining against his bonds. Ben ignored him and hauled out the shovel he'd brought from Brecon.

'I don't know what you're talking about,' Sinclair said.

Ben turned to face him. 'You don't know me, Sinclair. You just thought you did. I hope you all enjoyed the show.'

'We had a deal. You agreed to go away.'

'Linzi and Bev – were they on MI6's payroll too? By the way, I wouldn't have touched them with yours.'

'You're insane, Hope.'

'You don't know the half of it,' Ben said. 'But one thing I'm not is a fucking idiot. I never believed a word of your bullshit. I knew I could expect a little visit from your wet team the moment I got back to Brecon. I saw them even before they saw me. They left a trail like a rhinoceros.'

'You have to believe me,' Sinclair burst out. 'Whoever was sent to kill you, it's got nothing to do with us. I've never seen that man in my life before.'

'That's fine – then we don't need him,' Ben said. He pointed the CZ towards the open boot of the car and shot the team leader twice in the chest and once in the head. The gunshots shattered the stillness of the forest.

'Why did you do that?' Sinclair raged. 'You said you'd let him live!'

'I didn't say for how long,' Ben said. 'Lie to me again and you'll wish it had been you. Now, let's go for a walk.' He prodded Sinclair with the shovel.

An owl hooted somewhere among the trees as Ben marched the MI6 agent deeper into the forest.

'You're up Shit Creek without a paddle, Hope,' Sinclair muttered darkly.

'And you're in the middle of six thousand acres of woodland,' Ben told him. 'That's plenty enough room for a man to disappear. Nobody's going to hear you cry for help, so you'd better tell me the truth this time.'

'I've already told you the truth, you stupid bugger.'

'Like the part about the bomb capable of taking down a full-size airliner that went off inside a Trislander without blowing it into dust?'

'But that's what happened,' Sinclair protested. 'You must have seen the footage of the wreckage. It was completely destroyed.'

'Yes, it was,' Ben said. 'But not until a few moments after Nick Chapman had managed to crash-land it in the sea. He had time to call his daughter before he died. His call to her is the reason she was murdered.'

Sinclair stalled mid-stride and glanced back at Ben over his shoulder with a startled look that said very clearly, 'How did you know that?'

'I saw it happen,' Ben replied to his unspoken question. 'I'm sure you read the witness statement. Oscar Gillespie?'

'That was *you?*' Sinclair's eyes flashed in the darkness.

'Just one or two things I left out of it,' Ben said. 'For example, the fact that before she was killed, Hilary let me hear Nick's last message to her. It doesn't quite fit with your account, Sinclair. So I've decided to be generous and let you have another go in case you remember things differently this time. You can stop there.' They were deep among the trees, a long way from the car. 'Now, get talking or get digging.'

'What the hell do you mean, digging?'

Ben lobbed the shovel on the ground, still pointing the pistol at Sinclair's head. 'What do you think I brought this along for, to make mud pies?'

'You can't do this.'

'More and more people are opting for an ecological burial, Sinclair. You'd be doing your bit for the environment.'

'If you're going to kill me anyway, why should I talk to you?'

'I'm not going to kill you, Sinclair. I'm just going to bury you alive and let nature take its course. Unless you tell me everything, right now.'

'And if I do? You'll let me go? No tricks?'

'That depends on how convincing you are.'

'All right. All right. I'll tell you. There was some truth in what I said before. Larry Moss *was* one of our agents. And the CIC plane did go down because of him. But . . .'

'I'm listening.'

'But I lied about Moss making explosives. It was information that he was taking with him to London, nothing else.'

'What information?'

'Oh, Jesus . . .'

'What information?' Ben said again.

'It has to do with what happened in June,' Sinclair admitted. 'The Selfridges bombing.'

Ben frowned. 'Moss had information about the Selfridges bombing? Information for who? You mean his terrorist girlfriend and her gang carried it out?'

'You really have no idea, do you?'

'Nor have you. About what I'll do if you don't explain yourself pretty damn quick,' Ben said.

'There *was* no connection between Larry Moss and Al-Badr,' Sinclair said. It wasn't Muslim terrorists who blew up the ground floor of Selfridges in June.'

'Then who did?'

'We did,' Sinclair said.

Chapter 29

Ben said nothing. He couldn't speak.

'Now you know what nobody was meant to know,' Sinclair said.

Realising that the pistol had wavered way off its aim, Ben readjusted his grip and tried to focus his mind. 'You're telling me that the British government – that MI6 – set off a bomb *in the middle of its own capital city?*'

Sinclair shook his head. 'Not MI6. They wouldn't have a clue about that. That's something else I lied about. I don't really work for them.'

Ben thumped him roughly across the face with the pistol, beating him to the ground. 'Then who *do* you work for? Talk fast, Sinclair.'

Sinclair got to his knees and wiped the blood from his cheek. 'Tartarus,' he mumbled, then let out a hysterical laugh. 'There. I've said it. Now I'm completely fucked. Done for.'

Many years before, in a life that felt more like someone else's than his own, Ben had studied Theology at Oxford. It hadn't lasted long, before he'd gone his own way and ended up enlisting in the army. But he still remembered a few things from those days. Tartarus was from classical mythology, and also figured in the Bible's Book of Enoch: Tartarus, the dark, shady underworld, domain of wicked, fallen angels. 'Explain,' he said to Sinclair.

'Tartarus is a black ops arm of British Secret Intelligence,' Sinclair said. 'A department within a department. A ghost. Not even the Chief of MI6 knows about it, let alone the Prime Minister.'

'What kind of black ops, Sinclair?' Ben asked in a hard tone.

The agent looked up at him. 'Put simply, Tartarus stages incidents designed to be perceived by the public as acts of terrorism. Most of its international operations are low-grade exercises, not intended to produce casualties or significant damage, but to impact the media by scapegoating extremist terror groups – generally Muslim groups – and propelling them into the public eye. The unexploded car bombs that are always discovered by police just in time. The suitcase left in the train station that turns out to be full of Semtex. That kind of thing.'

'A fake terrorist organisation?' Ben muttered, dazed. He felt as if he were in a dream.

'It's not always entirely faked,' Sinclair said. 'And it's not that there are no real terrorists out there. It's not us setting off pipe bombs in Belfast or Londonderry. We leave the small potatoes to the handful of tin-pot fanatics scattered here and there throughout the world. But sometimes, when a real, existing terror group lacks the means or the funding to orchestrate effective attacks, which they very often do, Tartarus facilitates their ability to carry them out – either by infiltrating the group with trained agents who can pose as allies, or by making use of cultivated assets. It goes without saying that the daft buggers who blow themselves up in street markets in Iraq and Pakistan are only pawns in the game. They're either drugged-up deadbeats who don't realise what's going on, or dedicated fanatics who don't have the slightest inkling of who's behind the scenes.'

Ben said nothing. He hadn't the words.

Sinclair went on. 'In other cases, the groups blamed for terrorist acts never really existed. We only want the public to *think* they do. And to keep the illusion real, every so often the need arises to stage something more spectacular than a bomb scare at a racecourse or a few token casualties at a bus station in some place the British public neither know nor care about. Sometimes, it's necessary to make it feel that bit more real and close to home, to make people sit up and take notice. The Selfridges bombing certainly did that.'

'Why?' Ben said. 'Why?'

'Why exaggerate the terrorist threat? Why fabricate an enemy? For the same reason it was in the CIA's interest to perpetuate the myth of Soviet might during the Cold War. National security. Them and us. Keeping our flag waving and our state intact. It's simple, and it's been going on for centuries.'

Ben's teeth ground together so hard he could taste blood in his mouth. He had the pistol aimed right between Sinclair's eyes and every nerve in his body was telling him to squeeze the trigger. He'd fought and risked his life for this government. Now here was this man telling him that the country's rulers were capable of inflicting this kind of atrocity on its own people. Ben felt sick. 'And so Larry Moss was your trigger man,' he said. 'Is that what you're going to tell me?'

'No. Larry Moss spent thirteen years helping to engineer and carry out Tartarus missions across Europe, Asia and the Middle East. He was the best. But he had nothing to do with the London bombing. In fact, that's the whole point. Moss really did go rogue on us.'

Ben listened numbly as Sinclair described Moss's fall from grace. While cultivating contacts in Karachi, the Tartarus agent had fallen ill with a severe fever that had landed him in hospital for two weeks. There he'd met and befriended a Pakistani nurse called Salima – the beautiful young woman whose picture Ben had been shown on the flight from Grand Cayman to London. Sinclair was positive that nothing had happened between her and Moss, although there was a possibility that he'd developed a strong romantic attachment.

On his release from hospital, Moss had continued with his mission, which had culminated some weeks later in the very successful and well-publicised bombing of a nightclub in downtown Karachi. But when the names of the forty-seven dead were released, Moss had seen that his Salima's name was on the list.

'It was the first time he'd ever known one of his victims,' Sinclair said. 'And it had a profound effect on him that none of us understood at the time. It was only some weeks later, when Moss was summoned to the private Tartarus committee briefing where the planned London operation was revealed for the first time, that he snapped. It all came pouring out – his guilt over Salima's death, how it had changed him, how he'd started praying to God for forgiveness and all that.'

'You mean he'd suddenly grown a conscience,' Ben said.

'By the time the operation was ready to roll, Moss had been deemed unfit for a job of that scale and been removed from duty. We relocated him to a Tartarus safe house on Little Cayman, in the hope that he'd dry out and come to his senses. It was felt that he could still be a valuable operative, in a diminished role. But unknown to us, while he was on Little Cayman, Moss was plotting to blow the whistle on Tartarus. We intercepted a call to one Simon Shelton, a reporter for *The Independent*. Thankfully, Moss held back all the details over the phone, only saying that he could offer Shelton the biggest scoop of his life, a story that would bring down the government and change the world forever. He and Moss arranged to meet for coffee at Paddington Station on the afternoon of July 24. Far too public a place for any kind of intervention. Moss was going to tell him everything, *everything*. Preventing that rendezvous from taking place was given top priority. We were in a state of absolute emergency.' Sinclair paused uncomfortably. 'And so, the moment we learned that Moss was getting on the CIC flight off Little Cayman, the order was given.'

'The order.'

Sinclair nodded. 'On July 23, two Harrier Gr7s were deployed from a Royal Navy Invincible-class aircraft carrier stationed on Caribbean Patrol duty, ostensibly as part of the ongoing task of protecting the Virgin Islands, Montserrat and other British dependencies from drug traffickers. Their real mission was to intercept and destroy the CIC Trislander. The pilots and their superiors were given the same information as you: namely, that a known terrorist on board was threatening a strike against a major target.' Sinclair paused, glancing nervously at Ben. 'There was no warning shot fired. The first rocket blew away the Trislander's tail. The pilot somehow managed to belly-flop the plane down on the sea without it breaking up, and it grounded on the reef. The Harriers destroyed it outright on the second pass.'

Ben could visualise the horror of the reality behind Sinclair's matter-of-fact account. The terrorised screams of the passengers and their children. The flames, the smoke, the wail of the plane as it plummeted towards the sea. Nick's desperate determination to get his passengers down safely, overlaid by his sure knowledge that nobody on board was intended to survive the unthinkable attack. Even in that moment, with the certainty of death just moments away, he'd remained as much in control as humanly possible; and, when most men would have been thinking only of themselves, he'd thought to call his daughter to say goodbye.

'And when Nick's phone was retrieved from the scene of the wreck,' Ben said, 'you found the message he'd left Hilary and had her killed too.'

'You make it sound so personal,' Sinclair snapped. '*I* didn't have her killed. It's just politics. We couldn't have known what Chapman had told his daughter until we had hold of her phone. The message might have ruined everything. And we couldn't just steal the damn thing from her handbag – if she knew anything at all, it had to be silenced. As it turned out, we needn't have worried about the bloody message. It would never have stood up in court. But, as you know, you can't always predict these things.'

Right now, Ben was predicting how many blows from the blunt edge of the shovel it would take to separate Sinclair's head from his shoulders. 'You could have had a bullet put in Moss's head while he was still tucked away on Little Cayman. Nobody would have even known. Instead you ordered the deaths of sixteen innocent people.'

Sinclair shook his head vehemently. 'Too many people had already come into contact with Moss. If he'd suddenly turned up dead, washed up on a beach with his head blown off, who knows what might have come out? That he was a former secret service agent? That would have been sloppy. Tartarus doesn't *do* sloppy. This way, we could make him disappear completely. It was a perfect opportunity. Until you came along.'

'Who's Jennifer Pritchard?'

'That's not her real name. She's one of ours.'

'And you planted her at CIC to erase all trace of Moss getting on the plane.'

Sinclair nodded.

'And Shelton?'

'Eliminated the day afterwards. Carbon Monoxide poisoning. A leaky appliance at his flat in Hammersmith.' Sinclair shrugged. 'It happens all the time.'

'Another perfect opportunity,' Ben said. He was eyeing the agent closely.

Because something was happening.

When Sinclair had begun his forced confession a few minutes earlier, he'd been pale and shaking with terror. Now, a peculiar change had come over him. He was saying too much, too openly, and too confidently. The fear in his eyes had diminished, gradually returning to the same confident sparkle from when Ben had first met him. 'Perfect opportunities are what Tartarus specialises in exploiting, Major,' he said with a chuckle. 'And though you may not realise it, there's one developing even as we speak. Its outcome, needless to say, not so favourable for you.'

'Have you discovered a sense of humour, Sinclair? Forgotten the situation you're in?'

'You don't quite grasp what you're dealing with, old chap. There you are, thinking that you've brought me to this deserted spot where you could press the truth out of me and get rid of me. Whereas in fact it's *I* who allowed *you* to bring me to the perfect location for us to dispose of you.' Sinclair laughed. 'As you said yourself, six thousand acres is plenty enough room for a man to disappear.'

From somewhere among the trees a twig snapped, Ben looked sharply round to see a dark shadow step out of the forest. And a second. And a third. In moments, he was surrounded by armed men.

'I did tell you that Tartarus doesn't do sloppy,' Sinclair said with a smile. 'All our agents are trained to use code to indicate when they're under duress. Briggs back there told me a lot more on the phone than you imagined. "Ellis and Nash are down?" There *are* no Ellis and Nash. While I've been keeping you talking all this time, our people have been moving into position, using the GPS tracking device from that Audi you so cleverly decided to borrow from my men. Now, I'm afraid you're in rather more trouble than you're ever going to get out of.'

'Drop the weapon – down on your knees!' commanded a voice as more armed men came stalking out of the forest, approaching from all sides.

Ben sighed and tossed the gun. But if he was going to get shot, he didn't want the last thing he saw to be the cheesy grin plastered across Sinclair's face.

'Fuck it,' he said. And before anyone could react, the shovel was off the ground and spinning through the air. Its blade caught Sinclair in the mouth. Teeth and blood flew. Sinclair let out a crazed howl and staggered back, cupping his hand over his ruined lips.

'Something to remember me by,' Ben said.

Spitting gouts of blood, Sinclair snatched up his fallen CZ and aimed it at Ben. There was the same wild look in his eyes as there'd been in those of the Iraqi gunman in Basra who'd put the rifle bullet through Ben's ribs. Sinclair's finger tightened on the trigger and his bloody mouth opened in triumph. There was nowhere for Ben to hide.

The shot cracked loudly in the still night air.

Chapter 30

Ben staggered back a step and felt his knees go weak at the sound of the gunshot – but there was no impact, no nerve-jangling sensory alarm as the body registered extreme damage.

Blood spurted from Sinclair's open mouth. His knees buckled under him, and with a last look of pained confusion he collapsed on his face on the forest floor.

Ben looked down at Sinclair's corpse and raised his hands as the black-clad gunmen surrounded him, weapons trained on him from all sides. Suddenly they parted to make way for a grizzled, heavyset man in his late sixties, wearing a grey suit and holding a pistol.

Now Ben realised who'd shot Sinclair. The man gazed unemotionally at the body. 'Idiot,' he grated in a deep, throaty voice, then turned his impassive, strangely pale eyes towards Ben. 'I beg you not to compel us to use any further force, Major Hope. There's been quite enough violence tonight already, don't you think?'

Ben didn't reply. The man snapped his fingers and two gunmen stepped up to seize Ben's arms.

'I can walk by myself,' Ben said. At a nod from the man in the suit, they let him go. With two guns in his back they guided him through the trees, lighting the way with powerful flashlights, to where a pair of identical black Range Rovers and a plain, unmarked panel van were parked by the Audi. One gunman opened the back door of the van, another motioned for Ben to get inside. Before the van door was slammed shut, closing him in total darkness, Ben caught a glimpse of the man in the suit climbing awkwardly into the passenger seat of the lead Range Rover.

Instants later, the vehicles took off. Ben sat on the hard inner wheel-arch of the van and braced himself as it bounced over the rutted forest track. After a while they hit smooth road and the bouncing settled to a steady thrumming roar that went on for the best part of an hour before Ben felt the van turn sharply, as if passing through an entrance. He heard men's voices and the rattle of metal gates.

The van rolled to a halt. The back doors opened, and the light of dawn flooded inside. More guns pointing at him. A harsh order to get out.

Ben stepped down to the cracked, weedy concrete, flexed his stiff legs and looked around him in the early morning haze. The two Range Rovers and the Audi were parked a few yards away, already empty, hot metal ticking as it cooled. Judging by the journey time, he estimated they'd travelled about thirty or forty miles from the northeast edge of London to somewhere rural and secluded – Buckinghamshire, maybe, or Cambridgeshire. Wherever the place was, there was no mistaking the high wire security perimeter, iron gates and neglected-looking prefab buildings of a disused military base.

Ben was hustled indoors by his captors. In a large, neon-lit, otherwise completely empty room with no windows, the man in the suit was sitting on a wooden chair waiting for him. He peered over his spectacles as Ben was shown inside. The door locked, closing them in alone together.

Under the hard glare of the strip-lights, the heavyset old man looked even older. Deep lines creased his brow, and there were grey pouches under his eyes. It seemed to take him an effort to breathe. He gazed at Ben with those pale, unemotional eyes and spoke in his gravelly voice: 'Major, my name is one you won't have heard. I am Hayden Roth.'

'The head of Tartarus,' Ben said.

Roth nodded. 'I gather that Egerton Sinclair told you a certain amount about our organisation.'

'Is it true?'

'I felt there was no more reason for duplicity. Sinclair's instructions were that, if you survived the little initiation test we set for you – and I was confident that you would pass with distinction – he was to reveal to you the truth about the nature of Tartarus.'

'Then that makes you a murderer, Roth.'

No flicker of emotion showed in the man's eyes. 'None of us is immaculate. You included, Major. As you have aptly demonstrated, you're a highly efficient killing machine. One who happens to serve precisely the same masters as I do. We're all part of the same hypocrisy.'

'That's where you're wrong. I don't belong to your world.'

'Dear boy, if you knew how naive you sound. The orders that dispatch men like you all across the world to risk their lives and end those of others may come directly from our elected representatives in Whitehall, but not even they are aware of the larger picture. As a matter of fact, they are kept largely and deliberately ignorant.' Roth gave a chuckle that was as empty and humourless as his expression. 'I know what you're thinking. But it would be pointless to begin debating with me about democracy. If you were in my position, you would understand that democracy, party politics, the electoral process, are no more than a piece of theatre put on to appease the people, to make them believe they hold some power over the course of things. And I'm sure that even some of our worthy elected politicians share that same delusion. The fact is, Benedict – I may call you Benedict? – that irrespective of whichever political party the voters have chosen ostensibly to rule them, the real executive power rests in the hands of individuals whose names and faces are never made public, nor ever will be.'

'You mean people like you?'

Roth waved a hand. 'Oh, I'm really just a tiny, inconsequential component of the machine. As, indeed, is Tartarus itself. We fulfil a vital function, to be sure – but of necessity and for reasons you can now appreciate, we remain obscure to all but a precious few.'

Ben just stared at him.

'I understand this must all come as something of a shock to you, Benedict. You're a soldier, and as such your world is a relatively simple one. Your only responsibility is to the men under you. You don't have a country to run. You don't make the bigger decisions, so there's never any need for men of your station – should I say your current station – to see the bigger picture. Believe me, if you could, you'd understand only too clearly that the things we do, unpleasant as they may be, are a necessary evil that serve the greater good.'

'Like blowing up half of Oxford Street,' Ben said. 'Innocent men, women and children. Your own people. You're a piece of terrorist shit.'

Roth shook his head. 'I'm afraid that for all his efficacy as an agent, Egerton Sinclair had only the crudest understanding of Tartarus' mission. We are not terrorists. Lord, no. Our role isn't to create fear for its own sake, but to generate peace and social contentment among our citizenry. Exactly like small children, left to their own devices they will simply run out of control, ignoring their parents' wishes, all notion of discipline gone by the board. However, it takes only a little fright, a little pervading menace, to make them come running back to clutch at their mother's skirts for protection. At this moment, the people of London are more bound together by a sense of unity, and more responsive to the control of the state, than they have been in years. They object far less than they might have to the massive police presence on the streets, or to the cameras watching them from every rooftop. For the most part, they're deeply grateful for what freedom they're granted. Crime rates have dropped; the voter turnout at the next election will soar. The police haven't had to deal with a single peace demonstration since the day of the attack. Why? Only thanks to our humble efforts.'

Roth waved his arm. 'But I ramble on. Let's get to the point. I mentioned earlier that I had instructed Sinclair to tell you the truth about the department; what I didn't feel the need to make him aware of were my reasons for doing so. You see, I particularly wanted to have this discussion with you, Benedict. I've thoroughly examined your files. Your Oxford background caught my eye. You attended the same college as I did, as it happens.'

'If you've read the file, you know that I dropped out.'

Roth chuckled. 'No matter. The old boy network still counts for something in this decaying empire of ours. And believe me, it's considerably harder to get out than it is to get in. Then there's your superlative military record. Men of your qualities don't drop into our lap as often as I'd like. I believe you would find a career with us highly stimulating. Indeed, I think you'd be ideal material. In many ways, you remind me of myself, at your age.'

'That's nasty,' Ben said.

'I understand your reaction,' Roth said, peering at Ben with an almost affectionate expression. 'In some small way, I even admire it. But stop. Think. We could make you a very handsome proposition.'

'You want me to replace the likes of Moss and Sinclair.'

'You're still in your prime, Benedict. But the peak of physical fitness doesn't last forever. Sadly, I speak from experience. I was once a soldier much like yourself. The successive phases of a man's career must inevitably yield to change. Where do you see yourself, five, ten, twenty years in the future? Still running around the world's war zones, dodging bullets?' Roth motioned at Ben's injured side. 'Indeed, not always dodging them. There are other avenues for a man like you to pursue; and I think you ought to consider them carefully and wisely.'

'You can have my answer right now, if you like.'

'Don't be rash, my boy. *Ira furor brevis est*. That's Latin for . . .'

'I know what it means,' Ben cut in. '"Anger is a brief madness".'

'More educated than you give yourself credit for, Benedict. And it would indeed be madness to reject my offer out of mere rage. For your own sake, why don't you take the time to cool off and reflect objectively about your potential future with us?' Roth jutted out his chin thoughtfully. 'However, I'm afraid I can't just allow you to wander about freely during that time, pending an assurance of your commitment. It seems to me that our safehouse on Little Cayman would be the perfect relaxing environment in which to decide on your future.'

'Palm Tree Lodge?'

'Of course – you're already familiar with it. That's settled, then. I shall arrange for the Gulfstream to fly you to Grand Cayman in the next few hours. From there, my men will accompany you aboard a CIC charter flight to Little Cayman.'

'That's a bit rich,' Ben said. 'Or maybe there'll really be a bomb on board this time?'

'Nothing could be further from the truth. Rest assured you'll be well looked after. At a prearranged time on the third day, you'll be picked up by boat and brought out for an interview with the Tartarus committee to discuss the terms of your recruitment. This will take place aboard my sailing yacht, the *Hydra*. I have a personal fondness for the Caymans and often travel there to attend to financial matters.'

'I don't suppose Tartarus uses internet banking,' Ben said.

'There will be some further conditions,' Roth went on gravely. 'The phone with which you'll be issued will allow you to communicate with me, and me only. I shall require you to wear an electronic tag preventing you from venturing more than one hundred yards from the safehouse. Any attempt to tamper with it, or to make contact with anyone on the outside, will entail severe repercussions. Do you understand me?'

'Would you understand me if I told you to stick your offer up your arse, Roth? Or shall I do it for you?'

Roth looked at him. The pale eyes seemed to burn for an instant. 'That's a rambling old place you have there in

Galway. Your housekeeper, Winifred – perhaps a trifle elderly to be looking after it on her own? You must be aware of the potential risks. Accidents can happen. Fires are terribly common in these older properties. It doesn't bear thinking about, does it?'

Ben said nothing.

'Three days,' Roth said.

Chapter 31

Ben wished they'd picked a more companionable pair of goons to chaperone him. The older, less talkative one was rangy and bandy-legged, with a face pitted and bombed by acne and eyes as dead as a fish on a slab. The other had breath that smelled as if he chewed a pound of raw garlic a day. To make matters worse, he insisted on sticking to Ben's side the entire time and was sitting next to him as the Gulfstream sped from Heathrow to Grand Cayman. Ben was barely allowed to visit the bathroom on his own. When he came out, the guy was standing there, breathing all over the corridor, waiting to escort him back to his seat.

'What took you so long?' the goon said.

'I was looking to see if they had any industrial strength mouthwash for you, Stinker,' Ben told him. 'Maybe gargle with some neat bleach? That'll do the trick.'

Hemmed into the window seat, he dozed for most of the remainder of the flight. After landing at Grand Cayman just after midday, local time, his escorts steered him away from passport control and walked him under the hot sun to a waiting car that blasted northwards up the Seven Mile Beach road to Cayman Islands Charter.

Neither goon seemed to appreciate the irony as the three of them boarded the CIC Trislander. Ben noticed there were only five other passengers – business didn't seem to be picking up yet, and the gaunt face of the flight attendant, a dark-haired woman he took to be Jo Sundermann, showed that Nick's former colleagues were still stunned by his loss.

Sitting beside Stinker in the cramped interior of the Trislander was a good deal worse than aboard the spacious Gulfstream. Bandy Legs folded himself into the seat behind. Ben could feel the dead eyes boring into the back of his head. After the short, bumpy takeoff the flight attendant came round serving drinks. Ben had nothing. Stinker bought a can of Coke, cracked it open and took the occasional slurp.

Fifteen minutes into the flight, ignoring Stinker's astonished stare, Ben casually slipped his last pack of Jordanian cigarettes from his pocket, took one out and lit up with a flourish. He smiled and leaned back in his seat, watching the smoke drift across the aircraft's narrow interior.

A few feet away, a woman passenger twitched her nose, gave a little splutter and elbowed her husband as if to say '*do* something'. The guy twisted around in his seat and his face turned purple. 'Hey. Maybe you can't read, pal? There's no smoking in here.'

'It's for the smell,' Ben said, pointing at Stinker. 'I couldn't stand it any longer.'

A small argument broke out, during which Ben kept on puffing at the cigarette. It wasn't long before the flight attendant emerged from the front of the plane. 'Sir, I need you to put that out right now,' she said sternly. 'We operate a strict no smoking policy on board.'

'You're right. I'm sorry, everyone.' Ben dropped the half-smoked cigarette with a sizzle into Stinker's Coke can. 'And it's about time I gave up this disgusting habit. Would you mind disposing of these for me, please, Miss?' He held out the cigarette packet. The flight attendant looked at it hesitantly, glanced back at Ben and then took it from his hand. 'I'll do that for you, sir.'

'I appreciate it. The name's Ben.'

'That's enough chatting up the women,' Stinker muttered when she'd headed back towards the front of the plane. 'Don't pull any more capers like that again.'

'I won't,' Ben said. 'That's a promise.'

On arrival at Little Cayman airport, Ben's chaperones led him to another car. 'I guess you know the way,' he said as they bundled him into the back seat. They did, and a few minutes later he was making his second visit to Palm Tree Lodge. The damage to the door had been repaired and the fresh woodwork painted white. The goons opened the place up, marched Ben inside and made him sit on a chair while his right trouser leg was rolled up, his sock rolled down and the electronic tag clasped around his ankle.

'Don't even think about messing with it,' Bandy Legs warned him when the device was locked into place.

'Repercussions,' Ben said. 'I know the routine.'

'This is your phone,' Stinker said, laying a mobile on the sideboard. 'You can't make calls with it. Incoming only.'

'So the Little Cayman Sex Hotline is out?' Ben said. 'What I am going to do for entertainment?'

Thirty minutes later, he was alone. Wandering about the house with the tag weighing uncomfortably on his ankle, he found the fridge stocked full of provisions: nothing too fancy, mainly cold chicken legs and salads, but enough to keep him reasonably nourished for the next three days. There was a six-pack of mineral water, cartons of fruit juice and – delight of delights – even a few bottles of Red Stripe Jamaican lager.

Whoever had gone shopping for him had also been busy removing the TV, radio and landline phone and installing the base station for the tag device. The steel box that contained it was securely bolted to the living room floor. A red LED flashed more or less quickly depending on how far away Ben stood from it. He guessed it would trigger a remote alarm the instant he moved more than a hundred yards from that spot: just far enough to allow him to dip his toes at high tide and stroll a short distance up and down the beach. After studying the metal casing for a few minutes he decided there probably wasn't any way to deactivate either it or the tag without alerting his captors.

With nothing else to do, he grabbed a Red Stripe from the fridge and went to sit on the front steps to drink it. The bottle was small, amber glass, twelve fluid ounces in volume and nicely chilled.

As Ben sipped the cold beer and gazed out across the beach to the gentle blue waves, he pondered what he'd said earlier on about giving up smoking.

Chapter 32

Mid-afternoon on the third day, Ben was sitting barefoot on the warm sand in front of Palm Tree Lodge when he felt the tingle of the phone's silent ringer in his pocket and fished it out to answer.

'Have you made your decision?' said Roth's gravelly voice.

'I have,' Ben answered.

'Then what is it to be, Benedict: are you in or out?'

'You don't leave me a lot of choice, Roth. I'm coming on board.'

'Excellent. The *Hydra* is at anchor a couple of miles offshore. My colleagues are all looking forward to meeting you.'

'I'm looking forward to it too,' Ben said.

'The boat's on its way. Twenty minutes.' Roth hung up.

Ben padded across the sand to the house. Walking into the kitchen he tore two sheets of kitchen roll from the dispenser. When he'd finished with them he poured himself a glass of chilled grapefruit juice and drank it slowly. In the hallway he slipped on his shoes and laced them up, then left the house and walked back down the beach as far as the tag would allow, close to the lapping tide-line. The sea breeze ruffled his shirt and his hair. Shielding his eyes from the bright sun, he scanned the horizon.

Soon afterwards, a tiny white dot appeared on the sea and grew rapidly larger until Ben could make out the splash of foam from the motorboat's bows and the faces of the two men on board. A few yards from the shore, its pilot cut the motor and let the boat glide to a halt in the shallow water. Ben didn't recognise him, but the second occupant was familiar enough. Stinker gave a leer as he climbed out and crossed the wet sand towards Ben. The black rubber butt of a 9mm protruded from the holster in his waistband. 'Been a good little doggy?' he said.

'Good as gold,' Ben told him. 'You flossed today?'

Stinker's face reddened. He motioned for Ben to hold out his leg, took a key from his pocket and bent down and roughly undid the ankle tag.

'Let's go,' the pilot said, and fired up the outboard.

Ben splashed over to the boat and climbed in, his leg feeling strangely light after getting used to the lump around his ankle for three days. The pilot steered the burbling boat around and away from the shore. 'Pickup complete,' Stinker said into his phone. 'We're on our way.'

Ben sat quietly as the motorboat rode over the sea and Little Cayman shrank into the distance behind them. For the first few minutes of the journey, Stinker eyed him with suspicion; then, realising Ben wasn't going to be any trouble, he grinned smugly to himself and looked away.

That was when Ben slipped his hand in his pocket, took out the small package he'd carefully double-wrapped in kitchen roll, and laid it on the seat next to him. He started unwrapping it.

Before Stinker could take notice of what he was doing or react in any way, Ben had stepped across the boat towards him, drawn back his elbow and punched the pointed end of the four-inch sliver of broken Red Stripe bottle hard into the side of his neck, just below the ear.

Stinker would have let out a scream, but Ben's hand was over his mouth and once the razor-sharp glass sawing rapidly across his throat had sliced through the gristle of his trachea, he had no air to make a sound. Ben moved out of the way of the blood spray. He let the man's upper body flop backwards over the side and held onto his belt long enough to grab his phone from his pocket and the pistol from its holster.

The pilot hadn't heard a thing over the noise of the outboard, but sensing the rock of the boat he turned to see what was happening behind him. Ben shot him twice in the head and heaved his body into the water with Stinker's. The motorboat's wake turned frothy red. It wouldn't be long before the sharks turned up.

Taking over at the wheel, Ben used Stinker's phone to make a call. 'It's me. Everything ready?.

Chapter 33

The beautiful, stately three-masted hundred-metre sailing yacht had cost her present owner just a shade over eight million pounds. She was capable of twenty knots under a full spread of canvas, more if her massive auxiliary engines were brought to bear. At the moment, though, her loose-hanging sails crackled in the soft breeze and cast a welcome shade over the deck as she stood at anchor just out of sight of Little Cayman.

Lounging in that shade, sipping on tall iced drinks, chatting and laughing, most of them casually attired in shorts and sandals and polo tops or florid Hawaii shirts, were nine of the world's publicly least-known but most influential power-brokers: the senior committee of the organisation known only as Tartarus. Their ages ranged from early fifties to late seventies; between them they possessed over three and a half centuries' worth of experience at the highest, most secretive level of international politics, and the kind of knowledge that could tear a government down and reduce its country to rubble overnight. With the recent exception of Hayden Roth, not one of them had personally discharged a firearm at a living human being for many years – yet the total of the victims they'd claimed during their careers couldn't easily be counted.

‘Excuse me one moment, gentlemen,’ said Roth. He carried his clinking gin and tonic over to the chrome rail that lined the deck, and looked at his watch. The boat should arrive soon, he thought. His eyes shaded from the sun by the brim of his Panama hat, he scanned the blue horizon. No sign of it yet. Had there been some delay?

At that moment, his phone rang. He snatched it up. ‘Jenner, where are—?’

‘Jenner’s indisposed at the moment,’ Ben said on the other end of the line.

Roth was too thunderstruck to utter a reply.

‘Look up,’ Ben told him. ‘Due south. You should be able to see me. I’m that little yellow speck in the sky.’ He had to talk loudly over the thrumming rumble of the single radial propeller engine a few feet above him. From where he was sitting behind the Supermarine Sea Otter’s mass of dials and gauges, he could just about make out the majestic sails of the *Hydra* far below. He eased the joystick, bringing the aircraft down in a shallow dive closer to the waves.

‘Hope? What . . . y-you were supposed to meet the boat,’ Roth stammered.

‘I did,’ Ben said. ‘But there’s been a slight change of plan.’ He checked his readings: air speed, engine speed, flaps; the altitude gauge spun freely as the Sea Otter dropped another hundred feet, almost skimming the waves. She was so heavily laden that it would take all her power to get her up again. But that wasn’t Ben’s idea.

The *Hydra* was coming closer with every second. Ben could see the little matchstick figures on the deck. ‘Is that you in the dinky straw hat, Roth?’

'Hope, what the hell are you doing?' Roth's voice growled on the end of the line.

'I told you I was coming on board,' Ben said. 'That's what I'm doing.'

*

Things might have been different if Hayden Roth hadn't made one mistake: that night at the disused military base, he'd let it slip that it would be a CIC flight taking Ben to Little Cayman.

From there, the new plan had hatched quickly in Ben's mind. In the bathroom of the Gulfstream he'd used a pick-pocketed ballpoint to write a message to Tamara on the inside of his cigarette packet, asking her to get back to Grand Cayman as quickly as she could, and giving her the coordinates to fly Nick's Sea Otter to Little Cayman and meet him on the shore outside Palm Tree Lodge. A hastily scribbled footnote said: 'BRING DRUMS SPARE AVGAS. MANY AS POSS.'

On the outside edge of the cigarette packet Ben had written in block capitals the words: 'FOR TAMARA MARTÍNEZ, FROM BEN HOPE. URGENT!!', and below them the secret phone number on which she could be contacted. When he'd used his smoking ploy on board the Trislander later that day to get the attention of Jo Sundermann, the CIC flight attendant, he'd held the cigarette packet out in such a way that she was sure to see what was written on it. From the look on her face as she'd taken the packet, he'd been sure that she'd call the number. Tamara would surely realise that the message could only have come from Ben, and once she returned to Grand Cayman and Jo Sundermann showed her the cigarette pack, she'd recognise the unusual brand from the night they'd sat in her kitchen.

As to whether Tamara would respond to his call for help in time – that was something Ben could only hope for.

The first day of his captivity at Palm Tree Lodge had passed without anything happening. As the second day had dragged on, Ben had grown steadily more and more anxious and painfully aware of the far too many weaknesses in his plan: Jo Sundermann might have binned the cigarette pack without calling Tamara; or maybe Tamara hadn't answered her phone; or maybe she'd been too frightened to help. Maybe, maybe, maybe.

Towards sunset on the second day, just as he was starting to become despondent, Ben's heart had leapt at the rumble of the approaching aircraft and he'd hurried outside to see the bright yellow Sea Otter touch down on the water and taxi towards the shore.

Tamara had come running to meet him on the sand, and hugged him tight as she explained how she'd come rushing back the minute Jo had called her. Ben had returned her embrace with a real surge of affection.

'What's happening?' she'd asked him in alarm when she'd noticed the electronic tag on his ankle.

'I'll explain,' he'd said. 'Did you bring the fuel?'

'Just like you said. As many drums of 100LL avgas as I could carry. Even strapped one to the co-pilot's seat. Why did we need them?'

'You'd better sit down,' he'd said. 'I have a lot to tell you.'

They'd sat on the steps of the Lodge, and as the sun set across the beach he'd told her everything, watching her reaction shift from stunned disbelief to helpless tears to silent rage. When he'd reached the end of his long account, he'd described the idea that had been forming in his mind.

There had been no hesitation on Tamara's part. 'It's what Nick would have done,' she'd said. 'Let's do it.'

'We can hide the plane beyond those trees,' he'd said, pointing down the beach past Cuban George's open-air bar, to where the coastline receded out of sight into a hidden bay. 'You'll have to sleep on board and wait for my call tomorrow.'

*

Sometimes, the simplest plans worked out the best. Ben smiled to himself as the Sea Otter roared low over the waves towards the *Hydra*. He patted the drum of fuel strapped to the co-pilot's seat – 100LL avgas, one of the most highly combustible and explosive forms of petroleum fuel ever devised. The bright yellow Sea Otter, Nick Chapman's pride and joy, was about to crown its long career by going out in a blaze of glory.

Ben could almost hear Nick laughing.

The magnificent sailing yacht was just two hundred yards away and closing fast. On the sweeping, gleaming deck, tiny figures were scattering in panic: either desperately trying to lower the lifeboats or clambering over the side to take their chances in the water. Hayden Roth stood his ground in the middle of the deck, roaring like a bull into his phone. 'Hope! I order you to stand down immediately! You are a servant of Her Majesty's Government!'

'Not any more. I quit,' Ben said into the phone, and tossed it out of the window.

The Sea Otter was almost on the *Hydra*. The ship's expanse of white canvas sails blotted out the view from the cockpit as the aircraft swooped towards the deck. Ben caught a glimpse of muzzle flashes down below as Tartarus agents opened fire with submachine guns. Bullets raked the Sea Otter's fuselage and cockpit windows.

But there was nothing they could do to prevent what was about to happen. This one was for Nick, and Hilary, and all the other innocents who'd lost their lives thanks to the men aboard the *Hydra*.

At the last possible instant, Ben leaped out of the pilot's seat and dived towards the hatchway, grabbing the small rubber dinghy off the floor as he went. The rushing wind tore the inflatable out of his hands and snatched his breath away as he launched himself into space.

The stunning impact drove him deep underwater. Everything was a tumult of noise and confusion. Bubbles streamed from his mouth as he thrashed wildly to regain the surface.

His head and shoulders burst clear of the water at the same instant the Sea Otter hit the *Hydra* in a shattering, deafening collision of tangled wreckage and wings and sails and rigging and toppling masts. The explosion hurled Ben several yards back in the water and its heat seared his face as both aircraft and ship were engulfed in a gigantic rolling fireball that mushroomed high up into the sky.

Then the sea was suddenly burning, a slick of blazing avgas spreading rapidly across the water. Ben dived under the surface just before the carpet of flames burned him alive. Debris hit the water like a barrage of mortar shells and spiralled into the depths all around him as he swam like crazy away from the circle of devastation.

When he surfaced again, he turned to see a secondary explosion tear apart the shattered remains of the *Hydra*.

Nobody on board could have had any chance of escape. A column of acrid black smoke towered into the sky. Flakes of ash rained down like black snow. Treading water, Ben watched the blazing wreck sink slowly into the sea. Only when it had slipped beneath the waves did he turn away.

The little dinghy was bobbing on the swell nearby. Ben swam after it, clambered on board and unclipped the folding oar from its side. His ears were ringing badly from the noise of the explosion, and the skin of his face felt tender where the heat of the fireball had scorched it. It would probably take a while for his eyebrows to grow back – but then, he wasn't going anywhere. Not back to Credenhill RHQ, not back to Iraq – not any more, knowing what he knew. It was a different world for him now.

The burble of an approaching outboard made him look up and catch sight of the motorboat in the distance. Tamara's black hair caught the wind as she stood behind the wheel and waved at him.

Ben waved back with a smile and started paddling across the water to meet her.

SCOTT MARIANI

BRING HIM BACK

PROLOGUE

Somewhere in Europe
3 December 2003

Deep in the snowy pine forest, a young girl was running barefoot for her life.

She was almost fourteen. Her name was Kristina Braun, but for the last several months, she'd barely been aware of her own identity.

They had taken it from her.

They would strip your soul away, if you let them. *They* would steal your mind.

They. She had no idea who it was that had been holding her captive for so long and doing all these horrible things to her. She only knew that she must get away – and now, suddenly, after all these months of pretending to go along with them while secretly planning her escape, her one chance had finally come.

Except that they had no intention of letting her get away so easily. As she stumbled wildly through the snow, tree branches whipping her face and her bare arms torn by brambles and thorns, she could hear the voices of her pursuers close behind.

'I see her!' yelled one of them. An instant later, there was a muffled *crack* and something thwacked into a pine trunk just a few inches from her. Not a bullet, but some kind of dart. All she could do was keep on running. The trees seemed to thin out ahead. Could there be a road? Could there be a village?

Then, suddenly, there was nowhere to run. She skidded to a halt, teetered on the edge and almost fell, sending a shower of powdery snow down the sheer face of the ravine to the wooded valley far below. There was no road. No village. Just the stark, wintry emptiness of the mountains and forests all around her.

Shuddering with cold and fear, Kristina glanced desperately around her for another escape route. It was too late. The voices of her pursuers seemed to come from all sides. They'd cut her off.

She turned back to face the edge of the ravine. The freezing mountain wind whistled about her.

She knew what these people would do to her if they caught her, if she let them take her back to that awful place. The same thing they'd done to Angie. Perhaps something even worse.

No. She wasn't going to let that happen.

Kristina closed her eyes. Visualised the faces of her parents. These last months she'd often thought about how frantic and desperate they must be, wondering where she was, sometimes hoping she'd come back, perhaps sometimes thinking they'd never see her again.

And now she knew for sure they never would.

Kristina said goodbye and stepped out into the void.

Chapter 1

Near St Helier, Isle of Jersey
7 May 2004

The sun was melting into a golden shimmer on the water as another long, warm May day came to an end. As usual, the family who lived in the big house overlooking the bay were eating a late dinner at the long table in the conservatory dining room. As usual, too, these days, the fair-haired boy had said little during the meal. His mother sat opposite him, frowning as he toyed listlessly with the food on his plate.

The boy was twelve, and his name was Carl Hunter. The man sitting to his right with his back to the window wasn't his real father. And as the boy saw it, this wasn't a real family. It was a stupid pretend family and it wasn't the same any more. In all kinds of ways.

Carl laid down his cutlery and shoved his half-empty plate away from him. 'Finished. I want to go and watch TV.'

'You're not finished, Carl,' his mother said. 'And there's pudding to come. I made apple crumble.'

Carl shook his head and started getting up. 'Don't want any.'

'You should ask your mother properly if you can leave the table,' said the man who wasn't Carl's father.

'Please can I leave the table?' the boy muttered sullenly.

'No,' his mother said. 'You can't. This family sits down to eat together.'

Carl let out a short laugh. 'Yeah, right.'

'You keep on like that, young man, and you won't have a TV to watch,' his mother warned him. Her face was turning paler, like it always did when she was about to erupt.

The man laid down his fork and gently touched her arm. 'Jessica, it's okay.' Turning to Carl, he smiled and said, 'Hey, you know what I did today? Fixed the plug on your Novag. There was a broken connection inside. I've soldered it all up, so it should work fine now. How about that, eh?'

The Novag chess computer was one of Carl's favourite things, but he'd accidentally damaged the plug a few days earlier. If he was pleased it was fixed, he didn't show it.

'What do we say, Carl?' his mother said. 'That was very nice of Mike, wasn't it? Carl, what do we *say*?'

The boy gave Mike the frostiest scowl he could manage. 'Thanks, *Mike*.'

'It's on the table in the study,' Mike said in the same soft tone. 'Maybe you'd like to go and try it out, hmm? On you go, then.'

The boy left the room without a word. They heard him go stumping off towards the study to retrieve the repaired plug, then a moment later his footsteps on the stairs as he hurried up to his room. The door banged shut.

'Thanks so much for undermining me like that,' Jessica Hunter said tersely.

'I didn't mean to undermine you,' Mike told her. 'And I don't mean to spoil him, either. But he's been through a lot, you know? All the changes he's had to adapt to. Can't be easy for him.'

Jessica sighed and laid her hand on his. 'And you're trying so hard. I'm sorry.'

'Me too. I'm just trying to be a dad to him, that's all. I love him as if he was mine.'

'I know,' she said, and smiled.

From two floors above, they could hear Carl's music playing.

'Oh, I just remembered,' Jessica said, brightening up. 'Alison called earlier. We're invited to a party at their place next Saturday. I said we were free. Already booked the sitter. That okay?'

'Sounds great,' Mike said as he started clearing the plates. 'I'll fetch the pudding, shall I? You want cream or custard?'

'Better go easy on the cream,' she said. 'Have to get into a size eight by next week.'

He was about to make his usual 'you're not fat, Jessica,' remark when the sudden noise cut him short.

They both froze. Mike dropped the plates on the table. 'What the—?'

It had come from down the hall.

'That was the front door,' Jessica said in alarm, looking at him with big eyes. It was a thick, heavy door. Despite the almost nonexistent crime rate on Jersey, they kept it locked and bolted.

Carl's music was still blaring upstairs.

Before Mike and Jessica could say anything more, they heard the sound again.

A heavy thump. The splintering of glass. Someone was smashing their way inside the house.

They exchanged horrified glances, then Mike rushed out of the dining room and into the hallway. 'Stay there,' he yelled back at her. The crashing had stopped as suddenly as it had begun.

'Mike! No!' For a second she stayed in her chair, paralysed by fear. Then she leapt to her feet and ran out of the room after him. '*Mike?*'

Mike was standing in the hallway, staring towards the wrecked front door. There was a man in the entrance. A ragged figure. Crazed-looking. His beard and hair were long and straggly, like a tramp's. His eyes were wild and his fists were tight around the handle of the sledgehammer he'd used to break the door in.

'Oh my God,' Jessica gasped. 'Drew!'

The sound of music from Carl's room stopped.

The intruder let the sledgehammer drop from his hands. It hit the shiny hardwood floor with a clang. 'Hello, Jessica,' he said in a strangled voice.

Jessica gaped at the figure of her ex-husband. He was barely recognisable. His clothes were dirty and unkempt. He'd gained a huge amount of weight since she'd last seen him, that day in court when the restraining order had been put in place.

Shocked disbelief was quickly turning to rage. 'Have you gone out of your mind?' she screamed at him.

'What do you want, Drew?' Mike asked, his voice low and steady.

'I've come for Carl,' Drew replied.

Jessica drew a stunned breath. 'What do you mean, you've come for Carl?'

'You heard me,' Drew said. 'I've come to fetch him.'

'Have you been drinking? Are you completely *insane?* You can't come here like this. You can't come anywhere near Carl. The restraining order, remember?'

'Dad!' It was Carl. He was standing rigidly at the top of the stairs. Gripping the banister rail.

'Come down, son,' Drew said. 'I'm taking you away from this place.'

'Go back to your room, Carl!' Jessica shouted in a panicky quaver. 'You hear me? Right now!'

Carl hesitated. Then started making his way anxiously down the stairs. Drew nodded to him. He gave a twisted kind of smile through his messy beard.

'Carl!' Jessica yelled. 'What did I just tell you?'

The boy glanced at her, then at Mike, then back at his father. He paused nervously on the stairs.

'You're upset, Drew,' Mike said, moving warily towards him. 'We understand how much it's hurt you that you couldn't see Carl any more. But maybe it doesn't have to be forever. Let's talk it through like civilized people. Maybe we can come to an agreement.'

'Agreement,' Drew snorted in disgust. 'Like hell we will. Like I'd make an agreement with *you*.'

'You're frightening the boy,' Mike said. 'Don't you care about that, Drew? About his feelings?' He took another step forward.

'Don't you come any closer,' Drew warned. From the pocket of his jeans, he pulled a gun. It was a small semi-automatic pistol, black, ugly and purposeful, and its stubby barrel was pointing at Mike's chest. Jessica let out a cry.

'One more step,' Drew said to Mike. 'I'll blow a hole right through you. I *mean* it.'

Mike went very still. His gaze fixed on the muzzle of the small pistol in Drew's hand. It was trembling slightly. Drew was sweating and his breathing was rapid and ragged, clearly teetering on the verge of panic. Mike was very afraid of what might happen if he tipped over that edge.

'Come here, Carl,' Drew said, holding out his free hand. The boy paused, then slowly descended the rest of the stairs. 'Dad—' he murmured. Drew grasped him by the arm and held him close. Whispered something in his ear. The boy looked up at him.

'Let him go!' Jessica screamed. 'Drew! Please! Why are you *doing* this?'

Drew wagged the barrel of the gun down the passage that led past the stairs. The door on the right led down to the cellar. It was an old door, solid oak. The ring of a large iron key protruded from the lock. 'The two of you,' Drew said. 'Get in there.'

'You don't want to do this,' Mike said as Drew herded them towards the cellar. 'You know what's going to happen. Drop the gun. I said, *drop the gun*, Drew.' He spoke softly, calmly.

Drew blinked. He clasped the boy even more tightly to his side. 'Don't talk to me. Don't look at me. Get in there now! You first, you piece of shit. I'm not joking. You get in there now or I'll shoot you. I mean it. I will.'

'I'm begging you, Drew . . .' Jessica sobbed.

'Open the door.'

Mike turned the key with a sigh. The lock clunked. The door creaked open. Cool, slightly dank air wafted up from the dark space below. He reached slowly up to the light switch and turned it on to reveal the flight of concrete steps leading down to the cellar. There were packing cases and boxes, an old table, stacked chairs. Against one rough white-washed wall leaned the two bikes that Drew and Jessica had once enjoyed cycling around the island on. Happier times. Now they were gone.

Jessica was frantically weeping as she and Mike descended the cellar steps. Drew watched them from the doorway, still pointing the gun, his arm around Carl's shoulders.

'Mummy loves you, Carl,' Jessica sobbed. 'You hear me? Mummy loves you!'

'You harm him,' Mike warned Drew, 'and I swear you'll pay dearly for it.'

Drew made no reply. He slammed the cellar door, shutting off the anguished cry from Jessica. He turned the lock. Left the key in place, sideways so that it couldn't be pushed through from inside. There were wire coat hangers and all kinds of things in the cellar that could be used to pick the lock.

'Dad—' Carl said in a shaky voice.

Drew slipped the gun back into his pocket. He squeezed his boy's arm tightly. 'Let's get your things, Carl. We're leaving.'

'Where are we going?' the boy asked, staring up at him. He could remember all the times in the past when his father had been drunk, sometimes hopelessly inebriated, incoherent, reeking of booze, hardly able to stand. A miserable, heartbreaking sight that Carl had almost become used to.

But not now. Now he could see his father was completely sober.

'I have it all planned,' Drew said. 'Everything.'

Chapter 2

Fifteen days later
Saturday, 22 May

Ben Hope stepped out of the rented Ford Mondeo and looked up at the house. The warm sea breeze ruffled his thick blond hair, which he wore a little longer now that he'd been out of the military for almost a year. In the background, he could hear the waves crashing against the rocks. It was a sound that made him think of home.

The house looked just the way it had on the TV news, big and expensive. Not for the first time since he'd got the call, he wondered what would make a well-known, comfortably-off professional photographer decide to break into his former home, hold up his ex-wife and her new man at gunpoint and kidnap his own twelve-year-old son. Ben was keeping an open mind.

He took out his cigarettes, the blue pack of French Gauloises that he was smoking these days. He lit one from the fat orange flame of his Zippo, shielding it from the wind. Clanged the lighter shut, dropped the warm metal in the pocket of his leather jacket and started walking up the winding path between crisp expanses of manicured lawn towards the house.

The last desultory-looking stragglers left over from the army of media who'd been besieging the place since the news had broken two weeks ago were wrapping up their gear to go home. One of them, a wiry guy in a baseball cap and a Velvet Revolver T-shirt, was trying to ignite a cigarette with a match but getting nowhere in the wind. 'Got a light, mate?' he asked, seeing Ben's Gauloise. Ben paused, fished out the Zippo and helped him out.

'So, you a relative of the Hunters, then?' the guy asked eagerly, puffing smoke. 'Friend of the family, maybe? Care to make any comments?'

Ben just looked at him. He could see from the hungry glow in his eyes that he was desperate to milk a few more drops out of the two-week-old story that had already started fading from the news.

'Or are you with the cops?' the guy added hopefully. 'Come on, give us something.'

Ben shook his head. 'I'm just here to clean the swimming pool,' he said. He walked on. From behind him he heard one of them say, 'But they don't have a swimming pool, do they?' By then Ben was already climbing the steps to the front door. He flicked away the part-smoked Gauloise and rang the bell twice.

The woman who answered the door was tall, about five-nine, with long chestnut hair. Ben recognised her as Jessica Hunter. He knew she was only thirty-five, but the strain of the last two weeks had made her look older than her years, haggard with worry.

'Mr Hope?' she said, peering anxiously at him.

'Call me Ben,' Ben said.

Jessica Hunter's shoulders sagged with relief. She invited him in, then hurriedly closed the door to shut out the reporters, watching from a distance.

Ben followed her into a large, plush entrance hall. It was funny how money had its own smell that always imbued these kinds of places. Jessica walked briskly across to the foot of a broad flight of stairs and called upwards, 'Mike! Mr Hope is here.' She turned back to Ben. 'He'll join us in a minute. Please, won't you come into the kitchen? I was just about to make a coffee.'

She led the way into a large L-shaped space that was half kitchen, half breakfast room. Patio windows overlooked a well-tended garden with a tennis court in the distance. At one end of the room, deep wicker sofas covered in cushions faced one another across a low table. At the opposite end, an espresso maker was burbling on a shiny Aga range.

'So you live in Ireland?' she said with an effort to smile, just to make conversation and break the ice a little.

He nodded. 'Galway.'

'Nice there.'

He replied, 'I love the sea.'

'So does Carl,' she said, and her face tightened at the mention of his name, her brows knitting with emotion as if she might suddenly burst into tears. Collecting herself, she offered Ben a coffee. He declined politely and walked over to the wall where a large framed photo hung. The boy in the picture was eight or nine, sitting on a bike and beaming happily at the camera.

'His father took that,' Jessica said, glancing across with a grimace as she poured her coffee. 'Almost four years ago. It's the only photo of Drew's I still have on the wall. I can hardly bear to look at it any more.' She paused. 'Do you have any children, Mr Hope?'

'Ben,' he said. 'No. No children. No family. It's just me.' That wasn't something he liked to talk about. He pointed at Carl's picture. 'I'll need a smaller, more recent shot of him. Preferably one with you in it too.'

'Of course,' she said. 'May I ask why I need to be in it?'

'Because if I have to take him away from his father, having a family photo in my hand that he recognises means you sent me, and that he can trust me. It would also help to have one of Drew.'

She anxiously sipped her coffee, standing facing Ben and leaning against the kitchen worktop. 'It's such an incredible relief to hear you talk about finding him. Needless to say, there's still no word. Nobody's seen them. I don't even know *what* the police are doing.' She paused, looking at Ben with frightened eyes. 'You will find him, won't you?'

Before Ben could reply, a man walked into the kitchen. He was about Ben's height, just a shade under six feet, and around the same age. Despite the wire-framed glasses and the bookish look about him, he could almost have been Ben's more sedate, more urbane brother. His fair hair was neatly combed and parted, but there wasn't much he could do to hide the dark circles under his eyes from anxiety and lack of sleep.

'I'm Mike Greerson,' he said, striding over with his hand extended. 'We spoke on the phone.' Ben shook his hand. It was a good, dry grip.

'You've no idea how grateful we are to you for coming at such short notice,' Mike said. He waved towards the wicker sofas. 'Please, take a seat. You must be tired after your trip.'

Mike and Jessica sat together on one sofa, each with a coffee. Ben sat opposite. Mike Greerson might not be Mr Hunter, but from the way the two of them were sitting close together, fingers interlaced, and thighs touching, it looked very much as if he'd taken Mr Hunter's place.

'Let's recap,' Ben said. 'Your son Carl was forcibly abducted from home fifteen days ago by your ex-husband Drew Hunter, who threatened you with a firearm and imprisoned the two of you in the cellar while he made off with the boy.'

'That's correct,' Jessica said in a tight voice.

'We were locked in there all night,' Mike added. 'Until Sally arrived the following morning and heard us banging on the door.'

'Sally?' Ben said.

'Our housekeeper,' Jessica said. 'She lives in St Helier.'

'Is she here at the moment?' Ben asked.

Jessica shook her head. 'Nobody's been allowed into the house since that day. Except the officers dealing with the case, that is. And now you.'

'The moment we were let out of the cellar, we were on the phone to the police,' Mike said. 'To begin with, it looked as if they were being efficient. They were here within minutes, did everything they had to do and set up the trace on the phone. They even combed the island with sniffer dogs. But it's been over two weeks and they haven't turned up a single lead or shred of evidence.'

Ben was already familiar with every step the cops had taken to date. They'd done a lot of the things he'd have done himself, checking ports and airports on the assumption that Drew Hunter would have taken his son straight off the island on the evening of the abduction. The ferries to France had been checked, as well as every small boat charter outfit and every light aircraft shuttle service. Blanks had been drawn every which way. The only key development so far in the inquiry had been the discovery of the large cash withdrawal that Drew Hunter had made from the bank just minutes after opening time on Tuesday, 4 May, three days prior to the kidnapping. He'd emptied his entire account, walking away with almost sixty grand in a bag, which was all that remained of what had once been a much healthier balance. The only conclusion the police could draw was that this hadn't been a spur-of-the-moment crime.

'It's as if they'd simply vanished into thin air,' Jessica said, momentarily close to tears again. Sniffing, she went on, 'We soon realised that the investigation was simply going nowhere. That's when Mike suggested we call in someone from the outside. Someone who knows about these things. I understand you're from a military background?'

'I've been out of that coming up for a year,' Ben said.

'It isn't just any old military background, though, is it?' Mike asked with a knowing kind of tone.

'It's not something I really talk about a lot,' Ben said. 'I served with 22 Special Air Service. Which gave me experience in covert work and hostage rescue, among other things.'

'And since that time, you've been involved in a number of missing persons cases,' Mike said. 'The Italian kidnapping a few months ago, for instance. The girl was returned safely to her family, wasn't she?'

'I was barely involved,' Ben lied.

'And four kidnappers were jailed, one killed.'

'Nobody's going to get killed this time,' Ben said.

Jessica Hunter looked at Ben imploringly. 'Does that mean you'll help us? Please. I'm begging you. We don't know where else to turn.'

'I'm here,' Ben said. 'I'll do what I can.'

Chapter 3

'Thank you,' Jessica said, her eyes misting. She quickly wiped one of them. 'You don't know what it means.'

Ben had some more questions. 'So as far as you're both aware, apart from the boy's natural father, there's no other suspect involved in this situation?'

'Drew isn't a *suspect*,' Jessica said. 'His guilt isn't in question here. We both saw him snatch Carl away at gunpoint. And of course he's acting alone.'

'How long have you two been together?'

'Six months,' Mike said.

'Going on seven,' Jessica said, squeezing his hand.

'I take it that Drew wasn't exactly thrilled with the new domestic situation,' Ben said.

'He's jealous,' Jessica sobbed. 'He's all alone now and he can't stand it that I'm not. That's what this is all about. He's just trying to hurt me by taking away my child.'

'Seven months,' Ben said. 'The divorce was well over a year ago, wasn't it? Though I understand the marriage had turned sour long before.'

'You mean when he started drinking,' Jessica said bitterly.

'It's what I read,' Ben said.

'Nothing much escapes the reporters, does it? They get into your life like ants. They only care about their story.' Jessica paused, calmed herself and went on in a wistful tone,

'Drew hasn't been content with his life for a long time. I don't know what happened. He used to be. At least, he seemed to be. He had everything. Successful career, beautiful home. I thought we were a happy family, you know? Thought everything was fine. But obviously he was feeling restless and dissatisfied, deep down. It was about three years ago when he started drinking, and it got quickly worse from there. He'd always been so fit and active, but then he just seemed to let himself go. He stopped exercising, started not caring about the way he looked, or what he ate. He became moody and prone to outbursts of anger. Said what he was doing was bullshit. Said he'd trade it all – the money, the glamorous clients and friends, the cars, toys, all of it – to do what he really wanted to do.'

'Which was?'

'Wildlife photography,' Jessica said. 'That became his passion. Sneaking up on animals and getting pictures of them.' She snorted, her anger returning. 'He didn't give a damn that there was no money in it, that nobody was going to pay for a long-distance shot of some rare bird or other, even if he could stay sober long enough to snap the bloody thing. Didn't care that we might end up having to sell this house and live like a couple of paupers for the sake of his dream. He didn't even care about Carl's education. He was becoming more and more despondent and spending more and more time drunk, and I mean *drunk*. I couldn't take it any more. It simply tore us apart.'

Ben had already noticed the gold Datejust peeking out from under the sleeve of her silk blouse, and the diamond earrings that glittered through her hair. He wondered to himself how much it was the prospect of being married to a much poorer guy that had swung Jessica Hunter's decision to end it.

'What do you do, Mike?' he asked.

'I'm a development consultant for a specialist optics firm in Europe,' Mike replied. 'Custom applications for science and industry. I work mostly from home. But at the moment I'm taking time off to devote myself totally to supporting Jessica.' He squeezed her hand tenderly.

Ben nodded, and turned back to Jessica. 'Tell me more about your relationship between you, Carl, and Drew since the marriage ended.'

'He used to have Carl every second weekend,' she said, 'while things were still reasonably amicable between us and before the drinking got completely out of control. But then it did, and the arrangement couldn't go on. He'd turn up here reeking of booze, slurring his words – expecting me to hand Carl over to him in that state?' Jessica sighed. 'He was going more and more downhill. Living like a total slob. Carl said his place was a pigsty and all there was to eat there was frozen pizza and takeaway curry. Bottles everywhere, gin, whisky, vodka. He hadn't had a job in months and all he did was drink. The last straw was when he crashed the car with Carl in it. He'd tricked me, somehow managing to turn up relatively sober to collect him, and then getting plastered the moment he was away from here. When the police arrived at the scene of the accident they found Drew four times over the drink-drive limit and a half-empty bottle of spirits in the car.'

'Were they hurt?'

'Carl had minor bruising, nothing more serious, thank Christ. Drew dislocated his shoulder. That's when he was banned from driving and I had the restraining order put on him. Of course, I felt bad that it meant taking away his access to Carl completely. But I had no choice. It was the only thing I could do for my son's safety.'

'You said Drew had become prone to outbursts. While you were married, did you ever have reason to think that he could harm Carl?'

Jessica shook her head firmly. 'Never. Despite everything, I always thought he loved him as deeply as I do.'

'The night of the abduction, did it seem as if he'd been drinking?'

Jessica and Mike both shook their heads. 'That was the strange bit,' she said. 'He seemed completely sober. There was no smell of alcohol on him. He didn't seem discoordinated at all, and his voice was steady and clear. He knew exactly what he was doing. But he looked crazy.'

Ben asked, 'Crazy in what way?'

'I hadn't seen him since the restraining order,' Jessica said. 'He looked like a wild man. I can let you have a copy of the police artist's sketch, if you want.'

'That would be helpful,' Ben said. 'But if you can describe him to me, that would too.'

'His hair was all straggly and greasy. He had a beard. His clothes were dirty looking and he'd got so much fatter around the belly. It's like he's become a whole other person. A complete stranger.' Her voice choked up. Her lip began to tremble, and then she burst out weeping. 'How can a man who says he loves his son kidnap him?' she said through the tears. 'What's he going to do?'

Mike put his arm around her as she dabbed her eyes. 'I'm never going to see him again,' she sniffed. 'I just know it. Drew's never going to let me see him again.'

'What was Carl's reaction when his father turned up like that?' Ben asked, steering the conversation back onto neutral ground. 'Did he seem scared?'

'I think he was as shocked as Mike and I were,' Jessica replied, dabbing her eyes.

'So he didn't go willingly.'

'Drew was armed with a pistol,' Mike said, frowning. 'Who's going to argue with a half-crazed man waving a gun around? We did what he ordered. So did Carl. None of us had a choice.'

'Do you know where Drew could have got hold of a firearm?'

'I haven't the faintest clue,' Jessica replied. 'He's always hated anything to do with guns. Said the only thing he'd ever shoot an animal with was a camera.'

'The police have already been down that route,' Mike told Ben. 'They presume he must have obtained an illegal weapon from somewhere. They didn't find any leads. There isn't exactly a lot of arms trafficking on the island.'

'Plenty of places he might have got one in France,' Ben said. 'He could have smuggled it back on the ferry, or he could have sailed a boat across himself.'

Jessica shook her head and almost smiled. 'Drew couldn't possibly handle any sort of boat on his own. He's hopeless at anything practical that doesn't involve cameras, lenses and tripods.'

'Does he know anyone with a sea-going vessel of any kind?'

'We had friends with yachts, when we were married. They no longer speak to Drew. In any case, gun smuggling would hardly be their thing. Neither would helping to kidnap a child.'

'Look, the police have already been over this ground,' Mike said.

'And found nothing,' Jessica added, suddenly on the edge of tears again. 'Not a trace of my boy. Where is he? Where's Drew taken him?'

'Jessica, Mr Hope is here now,' Mike consoled her. 'If anyone can find Drew, it's him. Everything's going to be fine, you'll see.'

'Call me Ben,' Ben said. 'Now if you don't mind, I'd like to take a look at Carl's room.'

Chapter 4

While Jessica stayed downstairs, pacing and agitated, Ben followed Mike to the boy's bedroom. It was at the very top of the house, two floors up.

'Jessica can't bear to come near this room,' Mike said. 'Nobody's been in since the forensic people. It didn't take them long to find the DNA evidence that proves Drew was here.'

The door was slightly ajar. Ben swung it open a little wider and stepped into the large bedroom. He walked around, careful not to disturb anything. The bedclothes were rumpled. Drawers had been left lying untidily open where clothes had been pulled out. A lone sock lay strewn on the carpet.

'What do you see, Mr Hope?' Mike asked.

'After he closed you and Jessica in the cellar, Drew brought Carl up here to pack his things up. Looks like it was done in a hurry.'

'Why would that be?' Mike asked. 'He had us locked up good and proper down there. No way could I have smashed my way out, and he knew it.'

'Maybe he had an appointment to make,' Ben said.

'Such as?'

'Such as whoever he paid to take him and Carl off the island that night. With sixty grand in his pocket, there'd be a lot of people willing to help him, and no questions asked.'

Ben went on walking around the room, taking in details. Apart from its size, it was a more or less typical room for a kid Carl's age. Posters were clustered all over the wall around and above the single bed. A bookshelf was filled with books a twelve-year-old boy would read. There were model kits of fighter aircraft hanging on threads from the ceiling. A carefully painted plastic Tyrannosaurus Rex stood on a table next to a Sherman tank. Nearby was a collection of miniature enamel paints and some fine brushes standing in a pot.

'He likes models a lot,' Mike explained.

Spotting a small black object lying on the carpet, Ben crouched to look at it. It was a chess piece, a rook.

'That's from his chess computer,' Mike said sadly. 'I'd just fixed it for him, the night he was taken.'

'You won't mind if I hang onto this for now,' Ben said, picking up the rook and dropping it into one of the small polythene evidence bags he carried in his pocket.

'No, but any particular reason?'

'I like to have something of the victim's. So Carl's into chess?'

'Loves it, and he's an excellent player. Thrashes me every time. Even beats the machine. He's a very gifted boy. Very gifted indeed.'

Ben noticed the pride in Mike's voice. It could have been the real father talking. 'How do you and he get on?' he asked.

'He's a great kid,' Mike sighed. 'I've tried my best to be a proper dad to him, but it's hard. I know he resents me. I can't really blame him for that. It's normal in a situation like this. It's always tough on the kids when their parents split up, isn't it?' He glanced at Ben, then went on. 'I was hoping that in time he'd get to know me better. Now I don't even know if I'm ever going to see him again.'

'Don't think that way,' Ben said.

'I'm counting on you,' Mike said with sudden emotion. 'We have to have Carl returned to us. He's the most important thing in our lives. And I want that piece of shit Drew caught. I want him—' Mike swallowed whatever he was going to say next, as if he'd been going to say too much. 'What now?' he asked instead.

'I've seen enough,' Ben replied, and headed for the door.

'Where will you go from here?'

'Give me Drew's address.'

'The police have already—'

'I'm sure they have,' Ben said. 'I'd still like to take a look around the place.'

'Carl had a key,' Mike said. 'I think Jessica's got it somewhere.'

'Then I'd like that too,' Ben said.

'I can do that.'

As Ben was leaving a few minutes later, armed with the things he'd asked for, Jessica appeared in the hallway. She'd been crying again and her eyes were puffy and red.

'Take care. I'll be in touch,' Ben said, heading towards the door.

'Ben?' she said, and he stopped and turned.

She stepped up to him, reached out and clasped both his hands tightly.

'Please find him. Find my son. Bring him back.'

Chapter 5

Drew Hunter's abode since his divorce from Jessica had been a stark contrast from the family home the two of them had once shared. Ben parked a little way up the quiet street from the modest semi-detached suburban house on the outskirts of St Helier.

He didn't get out of the car immediately, because nobody could have failed to notice the police patrol car sitting right outside Drew's place. Ben sat at the wheel of his Mondeo, watching it. He could see the figures of two officers inside, in conversation with one another. With time passing and the kidnap becoming yesterday's news, he guessed that the cops would be downscaling their surveillance of the place, just dropping by now and again on the off chance that they could catch Drew sneaking back to his address.

As if he'd come near the place with a marked car plonked outside his gate, Ben thought. Not the best strategic policy in the world. But that was why they were the police.

A few minutes later, the patrol car drove away. Ben got out of the Mondeo, walked to the house and let himself in the front door using the key that Mike had given him.

As he went from room to room, he was keeping his eyes open for the telltale signs that Jessica had described and which hopeless drunks always left in their wake. Empty bottles lying about, unwashed glasses perched on every flat surface reeking of stale beer and spirits, dishes piled high in the sink, fast food containers overflowing from the bin.

But there were none of those. The house was tidy, everything in place, everything clean. Even the bed was made. One room was full of expensive photographic equipment, all carefully organised.

Ben spent the next half hour sifting through every piece of paperwork in Drew's study desk. Utility bills, tax documents, bank statements, insurance. Nothing beyond the mundane. Next, he went through every pocket of every jacket and pair of trousers in Drew's wardrobe. He found a small folding knife. Not exactly the weapon of a hardcore crook. A camera lens cleaning cloth, still in its packet. A bus ticket. A photography supplies business card. Lastly, there was a little yellow receipt from a business called 'A Stitch in Time', which sounded to Ben like a clothes repair shop. Below the place's address in St Helier was scrawled a collection date for the repaired garment: May ninth. Two days after the kidnapping, meaning that unless Drew was still on the island and crazy enough to go back to pick it up, it was still at the repair shop.

'A stitch in time,' Ben murmured thoughtfully as he left the study and continued his search of the house.

Returning to the kitchen, he checked the fridge and freezer. No beer, no vodka. Not even a frozen pizza. Surprisingly for a heavy-drinking deadbeat, it seemed that Drew had been living on organic health foods: tofu, lentils, wholegrain rice and pasta. 'Jesus,' Ben muttered to himself. He sniffed inside a plastic container: homemade vegetable soup. Give me army food any day, he thought.

Drew juiced his own fruit juice, too. A large bowl nearby was filled with oranges and grapefruit, some of them turning soft and discoloured with age. In a cupboard, Ben came across packs of dandelion and nettle tea, the kind of stuff hippies and alternative types drank. Along with them, sitting in front of stacked tins of organic butter beans and chickpeas, was a small brown bottle with a dropper top, which he took out and examined. It was some kind of herbal tincture. He wondered what ailment Drew had been using it for. That could be useful information. Sick people generally went to doctors, collected drugs at pharmacies. You couldn't do that without leaving a trail.

Thinking he might find more of interest in the bathroom cabinet, he went back upstairs to check. There was nothing in the cabinet apart from the usual everyday toiletries. A pack of soap. Band-aids. Nail cutters. A pair of scissors with specks of fresh orange rust on the blades. Ben closed the cabinet door.

Spotting another little brown bottle sitting on a crowded shelf near the bath, next to an empty glass that had probably contained a toothbrush before Drew had packed up and left home, Ben reached across to pick the bottle up. It contained lots of tiny white tablets and bore a simple label that read NUX VOMICA 6X. Ben replaced it on the shelf, then as an afterthought picked it up again. As he did so, his sleeve caught the glass, which dropped off the shelf, hit the bottom of the bath and smashed.

'Shit,' Ben muttered.

He was picking up the bits of glass when he noticed the hair clogging up the bath's plughole. He poked his fingers into the hole, pulled out a pinch of it and examined it. Drew Hunter was fair, like his son, and Ben had been told his hair was long and straggly. This was short and very dark, almost black. Definitely interesting. Ben carefully dropped some strands of it inside an evidence bag, sealed it and slipped it into his pocket.

'Milk Thistle?' the woman in the health food shop said some time later, peering through her thick spectacles at the bottle Ben was showing her. 'Why yes, it's very popular as a liver cleanser. A lot of customers come to buy it after Christmas and New Year, when they've been overindulging a little.'

'You mean, in drink?' Ben said, and the woman nodded. 'Would it help for hangovers, things like that?' he asked.

'Also to help support internal organs after a period of abuse,' she replied.

'So an alcoholic might use it?'

'If they were trying to detox themselves,' she said. 'Studies have been done that show how it can help regenerate the liver.

'Sounds like I need some more of it for myself,' he said dryly.

'Or people on a crash diet, to help protect against the release of toxins.'

'And what about this?' He showed her the bottle of small white pills he'd found in Drew's bathroom.

'Nux Vom,' she said, recognising it instantly. 'Same idea, only this is homeopathic, not herbal.'

'Does it work?'

'Oh, it works, all right,' she said. 'Just ask my husband.'

Ben bought another lot of each by way of thanking her for her help, and left the shop thinking about what he'd learned. First, no booze anywhere to be found in Drew's house. Now this. It looked as if the guy was pretty serious about cleaning himself up and purging the toxic effects of drink from his system.

As he walked up the street towards his car, checking the address for A Stitch in Time, Ben took out his phone and called Jessica at home. She answered on the second ring, as if she'd been hovering nearby waiting for a call.

'What have you found out?' she said breathlessly.

'Was Drew seeing anyone recently?' Ben asked.

Jessica sounded taken aback. 'As in, a girlfriend?'

'One with short hair, very dark brown or black.'

'I don't think so. I'm sure I'd have heard it through the grapevine. Who'd want him anyway, in the state he's in half the time?'

'What about friends who might have visited him?'

'I really don't know. Most of our friends stopped socialising with him when we broke up. Why are you asking?'

Ben told her about the hair in the bath. 'But what does it mean?' she said, sounding baffled.

'I can't be sure, of course. But I think he dyed his hair sometime not long before abducting Carl. And cut it, too. There were scissors in the bathroom cabinet. The blades were rusty, like they'd be if you used them to cut wet hair and put them away in a hurry.'

'But his hair wasn't short,' she said. 'It was long and straggly. I told you, I was shocked by his appearance. And you've seen the police sketch.'

'My guess is that he'd already done the job on himself by then, to save time, and that he was wearing a wig,' Ben said. 'And I'd bet that he's done the same for Carl, too, immediately after the snatch. Maybe at his place but more likely somewhere else, somewhere isolated and private, like a beach hut.

Dyeing the boy's hair wouldn't have taken long, maybe forty minutes from start to finish.'

'I can't even imagine what he must look like with dark hair,' Jessica said, sounding aghast.

'Exactly. So it's possible that they used the ferry after all. Drew's hideout could have been somewhere en route from your house to the port, so they'd have had time to do the job and still make the last ferry, well before you and Mike got out of the cellar and raised the alarm. That's how he managed to fool the cops when they reviewed the CCTV footage, because they only had your description of a fair-haired boy and a guy with straggly, sandy hair to go on.'

'Oh, my god,' she breathed. 'That devious . . .'

'I'll drop by the house later and let you have the hair sample I collected, so you can pass it on to the cops for analysis. I won't be surprised if it tests positive as Drew's. He's gone about this very cleverly, Jessica.'

A short drive across town, Ben found A Stitch in Time down a little alleyway. The bell tinkled as he walked in. The shop was filled with racks and hangers of clothing. A dumpy woman scowled up from behind a sewing machine.

He handed her the little yellow ticket he'd found at Drew's place. 'Picking this up for my brother,' he said.

She only had to look at the name on the ticket and put two and two together: Drew was all over the media and big talk on the island. But the blank look on her face told Ben that she'd either missed the news or didn't care one way or the other. She browsed through a set of hangers, pulled one out and laid it on the counter. It was a navy blazer, alpaca wool, pricey-looking. The woman showed him where she'd replaced a button and fixed part of the lining, then stuffed the garment in a bag. Ben tumbled coins across the Formica.

'I might need something repairing myself,' he said casually. 'Problem is, I'm going on holiday soon. How long does it take?'

She shrugged. ''Bout a week, normally, for a small job like this one.'

'Great. Be seeing you, then.'

Back at the car, he slipped the blazer out of the bag and looked at it. It somehow didn't look like the jacket of an overweight slob. Going by the description of Drew, it would have been impossibly tight on him.

Ben slipped off his own leather jacket and tried the blazer on for size. It wasn't too baggy even on his lean frame. He felt in the pockets. In the left one he found a piece of fluff. In the right one, a crisp and new-looking business card.

The name on the card was Paul Finley, and he was co-partner in a private detective agency in Dover.

Chapter 6

'Finley & Reynolds Investigations.'

'Can I speak to Mr Finley, please?' Ben said to the agency receptionist as he drove. He was heading back to Jessica's place, to give her the hair sample as he'd promised. The detective's card lay next to him on the passenger seat.

There was a pause on the line. 'I'm afraid that won't be possible,' she replied. Ben noticed the edgy tone in her voice.

'This is very important. When will he be available?'

'He won't. I'm afraid Mr Finley is no longer with us.'

'I see. Do you have a number for him?'

'He's dead.'

Now it was Ben's turn to pause at the unexpected news.

'May I ask who's calling?' the receptionist asked.

'My name's Ben Hope. I was calling on behalf of a mutual client. Was Mr Finley ill?'

Her swallow was audible on the line. 'Mr Finley was murdered.'

'I'm extremely sorry to hear that. What happened?'

'He was on his way back from London,' she said in a tight voice. 'Waiting for a train. These two thugs attacked him. Took his wallet, but obviously that wasn't enough for them. It never is these days, is it?' She sighed. 'They stabbed him, twice in the chest. He was dead by the time the ambulance arrived. Poor Mr Finley.'

'Did they catch the killers?'

She snorted. 'Do they ever?'

'When did this happen?'

'Nearly three weeks ago. It was late afternoon. Broad daylight. Can you believe it?'

'What date?' Ben asked, narrowing his eyes.

'May third,' she said. 'Monday. Why?'

The day before Drew had withdrawn all his money from the bank, Ben thought. Four days before the kidnapping.

'Perhaps I could speak to Mr Reynolds instead?' he said. 'It's about our mutual client.'

'I'm sorry, Mr, uh, Hope. There's no way Mr Reynolds or anyone else at the agency is going to discuss clients' affairs without prior written consent. Which I take it you don't have.'

Ben ended the call without saying anything more.

This time, as Jessica Hunter led Ben into the kitchen, he accepted a coffee from her. What he really wanted was some of the single malt whisky in his flask and a cigarette to go with it, but smoking and drinking weren't quite the thing inside a client's house. He sat at the breakfast bar and sipped the espresso she made him. Strong, black, no sugar. Coffee with a bit of welly to it, the way he liked. He took out the evidence bag containing the hair sample and laid it in front of her.

'This is for the police. A little something they missed, and I would have, too, except by chance. Like I said, ten to one they'll come back saying it's Drew's. In which case they have to start mounting a whole new search, if it's not already too late.'

Jessica picked the sample up and stared at it in horrified fascination. Just then, Mike walked into the room looking weary and drawn, and came to sit at the breakfast bar. 'Back again so soon,' he said. 'I can't believe you've only been on the case a few hours and already there's progress.'

'Let's take this one step at a time,' Ben said. 'I have a question. Does either of you know of any reason why Drew might have hired a private investigator?'

Jessica was startled. 'A what?'

'His name was Paul Finley,' Ben said. 'Based in Dover.'

'What on earth would Drew have wanted with a detective?'

'There could've been a few reasons,' Ben said. 'The most obvious being to watch you. It's not unknown for disgruntled ex-spouses to want to get the dirty on their former partners, especially when there are child custody issues involved.'

'Get the dirty?' Mike said, frowning.

'Incriminating information that might have enabled him to accuse you of neglect, as a way of getting custody himself. Did you two ever go out in the evening, restaurants, nightclubs, and leave Carl on his own?'

Jessica bristled. 'Absolutely not. I really resent the suggestion. And I'm frankly appalled that this man has been watching us like a couple of criminals.'

'You won't have to worry about him any more,' Ben said. 'He was stabbed to death in London before the kidnapping took place.'

'That's awful,' Mike said.

'It happens,' Ben said.

'Anyway, we have nothing to hide,' Jessica said angrily. 'There's no question of Carl being neglected or abused in any way. How dare Drew make those allegations? He's my son. I love him. *I'm* not the one who's falling about the place too drunk to take care of themselves.'

'It doesn't matter what Drew told the detective,' Ben said. 'What matters is that they were in touch in the first place. After Finley died, it's possible that someone else at the agency took over where he left off. That could mean that Drew was in contact with them right up until he took Carl, and maybe even since. It could help lead us to him.'

'Did you say they were based in Dover?' Jessica asked. 'Will you go?'

'Can't hurt to check it out,' Ben said.

'What if they won't talk to you?'

'I'm sure I can find a way,' he replied. 'I won't be gone for long. In the meantime, the police may have some work to do.'

'You're talking about this?' Mike asked, pointing at the sample bag containing the short, clipped lengths of hair.

Ben nodded. 'Forget the description you gave to the cops. It's leading us off the trail. I'm almost certain that we should be looking for a man with much shorter hair, black or close to it. And that's not all. If I'm right, the police should also change their suspect description from an overweight guy to one of slim-to-medium build. In other words, Drew has radically altered his appearance.'

'Hold on, we *saw* him that night,' Jessica said. 'Nobody can lose weight that fast. It's impossible.'

'That's true,' Ben said. 'But it's not impossible to fake being fat in the first place. In fact, it's pretty easily done.'

'I don't understand.'

'You said that you hadn't seen Drew for some time before the kidnapping. Not since the episode of the car accident.'

Jessica nodded. 'That's right. He was already getting out of shape then.'

'But between then and the day of the kidnapping, he had plenty of time to lose the pounds. Someone who's serious could get into good shape in that time.'

'What are you basing all this on?' Mike asked, looking doubtful.

'The clothes in his wardrobe,' Ben said. 'Every pair of trousers was a thirty-two waist. Shirts and T-shirts all medium size. Jackets all thirty-eight inch chest. Not whiplash thin, but hardly what you'd call porky either.'

'Obviously, they were his old clothes,' Jessica said impatiently. 'I told you, he was quite slim and fit when we were first married. He wouldn't have packed those things when he went on the run with Carl, if he couldn't get into them any more.'

'That was my thinking, too,' Ben said. 'That he'd have taken all his large-size clothes with him, especially if he wasn't planning on coming back. I assumed he mustn't have worn the other stuff for quite some time. But then, why keep it? It's taking up a lot of wardrobe and drawer space. That interested me. Then I saw the way he's been eating lately. All health food. A man can starve pretty fast on that stuff. No beer, no booze of any kind. He'd been cleaning himself up, even using herbs and homeopathic medicine to cleanse his liver and protect himself from the flood of stored toxins that can be released when people go on a crash diet after a prolonged unhealthy lifestyle. Looks like he was committed to it.'

'But that's just a theory,' Mike said, still perplexed. 'It doesn't prove that he actually did lose weight.'

'No, but it got me interested in finding out more. Not long before the kidnap, Drew took a blazer to be repaired at a little clothes alterations place in St Helier.'

'How do you know?'

'Because I've just been to collect it.' Ben opened up his bag, pulled out the blazer and showed them.

'That was a birthday present for him, years ago, before all the troubles began,' Jessica said.

Next, Ben took the police artist's sketch from his pocket. 'You agree there's no way the man in this picture could get into that blazer?'

'I doubt it,' Jessica said, raising an eyebrow.

'Right. Then how do we explain why he'd have a missing button and a ripped lining fixed on a jacket he couldn't wear any more?'

Mike and Jessica looked at each other. 'I don't know,' she said.

'Simple explanation,' Ben said. 'He isn't the man in the picture. He just wants us to think he is. The blazer repair tells us two things. One, he didn't just fake his hair and beard when he came here for Carl. I think he was all padded up to make himself look overweight, to mislead the police. He could easily have disposed of the padding, the wig and the beard afterwards. Based on how carefully he's gone about the whole thing, I'd say he burned them.'

'And the second thing?' Mike asked intently.

'The blazer's been ready for collection since two days after the abduction. The repair took about a week, which tells us Drew took it in about five days before snatching Carl: let's say the second of May. Now, we also know that *four* days before snatching Carl, probably the day after taking the blazer in for repair, he withdrew all the money from the bank.'

'That just indicates he was acting randomly, without logic. Like a crazy person,' Mike said.

'No, I think it indicates that the scheme to snatch Carl all came together quite suddenly,' Ben replied. 'Why would he have bothered with the clothes repair, if he'd known he wouldn't be around for the collection date? That suggests he hadn't been planning the kidnapping for very long. Something triggered him off, and we can narrow down the moment that happened to sometime between his taking the blazer for repair to the time of the cash withdrawal first thing on the fourth of May. That's a pretty tight window. He was suddenly in a hurry.'

'But you said he'd been working on losing the weight all this time,' Jessica said, confused. Doesn't that sound like he was planning it all long in advance?'

Ben nodded. 'Like you said, weight loss doesn't happen overnight. It's been a medium-term goal for Drew. But I don't think he was doing it as part of his kidnap plan. He was doing it for the same reason anyone else would. To become healthier, to get himself together, sober up, clean up his act and maybe, in time, be allowed to see his son again. Then something else happened. Something that made him take this sudden drastic action.'

'But what?' Jessica asked. Tears were forming in her eyes.

'That I don't know,' Ben said.

'This is all guesswork,' Jessica burst out. 'We're just sitting here speculating over tiny details, when Drew is out there with Carl, God knows where, and getting further away every minute.' She was glaring angrily at Ben.

‘They’re not tiny details, Jessica,’ Mike said, putting a hand on her arm. ‘Ben has done some great work here. If this is right, and we can give a much more accurate description to the police, we stand a far better chance of finding them.’

‘I can’t take this any longer,’ Jessica said in a choking voice. Getting up abruptly from her stool, she excused herself and ran from the room, leaving Ben alone with Mike. A door slammed. They could hear the sound of her crying inconsolably from another room.

‘I’m sorry about that,’ Mike said. ‘She’s under so much strain.’

‘I don’t blame her for a minute,’ Ben said.

‘I think your ideas make sense,’ Mike said. ‘And I’m also thinking I might know what triggered Drew. Don’t tell Jessica I said this, because it’s a sore subject and I don’t want to upset her any more than she already is. But shortly before Carl was taken, I’d been trying to persuade her to sell up here and leave Jersey. Fresh start, you know? A new life, just her and me and Carl, leaving behind the past and all the painful memories. Not to mention that I wasn’t happy living in the house she’d shared with Drew. Sleeping in the same bed.’

‘I understand,’ Ben said.

‘It’s sensitive, you know? We argued a lot about it. Jessica didn’t want to leave, and thought I was trying to force her unfairly. Now, I’m thinking that what if Carl overheard us arguing? What if he’d mentioned it to his biological father? He could easily have called him behind our backs. Couldn’t that have prompted Drew to want to take him away sooner rather than later, before he lost touch entirely? Maybe it drove him into a panic.’

Ben thought about it, and nodded. ‘It’s possible.’

'And if it's true, then it means . . . it means I'm partly to blame. If I hadn't put that pressure on her . . .'

'Don't beat yourself up,' Ben said. 'It was Drew who took him, remember.'

Mike looked relieved. 'Thanks, Ben. Keep us posted, won't you?'

'Of course,' Ben said, opening the door.

'I really appreciate what you're doing for us,' Mike said. 'I know you're going to find him.'

Ben just nodded, and left.

Chapter 7

The Dover base of Finley & Reynolds Investigations Ltd was situated at the end of a tree-shaded terrace of tall three-storey Victorian houses that were now mostly offices apart from one or two residential properties, on a narrow street on the edge of town. Ben had come across quite a few low-rent gumshoe private dick operations in his time, but Finley & Reynolds wasn't one of them. A sporty Jaguar was among the cars parked in a railed-off area in front, and a wall plaque engraved with the company name glittered in the late-afternoon sun.

He'd known even before leaving Jersey that these guys wouldn't talk to him. Improvisation was the key in such cases.

He climbed the steps to the front door, which sported a handsome, gleaming brass lion's-head knocker below a stained glass window panel. More olde worlde charm, doing a fine job of offsetting the stigma that was hard to detach from the sometimes inevitably seedy domain of private investigations. Ben pushed through the heavy door and found himself in a spacious white lobby filled with artificial plants. A woman smiled at him from behind a desk as he walked over.

He didn't smile back at her. Instead, he clasped a hand to his cheek and twisted his face as if in terrible pain. 'Think it's a bloody abscess,' he said indistinctly. 'How quickly can I be seen?'

The woman stared blankly at him for a second, then understood. 'I'm so sorry,' she said with a frown of sympathy. 'You've got the wrong place. The dental surgery is next door. But I think they're shut on a Saturday.'

Ben mumbled a tortured apology and hurried out. By the time he'd reached the door, a quick sideways glance had told him the location of the alarm system control box a few feet from the entrance, what type it was and how to disable it. This kind of stuff wasn't exactly new to him.

But it would have to wait a few hours. Toothache miraculously vanished, the patient walked the half mile back to the bed and breakfast he was staying in. There he sorted through some of the kit he always carried in his bag: the mini-Maglite; the set of locksmith's picks made to resemble an innocent ring of Allen wrenches; the Yale universal bump key that looked just like an ordinary house key and was disguised on a ring of real ones, capable of opening most locks; and a pair of thin leather gloves. Nothing that could mark him out too obviously as a burglar, should a nosy cop decide to take a look inside his bag.

Ben bided his time quietly until early evening. Having never liked breaking and entering on an empty stomach, sometime after seven he made his way to a nearby pub, ordered a steak and lingered for a long time over a couple of pints of Guinness when what he really wanted was whisky.

He was the last to leave the pub at closing time. From there, he took a long stroll along the seafront, then made his way down onto the beach where he leaned back on a bench and watched the lights twinkling on the water while he chain-smoked the last of a packet of Gauloises. It wasn't quite his own little secluded stretch of shingled Galway beach, though, and the intrusive Saturday-night thump of music drifting down from a nightclub on the esplanade kept reminding him how he missed his sanctuary in Ireland. When the green glow of his watch dial read one-thirty, he shouldered his bag and began making his way back towards the detective agency.

The parking area in front of Finley & Reynolds' offices was empty now, the rails gleaming dully by the amber glow of the streetlights. Ben slipped on his gloves as he neared the steps. A plain white van and a couple of residents' cars sat along the kerbside, but other than that, the street was deserted.

He didn't pause at the bottom of the steps to glance about, or go darting quickly up to the door. The furtive ones were always the ones who got spotted. With all the casual ease of someone who'd worked there for years and was just popping back late to pick up some documents they'd forgotten, he approached the door and took out his bumper key. If that didn't work, the lock picks would make fast work of it. Once he was inside, the thirty seconds' delay before the alarm system sounded would be ample time for him to open up the alarm control box and disable the power and phone wires. He'd reconnect them before leaving, so that nobody would ever know he'd been there. In and out: the SAS way, except without blowing anything up.

The bumper key slid into the lock. He felt the serrations engage in the cylinder. Just one twist, and he'd be in.

But just as the lock was about to open, the side door of the van parked at the kerbside slid open with a scrape and a clang. Three dark figures piled out and instantly raced across the pavement to the steps of the building. Figures clutching impact weapons.

Ben instinctively ducked the object that came slicing towards him. The tapered aluminium shaft of the baseball bat swooshed through empty air where his head had been half a second earlier, and smashed into the stained glass window panel on the door, instantly setting off a high, keening alarm.

'That's just great,' Ben said. But he couldn't afford to worry about that now. The strike that had just been aimed at him would have killed him if he hadn't moved fast. And that was upsetting. So was the sight of the knife in the hand of one of the other attackers.

At times like these, Ben didn't have to think about what to do. Thinking was too long-winded a process. Thinking got you killed. So he simply reacted. Fast. Faster than anything any of the three had ever seen before, or could even have imagined.

In less than a second, he'd gained control of the thick end of the baseball bat and jabbed the handle end hard and fast towards its wielder, aiming at the strip between the eyeholes of the ski mask. The round pommel of the bat hammered into the bridge of the guy's nose with a soft crackling crunch and sent him sprawling backwards down the steps, knocking down the man behind him. The third attacker managed to dodge out of the way and came at Ben with the knife. Ben saw it coming, that slim little four-inch blade glittering like a tongue of flame under the streetlight as it darted towards his stomach.

With his back to the door and nowhere to retreat, he twisted aside; the knife missed him and the force of the stab sent its sharp tip thunking into the wood. Before the man could wrench the blade free, Ben had broken his wrist. Then, without hesitation, he grasped the collar of the man's jacket and drove his head so hard into the iron railing alongside the steps that the bars bent.

Ben let him collapse in an unconscious heap, plucked the knife out of the door and turned to face the other two, who'd picked themselves up. The one with the smashed nose was unsteady on his feet and pouring blood from under his mask. The other was brandishing his bat but looking much less sure of himself now that it was all on him to finish the job. Ben saw the fear in his eyes, and knew it was over. With barely a glance at their stricken comrade, the two of them retreated quickly to the van. The uninjured one leapt into the driver's seat, twisted the ignition and hit the gas. The van took off with a wheel-spinning screech and a roar, and went snaking wildly off up the street.

The alarm went on keening, shrill and insistent. Ben's plan was already blown – now he had just a short time to press some truth out of his remaining attacker. 'Wakey, wakey,' he said, slapping him hard about the face and shaking him. The man's eyes fluttered groggily open in the holes of the ski mask.

'Nice to know who your friends are, hmm?' Ben said to him as the escaping van skidded round the corner out of sight. As the man put up a half-hearted struggle, Ben kicked him all the way down the steps, hauled him roughly upright, slammed him hard up against the wall and ripped the mask off his head. He was about thirty. Crew cut, brutish features, scarred cheek. 'They find you in the pages of a comic book?' Ben said.

Lights were coming on in the residential part of the street as the alarm began to draw attention. Time was getting shorter by the instant, and Ben wasn't going to waste words. The guy gasped in terror as the edge of the blade pressed against his windpipe with just enough pressure to break the first layer of skin. The broken wrist and fingers were all but forgotten now. He looked into Ben's eyes and saw the look that left him in no doubt: here was someone who would not hesitate to saw his head off if he didn't talk, and fast.

'Who sent you?' Ben demanded. Over the shrilling of the alarm came the sound he'd been afraid he'd hear any moment. Saturday night in Dover with little to do, the cops were on the prowl. The siren wasn't too far away. They'd be here in a minute.

'I said, who sent you?' A little more pressure with the blade. Another layer of skin. The thin trickle of blood looked black in the street light.

'Hunter!' the man wheezed in panic, desperately trying to pull back from the touch of the blade.

Ben frowned. 'Drew Hunter?'

'Yeah—'

'Where's the boy?' Ben rasped, his eyes just inches from the guy's. He ground the blade's edge harder against his throat. Any more, and it would sink in so deep that he wouldn't ever talk again.

'Aagh! I don't know!'

The howl of the siren was drawing close. Ben took his eyes off his captive for an instant and saw the swirling blue halo and the blaze of headlights at the end of the street. Time to leave. He let the guy slide down the wall and slump bleeding to the pavement. Picked up his bag and slipped away round the side of the building just as the police car came tearing into sight. There was a little fenced yard at the back, a screen of conifers between it and the neighbouring property. Ben tossed the knife, vaulted over the fence. Without a sound, he merged into the shadows and was gone.

Chapter 8

Back in his digs across town, Ben threw open the window, leaned out and lit a Gauloise. He washed the first deep draw of smoke down with a sip from his whisky flask to quell the last of the adrenaline rush still pumping around his system. There was a small shard of glass in his hair. He picked it carefully out and laid it on the windowsill, gazing thoughtfully at it and trying to understand what the hell was going on.

The anomalies were stacking up. There were more questions than answers, but one thing was for sure: this case was about more than just a kidnapping. If Drew Hunter had sent in a bunch of heavies to take Ben down, it could only be for one reason: to stop him from finding out too much about whatever business Hunter had had with the private detective. But what, and why?

Ben was as expert at following people as he was at telling when he was being followed himself – and he was certain he hadn't been. Yet somehow, Hunter had known where to find him. The man was full of surprises. Was he also behind Paul Finley's death? It was a worrying thought. If Hunter was a killer as well as an abductor, then Carl might be in more danger than anyone, even Ben, had anticipated.

More certain than ever that the files of Finley & Reynolds held an important key to all this, he resolved not to leave

Dover until he knew more. And when he returned there the following night he'd be ready for the unexpected.

Ben awoke the next morning knowing that today was going to be a waiting game. He gulped down breakfast and then spent a while in his room, going over his case notes in an attempt to make sense of them. Around lunchtime, he returned to the beach, biding his time, quietly smoking, watching the tide. Waiting was a skill he'd perfected in the SAS. He'd learned how to remain still for long periods, outwardly so calm that an observer might think he was in a trance – while mentally he was ultra-alert, aware of everything around him and analysing a thousand details at once.

It was afternoon when his phone rang. It was Jessica, sounding in a high state of agitation. 'Where are you?'

'Still in Dover,' he replied. 'Something came up.'

Strange that she didn't seem interested to ask what, he thought. In the next moment, he understood why.

'We heard from Carl.'

Ben's eyes narrowed. 'What do you mean, heard from him? When?'

'He phoned us. Just half an hour ago.'

'You talked to him?'

'No,' she groaned. 'We weren't here. We were only gone twenty minutes, to get some shopping because there wasn't a scrap of food left in the house. When we got back, there was a message on the answer machine. We'd only just missed him. We tried calling the number back but it didn't come up. It sounded like a mobile.'

'He didn't say where he was calling from?'

'He wasn't on the line long enough. We called the police right away. They're working on tracing the call. Ben, you've got to get back here.'

This changed everything.

'I'm on my way,' he said.

'The police just left a few minutes ago,' Jessica told him when he arrived at the house just over three hours later. He wasn't entirely sorry to hear that he'd missed them. Cops were as uneasy in his presence as he felt in theirs. It wasn't a harmonious relationship he had with them, never had been, never would be.

'There have been developments since I called you,' she said. Jumpy with contained excitement, she led him into a huge, plush living room where a phone sat on a low table. Moments later, Mike joined them. 'Ben, thank Christ you're here. Sorry we had to call you back from Dover so urgently, but under the circumstances . . .'

'What's happening?'

'Since we called you earlier, lots. The mobile number turned out to be a foreign one. Interpol are involved now. They've traced the phone's owner. It's registered to a man called Barberini. Gianni Barberini. Apparently, he's a doctor in Turin.'

'A dermatologist,' Jessica corrected him.

'What do the police make of it?' Ben asked.

'They seem as baffled by it as we are,' Mike replied. 'Last we heard, they were still trying to track down this Dr Barberini's whereabouts. He's not at home. His wife told them he was away at some medical conference in Milan, but she's not heard from him. We've been waiting for more. And hoping you could make sense of this.'

'Let me hear the message,' Ben said.

Mike replayed it from the answerphone. The line was a bad one, with an echo and lots of background noise. *'Mum? It's me,'* said a boy's voice.

'That's definitely him?' Ben asked Jessica, and she gave a quick, certain nod.

'Mum, I'm . . . I'm okay,' Carl blurted, speaking in hesitant snatches over the background noise, which sounded to Ben like voices, as if the boy had been calling from the middle of a crowd of people. But there was another noise too, distorted and hard to identify. A kind of screech, followed by what sounded like a muffled bang. Ben couldn't make it out at all.

'I just wanted to say . . . I love you, mum. I—' Carl's voice was lost for a second amid some kind of commotion. *'I've got to go,'* he said suddenly. And there the message ended.

Jessica was looking fraught and gnawing at her thumb. 'That's all there is,' Mike said anxiously. 'What do you make of it, Ben?'

'It's definitely some kind of public place,' Ben said. 'Indoors, and crowded. A bar, maybe, or a café. But that other sound . . . let me hear it again.'

Mike replayed the message. Ben closed his eyes, concentrating hard on the strange noises in the background. They seemed to be coming from further away, which meant they must have been pretty loud. 'What is that?' he muttered to himself.

'The police think it might be fireworks,' Jessica said. 'The high-pitched screech, then the loud bang. What else makes a sound like that?'

'Maybe,' Ben said. 'But in the middle of the day?'

'They have technicians working on it,' Mike said. 'Apparently they can separate out the frequencies or something, and use filters to clean them up.'

Ben looked at his watch. It was getting late, but there was still time if he hurried. He pulled out his car key.

'Where are you going?' Mike asked.

'Turin,' Ben said.

Chapter 9

It was getting towards midnight by the time Ben's flight touched down at the Aeroporto di Torino in the middle of a rainstorm. As he was leaving the airport, Jessica called again.

'They found Barberini,' she said, and for a second Ben thought she was going to tell him that he was dead, too. 'Found him?' he asked.

'I mean, they have him. He turned up at his home in Turin at eight o'clock this evening, and the Italian police were waiting for him there. They took him for questioning. As far as we can tell, they're still talking to him.'

'Any feedback yet?' Ben asked as he spotted the car rental place across the way and began heading for it, head down through the lashing rain.

'They're keeping us updated. I don't think he's been charged with anything. It's been confirmed he was on the list of delegates at that conference, and his alibi checks out. He totally denies any involvement in the abduction. Says he's never heard of Drew or Carl, and doesn't know anyone from Jersey. But listen to this.'

'I'm listening.'

'They found fingerprints on his phone. The police faxed Interpol a set of Carl's taken from his room, and we had a call twenty minutes ago saying they're a match. So Barberini's lying. He was involved.'

'Or else Carl just used his phone to make the call,' Ben said. 'With any luck, we'll soon find out.'

*

At nearly twelve-thirty a.m., a very resentful and sullen Dottore Gianni Barberini was finally released from police questioning, demanding to be taken home in an unmarked car so that his nosy neighbours wouldn't take him for some kind of a damned criminal. The pouring rain just pissed him off all the more. All the way from the Posto di Polizia to his villa in one of the more affluent neighbourhoods of the city, he grumbled sourly at the plain-clothes driver, who was just as irritable as he was for having to ferry this arrogant prick home, and made no reply.

It was ten to one by the time Barberini climbed wearily out of the car and tramped up his long, curving driveway, cursing the rain and glancing up at the master bedroom windows to ensure that Germana hadn't stayed up waiting for him. The lights were all off – thank God. His wife could be a terrible bitch if she was disturbed late at night. In fact, he reflected sourly as he approached the house, she'd been a terrible bitch for most of the miserable thirty-two years he'd been married to her.

Rather than risk waking her and face all kinds of wrath and yet more goddamn inquisition that night, he made for the separate entrance to the suite of rooms he used for his private dermatology practice here at the villa. Above it was his little sanctuary, his personal den, where he often slept on the sofa bed after working late, or sometimes just to get away from Germana. He loved it in there, undisturbed, just him and his collection . . . He paused at the door, fumbling keys with one eye on her window, dreading that her bedroom light might come on at any moment. Where was the key? Ah – got it.

'Gianni Barberini?' said a voice behind him.

Barberini whirled around and his eyes opened wide at the sight of the stranger standing there. He hadn't heard anyone sneak up behind him. The guy had moved like a ghost. 'Who the hell are you?' he demanded indignantly.

'Someone who's going to ask you a few questions.'

Barberini glared at him. The blond-haired stranger didn't look much like an Italian. Didn't sound like one, either. He spoke the language fluently enough, but the accent was foreign. A Swiss, maybe? A Kraut? 'What's the matter with you people? I've just spent the last seven hours giving my statement over and over. That not enough for you bastard cops?'

'I'm not a cop,' Ben said. 'But some people say I'm a bit of a bastard, so you'd best get talking to me before I start to get nasty.'

Barberini stared at Ben for a moment, the cocksure belligerence in his eyes turning to uncertainty.

'Lead the way,' Ben said, motioning towards the door.

Barberini hesitated, then did what he was told. They walked through a comfortable little waiting area into the consulting room, then through that to a nicely decorated office lined with medical certificates and books. At the far end of the office, an open-tread stairway led upwards to the floor above.

'We can talk in here,' Barberini said nervously as they emerged in his den.

Ben looked around him at the room. 'Very cosy. So this is your little hobby room, is it?'

'Look, whoever you are, I don't know anything about a missing kid. I swear it. I'm telling the truth, just like I told the cops. I got the rail tickets to prove it. Hotel bill. Everything.'

'You were in Milano for a conference?'

'Yeah, for two days. A European Society for Pediatric Dermatology seminar. Top of the agenda was the latest research from Kiel University into infantile haemangiomas.'

'You can spare me the jargon. I take it you weren't one of the speakers?'

'No, I was just attending it. First day was good. Afterwards I spent the evening with Davide Gagliardo, a medical colleague from Bologna. He's already corroborated my story. Second day wasn't so interesting, so I left for a while and went to a coffee bar for a break. I called my wife from there to tell her not to wait up for me tonight because I'd be home late. I didn't think it would be *so* fucking late.'

'Go on with the story,' Ben said, with just enough menace in his voice to keep Barberini on edge.

'Anyway, so that's why I had my phone out, see? I'm sitting there finishing my coffee, then I see this guy at the next table eating a cannoncini alla crema – that's a pastry.'

'I know what it is,' Ben said, eyeing him coldly. When people recounted their stories in this much elaborate detail, they were usually full of shit.

'Right. I'm thinking how I'd like one of those myself. The waiter's right across the room and I'm in a hurry, so I go over to the counter to order one. Left my stuff at the table. My back was turned maybe a minute, maybe two. When I come back, I notice how the phone isn't where I left it, like someone had moved it. I thought maybe a waiter or someone had nudged it as they passed by.'

'So you wouldn't know if a twelve-year-old boy picked it up while your back was turned?'

'Hey, listen. The place was full of people. I didn't even see a kid, let alone speak to him or have anything to do with him, okay? That's the whole truth, and I've got evidence to back up all of it. The first I heard about this kidnapping business is when I got home tonight and the police were waiting for me.' Barberini's face was flushed. 'That's it. You've heard all there is to hear. So now would you kindly leave my home, before I call the cops? Hey, be careful with that. It's extremely valuable. Please, put it down.'

As Barberini had been talking, Ben had gone over to one of several trophy cabinets that lined the walls of the Italian's little den. Except they weren't filled with trophies. From the moment they'd come in, Ben had noticed the large collection of old motor racing memorabilia that cluttered the room. 'What, this?' he said innocently, holding the racing helmet he'd picked off a display unit.

'Yes, that,' Barberini said, turning pale. 'It's the helmet Mario Andretti wore when he won the South African Grand Prix in 1971.'

'Really?' Ben lobbed it casually across to him, like a ball.

Barberini leaped forward with a squawk to catch the helmet, and clutched it to his breast as if he'd just rescued a holy relic from the barbarian hordes. 'Don't mess with my collection,' he muttered.

It was far from being the only holy relic in the room. On one wall was a giant signed poster of Ayrton Senna. A steering wheel was encased behind glass, with a photo of a beaming, goggled Jim Clark in the cockpit of a sixties'-era Lotus. A whole corner was dominated by a vintage twelve-cylinder Ferrari demonstration engine on a stand, part of its casing cut away to reveal its lovingly oiled innards. Pictures everywhere. Cars, cars, cars. You could almost smell the high-octane fuel and burning rubber and hear the shriek of high-performance engines revving sky-high.

Ben was putting it together in his mind. 'Quite the racing car freak, aren't you, doctor? You must spend a lot of time and money on this stuff.'

Barberini reverently replaced the precious helmet on its unit and turned angrily to face Ben. 'Never mind what I am,' he blustered. 'You haven't even told me who you are. You better show me some ID. What right have you got to come in here, asking me all these questions and manhandle my property like that?'

'I never did think it was fireworks,' Ben said.

'Fireworks?' Barberini snarled at him. 'I don't know what the hell you're talking about. But there'll be some fireworks in a minute if you don't get out of my house.' He stamped over to a desk, yanked open a drawer and pulled out something small and black.

'I wouldn't do that,' Ben said, eyeing the little Beretta .25 auto that Barberini was pointing at him.

'And I wouldn't come a step closer,' Barberini said with a twisted smile. 'Unless you want a keyhole in your belly.'

Chapter 10

Ben stood very still, staring at the gun.

'Not so tough now, are we?' Barberini chuckled.

'You can't shoot me,' Ben said.

'Want a bet? Self defence. The cops will drag you to the morgue and give me a medal. One less scumbag in the world.'

'No, I mean you can't shoot me because the safety's on,' Ben said, pointing. 'Let me show you how it works.' In two steps, he'd walked up to the gaping Barberini and twisted the gun sharply out of his hand.

'Aagh! You son of a whore! You broke my finger!'

'You're a doctor,' Ben said. 'You should know it's not broken. Now *this*,' he went on, holding up the tiny pistol, 'is what we call a mouse gun. Probably wouldn't have pierced my jacket. Not very accurate, either. I'll bet I couldn't even hit that signed Ayrton Senna poster from here. Let's have a try.' He flicked off the safety catch and took careful aim.

'Please!' Barberini cried out. 'Not that! It's irreplaceable!'

'I imagine so,' Ben said. 'All right, then let's see if we can put a dent in a Ferrari flat-twelve cylinder head. I doubt it, personally.' He pointed the gun at the engine on the stand.

'No! I beg you!' Barberini was virtually crying.

Ben lowered the pistol. 'Not that either? Then tell me, doctor. How was the Grand Prix?'

There was a moment's dead silence in the room. Then Barberini, ashen-faced and trembling, said, 'I know who you are now.'

'You do?'

'Yes, I do. You're not searching for any missing kid. You're a fucking private eye. Germana hired you, didn't she? My darling wife. And I suppose you know all about Claudia?'

Ben shook his head. 'I'm not interested in some pretty young thing you ran off to meet when you were pretending to be in Milan and getting one of your doctor buddies to cover up for you. The hotel bill – that was a nice touch, by the way. Fooled the police, at any rate.'

'Then what do you want?' Barberini moaned, nursing his twisted finger.

'Not all your story was a lie, I'll give you that,' Ben said. 'I believe that you were in a café. I believe you turned your back for a moment, and that the boy happened to be there and took the opportunity to use your phone. But you weren't there by yourself, and you weren't at any conference. While the boy was calling on your phone, there was a noise outside. Hard to tell what it was at first. It was a car crash, and no ordinary car, either. Sounded like quite a smash. Was the driver badly hurt?'

Barberini knew there was no longer any point in pretending. 'He walked away from it,' he muttered. 'A few cuts and bruises. He was lucky.'

'I'm pleased to hear it,' Ben said. 'Now, I can easily find out what Grand Prix took place this afternoon within driving distance of here. But you're going to save me the trouble. Aren't you, doctor?'

'Monaco,' Barberini groaned, shoulders sagging. The admission was obviously a lot more painful than his twisted finger.

'You were in Monaco this afternoon?'

'Yeah, yeah. You got me. I wasn't in Milan. I never went to the conference. You were right, I got my pal Davide to cover up for me so I could spend some time with Claudia and catch the GP. We were at medical school together. I cover for him, sometimes.'

'So he's another one who cheats on his wife,' Ben said.

'Look, you don't know Germana,' Barberini protested. 'She makes my life a misery.'

'I suppose Davide says the same about Mrs Gagliardo,' Ben replied. 'The fact is, I really don't give a shit about your domestic affairs. But I'm betting Germana would be interested to know what you've been up to. I know she's at home, because I saw her at the bedroom window earlier. So unless you want me to go and wake her up and have a little chat with her, you're going to tell me exactly where you were when the crash happened this afternoon in Monaco.'

Chapter 11

It was less than a three-hour drive from Turin to Monaco, especially the way Ben drove, and at that time of night the motorway was virtually deserted. He called Jessica's number from the road.

'Sorry to wake you in the wee hours,' he said when she picked up.

'I wasn't sleeping anyway. I hardly do these days.'

'Any more news?'

'Carl hasn't called again. Nothing from the police. What's happening at your end?'

'Tell me,' he said. 'Is Drew a race fan?'

'Horses?'

'Cars.'

'No, he could never stand motor racing.'

'What about Carl?'

'Never expressed an interest. Why are you asking? Have you found something?'

'Get some sleep, Jessica. You sound knackered.' Ben ended the call and went back to wondering what the hell Drew Hunter was doing in Monaco. And how a kidnapped boy had been able to walk into a café and make a phone call to his mother. This case was getting stranger by the hour.

'Fuck it,' he muttered to himself as the car sped into the night. There was nothing for it but to keep pushing on and see where the trail led him.

*

The tiny principality of Monaco, all two square kilometres of it, went about achieving its enviable record as the safest and most crime-free corner of Europe, even of the world, by means of a virtual police state. The heavily armed cops didn't tolerate vagrants, any more than they would look kindly on unshaven, slovenly-looking former British Special Forces soldiers kipping in their cars with the remnants of a flask of malt whisky between their knees and a 'borrowed' .25-calibre semi-auto pistol in their pocket. Sometime before dawn, Ben found a secluded spot in the wooded hills overlooking the small city and its moonlit harbour, and settled back in his reclined driver's seat for a couple of hours' nap.

By the time he'd awoken, feeling none too refreshed, cleaned himself up as best he could, revitalised himself with the first Gauloise of the day and driven down into the winding streets of Monte Carlo to find a parking place, the place was already buzzing. Yesterday's Grand Prix was now winding up, but in the aftermath of the huge annual event the streets were still crowded and crackling with the excitement of thousands of spectators from all over Europe and beyond. Crews of race personnel were busily dismantling the crash barriers that lined the streets; in just a few hours one of the most famous race circuits of all time would revert back to being simply one of the wealthiest and most fashionable resorts in the world.

Ben now knew the exact spot where the Argentinian driver Enrique Hernandez had spun off the track and totalled his McLaren, in what had been the only real dramatic incident of yesterday's Grand Prix. Debris from the accident was still being gathered up and loaded onto a trailer as he walked by. The crash had happened on the approach to a hairpin bend at the end of a narrow straight that ran within sight of the harbour. Anyone living in the snazzy apartments overlooking the narrow street would get a stunning view of the race, if they could stand the din of the cars rocketing past below their balconies.

Ben walked on. It was warm. The scintillating morning sunshine glared off the white buildings. Blue sky, blue water, lazy yachts and whispering palm trees. The place must have had some real allure once, he thought, before it had become a haven for the self-consciously rich who lived only to flash their toys, their tans and their starvation-diet bodies, immaculately groomed and preened down to the last designer thread. He knew he stood out like a sore thumb here among the beautiful people. Every second vehicle was a Rolls or a Lambo. Perhaps inspired by the thrill of the Grand Prix, all the moneyed young bucks were out in force, cruising the drag in their aviator shades, arms dangling from the windows of their gleaming red sports cars and trying to look all aloof and studly for the preternaturally large numbers of attractive young females on the street.

Fifty metres up from the crash site, right on the hairpin bend for which Hernandez had been braking when he lost control, was the café from where Carl Hunter had made his brief phone call home. Scantily clad women in sunglasses and men with gold watches the size of wagon wheels were taking their morning coffees and champagne breakfasts at parasol-shaded tables on the pavement outside.

Ben flicked his unfinished Gauloise into a vacant ashtray, strolled into the bustling café and glanced about. He approved of the John Coltrane jazz playing in the background; other than that, the place was way too glitzy for his tastes, but he hadn't come here to appreciate the decor. Second alcove on the right: that was the table where Gianni Barberini had been necking distractedly with his girlfriend when Carl had managed to snatch the mobile phone from the table for a few moments.

'Can I help you, sir?' asked a waiter.

'Maybe,' Ben said. 'Were you working here yesterday?'

'Sure. It was crazy.'

Ben took out the photo of Carl to show him. 'Did you see this boy? He may have dark hair now.'

The waiter peered closely at Ben. 'Police?'

'Scotland Yard,' Ben said, and flashed an old military pass at the guy. 'What about this man?' he asked, taking out the photo of a slightly younger and much slimmer Drew Hunter that Jessica had given him. 'Again, dark hair now. We think he may be living locally.'

'What'd he do, default on his taxes?' the waiter asked with a grin.

'Terrorist bomber,' Ben said.

'No shit.' The waiter studied the pictures for a moment, then shook his head. 'Can't say they look familiar to me.'

'Think I might show these to a couple of your other staff here?'

'Sure, no problem. See Valérie over there? Go ask her.'

But Ben drew a blank with Valérie and the other three members of staff he quizzed. He downed a quick espresso at the bar, then walked back out into the sunshine and gave a sigh.

'Fine,' he murmured aloud. 'Then we do this the hard way.'

The hard way was to go hoofing it door-to-door, and just keep trying until, with any luck, someone recognised either Carl or Drew from the photos. It was gruelling and time-consuming work, but Ben didn't have a lot of choice. The only question was where to start. He glanced left, glanced right, and began making his way back down the busy street towards the apartment buildings near the crash site.

He walked briskly, deep in thought. He passed a boutique. Then a little charcuterie. Next door was a bakery, emanating the wonderful odour of fresh baguette still warm from the oven. A man stepped out of the bakery, dressed in Bermuda shorts and a white polo shirt. He was slim and clean-shaven, with dark glasses and a Panama hat. He had a shopping basket in one hand and a couple of baguettes wrapped in brown paper tucked under his arm. His son followed him out of the bakery, a pre-teenage boy who looked like any other Mediterranean kid: tanned, black hair.

They were Drew and Carl Hunter.

Chapter 12

Ben barely paused in his stride, even though every nerve in his body was jangling like an alarm bell at the sight of them. Covering his reaction perfectly without a flicker of emotion showing on his face, he walked on a few steps and then paused and gazed in the bakery window, ostensibly to admire hungrily a rack of ornate chocolate-laced delicacies on display.

Drew and Carl passed within just a couple of feet of him and then went walking on up the street. Ben waited a few tantalising seconds, watching them from the corner of his eye as he allowed a little distance to come between himself and the pair, then moved away from the window and began to follow them.

They didn't seem to be in a hurry, just ambling along at a pace that allowed Ben to merge into the slow-moving crowds about twenty yards behind. Watching them, they could have been any father and son on earth. Nothing whatsoever in Carl's body language suggested any of the unease or distress Ben would have expected to see in a kidnap victim. What was going on?

But he didn't have long to dwell over the matter. Because without warning, Carl turned, picked Ben out of the crowd of people and looked right at him.

Ben's heart skipped a beat. Again, he managed to cover up his reaction, avoiding eye contact and pretending to be gazing at something across the street. For two seconds that felt like minutes, he could feel the boy's eyes on him.

Finally, Carl turned away and kept walking alongside his father, who didn't seem to have noticed anything.

It must be a fluke, Ben thought. Okay, so maybe he didn't quite fit the Monaco image and looked a little rougher, a little less manicured, than the typical good citizen of the place. But surely he didn't stand out *that* much. There was no way anyone, let alone a twelve-year-old kid totally untrained in the art of counter-surveillance, could jump to the conclusion or have any inkling that they were being trailed.

He went on following them. Now father and son were in conversation about something. Ben relaxed, certain that he hadn't been spotted after all.

And then Carl turned again. This time, he whirled around very quickly, too suddenly for Ben to look away until it was too late.

Carl stared right at him. He seemed to know. But how? Had the boy phoned Jessica again that morning? Had she let slip about Ben?

Carl started nudging his father and tugging at his sleeve, pointing back in Ben's direction. 'Oh, shit,' Ben said, and turned to peer in another window. But it was pointless. He was blown.

Drew turned and looked in the direction Carl was pointing, right at Ben. He frowned questioningly down at the boy. The boy nodded up to him, as if to say 'I'm sure'. Now they were both staring at Ben. The game was up. Fear was in the air. Drew Hunter dropped his shopping basket and his baguettes where he stood. He grabbed his son by the arm, and they took off.

'Shit,' Ben said again, and broke through the slow-moving pedestrians to give chase. Drew and Carl dashed across the street, weaving between honking traffic. Ben went after them. Too late, he saw a motorcycle bearing down on him, tried to dive out of its way and lost his footing, falling and grazing his knee. The rider braked hard. Too hard. With a screech, the front wheel locked and washed out from under the machine as it toppled over with a scraping clatter. The rider tumbled to the road, but sprang up again almost instantly, and Ben could see he wasn't hurt. No time to hang around and help the guy straighten his bent handlebar. Drew and Carl were getting away.

Cursing and ignoring the pain from his scraped knee, Ben ran on after them. People stared and pointed. The motorcyclist yelled after him. Ben lost sight of the father and son among a crowd of shoppers, then saw them again, fifty yards further up the street, battling against the tide of pedestrians. Drew had lost his hat, revealing the black-dyed hair beneath. There was nowhere they could run. Ben sprinted up the road, avoiding the pavement. He could catch them.

A guy in a florid shirt was getting into a white open-top Ferrari that was parked at the kerbside. Drew grabbed him by the collar, spun him away from the car, snatched the key from his hand and leapt behind the wheel, dragging Carl in with him. The car roared into life and took off with a squeal, leaving snakes of rubber on the road and its owner standing bellowing and shaking his fist.

The Ferrari came belting down the street towards Ben, and he bounded onto the kerb to get out of its way. He caught a glimpse of the boy gaping at him from the passenger seat as the car streaked past, heading back the way they'd come, towards the straight and past the scene of yesterday's crash.

Ben stood in the gutter, helplessly staring at the disappearing car. People were looking and pointing in alarm. The Ferrari's owner was screaming murder. It wouldn't be long before the police turned up, bristling with weaponry.

Ben had little chance of catching Drew now, but went sprinting down the street after the Ferrari anyway, yelling at frightened pedestrians to get out of his way and making them scatter. Ahead, a little old woman emerged from a fashion boutique laden with boxes, and he almost ran right into her. 'Watch where you're going, asshole!' she shrieked at him. Across the pavement, a chauffeur in uniform and cap was opening the back door of a stately Rolls Royce to let her in. Its engine was purring softly.

'Thanks for the ride,' Ben said to her, and before the chauffeur could stop him, he jumped into the Rolls and floored the accelerator. The car was ungainly but powerful, and Ben was pressed into the red leather of the driver's seat under the acceleration. The swinging open back door scraped a lamppost and crashed shut. Glancing in the mirror, he could see the little old woman and the chauffeur standing speechless on the pavement.

The Ferrari had long since vanished around the hairpin bend at the bottom, past the café. Ben gunned the Rolls down the straight at full throttle, overtaking everything in sight as if he was trying to re-enact the Grand Prix. But it was no racing car. As soon as Ben entered the bend and felt the heavy bodywork begin to pitch on its soft suspension, he knew it was about to go into a slide. He eased off the gas and changed course, clipping the corner and mounting the kerb. There was no avoiding the empty café tables in his path. The Rolls trampled several of them down. Another flew up onto the bonnet, smacked off the windscreen and went tumbling in his wake.

He hit the gas again as the road straightened up ahead. Still no sign of the Ferrari. Unless—

Yes, there it was, a long way up the road, speeding past the traffic. Ben was still in the chase. As he raced after it, he saw its brake lights flare as it stopped for a red light. Drew wasn't exactly schooled in the art of urban high-speed pursuit, which only helped even the odds a little in Ben's favour. The Rolls quickly caught up. He was thirty yards behind the Ferrari when the lights changed and he heard the rasp of its exhausts before it took off again like a bullet fired from a rifle.

The Rolls sped through the junction after it, narrowly avoiding an oncoming car as Ben held the pedal to the floor and struggled to keep this overpowered barge in a straight line. The Ferrari was a shrinking white dot in the distance. There was no way Ben could stay with it. He saw it vanish around a right-hand bend a hundred and fifty yards away, and knew that might be the last he'd see of it.

He couldn't afford to lose Drew and Carl. Not now that they knew he was after them. They'd simply go to ground and he'd never find them again.

It was time for a short cut. Ben saw the little sidestreet flashing up on his right and took the gamble, turning into it with a squeal of tyres and roaring through the narrow space between the houses. Never mind the no vehicular access sign. If his hunch was right, this would cut off a corner and he'd have a sporting chance of catching the Ferrari at the other end.

Or perhaps not. The sidestreet came to an abrupt end up ahead.

'Christ,' Ben muttered as he went to hit the brakes; then he saw it wasn't a cul-de-sac. It was a steep downward flight of steps, bisected down the middle by an iron hand railing.

There was nothing for it. Ben steered right for the steps, keeping his foot down hard on the gas. The brink flashed towards him, like the edge of a waterfall that was about to tip his boat vertical and send it plummeting down to the bottom. He aimed the big square nose of the Rolls at the gap between the iron railing and the stone wall. Felt his front wheels run out of road; then they seemed to fall into space for a second before hitting the steps with a violent jolt that almost pitched Ben through the windscreen. The space between the railing and the wall was perhaps half an inch wider than the Rolls. With a screeching rending of handbuilt coachwork on stone on one side and solid iron on the other, the car hammered unstoppably down the steps.

All Ben could do was hang on. He braced himself for impact as the bottom of the steps raced closer. The Rolls crunched down at a forty-five-degree angle, bouncing all over the road in a shower of sparks, trailing its badly twisted front bumper and leaving the shattered remains of a headlight behind it. Ben sawed wildly at the wheel and stamped on the accelerator. If the old tank was as solid as it felt, it could take a little abuse. This was nothing.

And there was the Ferrari, dead ahead. Ben's gamble had paid off. He smiled grimly as he saw Drew glance back with a look of astonishment. 'You don't get away that easily, matey boy.'

Moments later, they were approaching the limits of town and roaring into the hills. The last of the buildings gave way to verdant countryside, the road twisting upwards between the trees as they climbed over the town. Once again, the Ferrari's huge speed advantage quickly began to tell as it shrank smaller and smaller into the distance ahead. Ben swore. Drew was going to leave him far behind, and that would be it. Then all hopes of catching him would have to be pinned on the French and Italian police.

Ben clenched his jaw as he finally lost sight of the tiny white speck of the speeding sports car. He eased back on the throttle, and the Rolls engine settled down to a smooth purr. The chase was over and he'd lost.

Chapter 13

Ben was wondering what the hell to do next when he rounded the next bend, tighter than the others, and saw smoke drifting on the breeze up ahead. His heart began to thump.

Piled into a tree at the side of the road was the buckled wreckage of the Ferrari, deep trenches cut into the verge where it had skidded out of control. The twisted-up tyre marks were all over the Tarmac.

Drew Hunter was sitting on the grass near the wrecked car, blood trickling from a cut on his temple. Carl was bent over him, apparently quite unhurt and dabbing attentively at his father's wound with a handkerchief. They both turned to look as the Rolls appeared. Ben saw Drew lay a hand on the boy's shoulder, as if to say, 'I'm sorry, son. I tried.'

Ben screeched to a halt. He had to push hard against his battered driver's door to open it. 'Carl, are you okay?' he called out.

'I'm okay,' Carl replied in a small voice. There was resentment in his eyes as he looked at Ben.

'You're all done, Drew,' Ben said as he walked over to them. 'It's time to go home and face the music. Jessica wants her boy back.'

'Jessica sent you?' Drew said. He staggered to his feet as Ben approached. He reached into his trouser pocket and came out with a pistol.

'Not you as well,' Ben said. He could have got Barberini's .25 auto out a lot faster and put half the magazine into Drew, but his job was to take the guy back to Jersey, not shoot him. Besides, something about Drew's gun didn't look right. Ben snatched it from him, without twisting any fingers this time.

Just as he'd thought. It weighed nothing in his hand. Pressed tin and plastic. It was just a non-functioning replica, little more than a toy, totally harmless and, at least to a trained eye, absolutely unrealistic. 'You kidnapped your son with this?' Ben said in bemusement. He didn't understand. How could a man with a toy gun be the same guy who'd hired heavies to kill him? The same guy who'd orchestrated the stabbing of Paul Finley?

'I didn't kidnap him,' Drew retorted. 'I rescued him.'

'Tell that to Jessica and all the cops who're hunting for you,' Ben said.

Drew shook his head in defeat. 'I can't believe you found us.'

'The moral is, don't phone home. Calls have a habit of being tracked.'

'Don't *what?*' Drew said. 'Nobody phoned.'

'It was me,' Carl admitted, flushing.

Drew looked at him. 'Oh, son, what have you done?'

'I'm sorry,' Carl muttered guiltily. 'I just missed mum so much. Just wanted to talk to her . . .' He sniffed, looking as if he was about to cry.

'It's okay, son,' Drew said, and clasped the boy tightly for a moment. 'It's okay. I understand. Daddy doesn't blame you.'

'I hate to break up a family scene,' Ben said. 'Now let's go.'

'You don't realise the harm you're doing,' Drew said to him in an agony of emotion.

Carl was peering at Ben, a strange look in his eyes. 'Dad, I think he's all right.'

'Stop messing around,' Ben said. 'I'm here to take you back. Carl, you have to go home. Your father's in quite a bit of trouble.'

Drew shook his head and put his arm tightly around Carl's shoulders. 'Please. You can't do that. You can't let him go back there. If you could only understand . . . wait, what are you doing?'

Ben had taken out his phone and was dialling. 'You want to talk to your ex-wife?'

'Don't do that!' Drew cried out. 'Please!'

Jessica answered. 'I have them,' Ben told her. 'Both of them. Carl's safe and sound.'

There was an explosion of relief and joy at the other end of the line. Ben smiled to hear it. 'I'll be bringing him home to you soon. Stay near the phone, I'll call again en route.' He ended the call.

'Why did you do that?' Drew groaned. 'You shouldn't have done that.'

'It's my job. To find you and take you back.'

'You fool. You have no idea . . .'

Ben motioned at the Rolls and snapped his fingers. 'Enough. In the car,' he commanded.

'No,' Drew said.

'Don't be stupid, Drew. You'll get in the car, if I have to stuff you in the boot. You really want to do this the hard way?'

'Twenty minutes,' Drew pleaded. 'That's all I ask. I'll explain everything to you. Then you'll know why I can't let my boy go back there. I just can't.'

'You've got ten. Starting now. I'm listening.'

'Ten, then. But not here,' Drew said.

'Here's as good as anywhere.'

'No, no. We have to go back to the apartment,' Drew insisted. 'You'll understand. Trust me. Please.'

Chapter 14

The police sirens ululating over Monte Carlo signalled that the cops were furiously searching for the stolen cars and the thieves who'd made off with them in broad daylight. Their transport was just a little too conspicuous, so rather than risk getting caught Ben ditched it in a backstreet right on the edge of town. He and his two charges walked a little way and then hailed a taxi to take them to Drew's apartment.

Ben knew he was being soft by letting Drew bring him here, but there was no possibility now that the guy could make a break for it and hope to get away from him again. The man seemed so forlorn and broken that Ben couldn't bring himself to play hardball with him. If Drew had something to say, he at least deserved a few minutes to get it off his chest before he was carted home to face justice.

The apartment wasn't exactly a typical desperado hideout. A penthouse crowning an exclusive block overlooking the harbour just a couple of minutes' walk from where Ben had found the two of them, it was as palatial in size as it was luxurious. The place had more antiques than Sotheby's, and some of the Oriental rugs draped over the polished marble floors were probably worth as much as the Rolls Royce Ben had trashed that day.

Seeing Ben's surprised look, Drew explained that the apartment belonged to a former client, Prince Al-Naseem.

Some years ago, Drew had travelled to Saudi Arabia to do a photo portrait of his prized pair of hunting goshawks. The Prince had been impressed enough with the result to grant him free use of the luxury apartment in Monaco whenever he needed it. 'I never told Jessica about it,' Drew sighed. 'Never thought I'd ever use it.'

'You'll get your chance to tell her before too long,' Ben said. 'Now, ten minutes. Remember?'

Sitting on a plush sofa with Carl next to him, Drew took a deep breath and began to tell his story.

'If Jessica's hired you, then you probably know all about me. I was a drunk. I admit it. I was a bum. It's not something I'm proud of. And when Jessica started seeing that Mike character, I got even worse. Like a fool I went and got myself so sloshed that I crashed the car that day. For the first time,' he added, shamefaced, touching the fresh cut on his brow.

'Wasn't your fault, Dad,' Carl said softly.

Drew lovingly caressed his hair. 'Maybe not this time, son. I'm not much of a getaway driver. But the first time *was* my fault and I hate myself for it.' He paused. 'Carl, why don't you go and play with your chess set while I talk to this man?'

'*Dad . . .*'

'Please, Carl.'

With the boy reluctantly gone from the room, Drew was able to speak more freely. 'I felt like drowning myself after the accident. I'd not only risked Carl's safety, the repercussions were devastating. Next thing I knew, Jessica had the restraining order slapped on me and I couldn't even see my boy any more. Maybe I was being irrational. I know I was. But I blamed *him* for it.'

'Mike?' Ben asked.

Drew nodded. 'That fucker was the reason I'd hit the bottle so hard this time. I wanted some kind of revenge. So even though I was banned from driving, I bought an old banger for cash, no tax or insurance, and started hanging about the house. I'd hide in the trees and spy on the place with binoculars. Saw *him* playing with *my* boy in the garden. I knew Carl didn't like him either. He'd told me so. I suppose that could have been a consolation to me, but it just made me feel worse knowing that this slimy prick had taken my place. My role. My life. It was like he'd erased me, like I didn't exist any more.'

Drew paused to reflect sadly. 'God, I was so down, I could've just drunk myself into the ground at that point. But then, I don't know, I just somehow focused. Look at this guy, I thought. What's he got that I haven't got? The answer was obvious. He was better looking than me, he was thinner than me, and he was probably a damn sight richer than me now that I'd squandered most of my money. Not to mention that he wasn't a pitiful stumbling piss-artist, either. So I realised what I had to do to better myself. I poured all the booze down the drain and vowed I'd never touch another drop. Same with all the junk food. Off with the beard, the hair. I started exercising like crazy to lose weight, tried to eat right.'

'And you started on the detox medication,' Ben said.

'You knew about that? It's true. Christ, I'd have done anything to better myself. As time went by, I kept hanging about the house. Couldn't help myself. I looked so different I don't think they'd have recognised me, but I still made sure they never spotted me. I'd noticed the way Mike would often go off on his own for hours at a time, and I got this idea in my head that I should follow him and see what he was up to. I became obsessed with the idea that he was cheating on Jessica, seeing some other woman on the island. It made me so furious. I might have been a shit husband, but I'd never once been unfaithful in all the years we were married. I hatched a plan that if I could catch the scumbag at it, I could get him out of the picture. Then maybe, just maybe, Jessica would see how I'd changed and she'd take me back in and I'd have my family again.'

Ben could see the raw emotion on Drew's face. He was being completely sincere.

'So I started tailing Mike. And I found out where he was going. He wasn't seeing another woman. He was meeting up with men.'

'Meeting men?' Ben echoed. 'You mean—?'

'Uh-huh. Well, that was my initial thought, at least. They'd meet up in cafés, on the ferry. I took pictures with a long lens. There were two different men, but it was always a one-on-one meeting. I never saw them going into hotel rooms or anywhere private like that, but I was sure there was more to it. That's when I brought on board a detective from the mainland.'

'That would be Paul Finley in Dover?'

Drew glanced at Ben in surprise that he knew. 'That's right. The agency specialised in divorce and custody cases, infidelities, that kind of stuff. If someone was cheating on their wife or partner, they'd know about it. I went to Dover and hired them on the spot. I was convinced that we could nail Mike, and that Jessica would throw him out. Anyway, a while went by without contact. Then Finley phoned me to say he'd seen what I'd seen. He was keeping track of Mike's mysterious little meetings. But he'd managed to get closer than me, and he didn't think it was a gay affair at all. He said he thought Mike was passing *information* to these guys.'

'What kind of information?'

'Finley couldn't tell. At least, not at first. Time went by and I didn't hear anything from him. Then one day, he called me. Sounded excited, and anxious too. Said he'd found something out. Something very strange and disturbing. Those were his words. He wouldn't say any more over the phone. What he did say was that he believed it had something to do with Carl.'

'With Carl?' Ben said, narrowing his eyes.

'He warned me that Carl might be in danger. Promised to meet me and explain everything, when he'd found out more. And that's the last I heard from him. Next thing I knew, he was dead.'

Ben looked carefully at Drew. He seemed to be telling the truth.

'A mugging gone wrong,' Drew went on. 'Just another statistic. There are so many fatal stabbings in Britain these days, what's one more? But I knew that this was connected. And I knew that Finley had been right and that Carl was in danger.'

Ben frowned, but said nothing and went on listening.

'That's when I decided I had to get him out of there. If I'd still had parental access, it would have been so much easier. Instead, I had to plan this whole kidnap thing, as fast as I could. I found a forger in Brittany who could do the false passports. Dyed my hair for the photo and used Photoshop to doctor Carl's picture. I took all my money out of the bank. Bought a wig and a fake beard that made me look like I used to before I'd cleaned myself up, and a load of padding that I could stuff under my clothes to make me look fat. Paid six months' rent to this old farmer for a static caravan in a field overlooking Bonne Nuit beach. Very secluded, the perfect place I could take Carl after the snatch.' Drew shrugged. 'Then all I needed was a weapon of some kind. I'm not the most physical guy. I needed to be able to intimidate Mike somehow and get him into the cellar. I thought about using a knife, but what if there was a struggle and somehow Carl got hurt? That's when I thought about using a fake gun. Not,' he added, 'that I'd have had the faintest idea where to get a real one. But that way, I could carry off the kidnapping without any risk of anyone being injured if it all went horribly wrong. I found one in a second-hand shop that looked real, at least to me. And it worked on Mike, too. Everything went exactly as I'd planned. Carl played his role very well.'

'He knew?'

'Oh, yes. We were secretly in touch the whole time, by phone. He wanted to get away as much as I wanted him out of there. So off we went. I hated having to lock Jessica in the cellar, but I'd no choice. After we left the house, I drove Carl straight to the caravan. I burned the wig, the beard and the body padding. Quickly dyed his hair to make him look like the passport photo. I'd timed it all so that we could catch the last ferry. If by some chance Mike and Jessica had got out of the cellar by then and raised the alarm, the police would be looking for an overweight bearded guy looking like a dosser, accompanied by a little fair-haired boy. It didn't happen. Nobody looked twice at our passports on landing in France. It was so easy. We jumped on a train and came down to Monaco. I'd planned to stay here a few more weeks and then move on somewhere more permanent. We'd have started a new life.' Drew shook his head forlornly. 'And I was sure we'd made it. Until today, when you came along.'

Ben thought for a moment. 'So this whole plan came about because you thought that Carl was in danger from Mike?'

Drew nodded. 'I'm still certain of it.'

'And you couldn't just have told Jessica, instead of resorting to kidnap?'

'What, you think she'd have believed me?' Drew snorted. 'She'd have seen it as a ploy, that's all.'

'Fine. Let's talk straight here, Drew. You've told me about Mike's meetings with these other men. The way he seemed to be passing on some kind of material that somehow related to Carl. Then there's whatever it was that Finley found out that made him think Carl was at risk. Are you saying that Mike belongs to a paedophile ring? Was Carl being abused?'

Drew shook his head. 'No, he wasn't being abused. It's not that. It's something else. Something even worse. Carl knew all along that Mike wasn't what he seemed to be. The creep was always asking him all these little questions. Playing mind games, like he was observing his responses. Studying him like a lab rat, Carl said. Carl couldn't get into his head. Which is odd. But he could sense something about the guy that made him uncomfortable. I believe that Finley discovered the truth behind it all.'

'What do you mean, Carl couldn't get into his head?' Ben asked, totally baffled. 'Sensed what?'

'That's why I needed you to come here,' Drew said. 'There's something I have to show you.'

Chapter 15

Ben waited, confused and impatient, while Drew fished a video cassette out of a bag and fed it into a VCR. Prince Al-Naseem's giant TV screen flashed into life. 'What are you showing me, Drew?' he asked. The ten minutes had been up long ago.

'Just watch,' Drew said. As the video began to play, Carl put his head round the door and came back into the room. 'Is this—?' he began, and his father nodded.

Ben quickly realised that he was watching a high-quality home video. The image was steady, as if the camera had been mounted on a tripod in the hands of an expert. 'Did you film this?' he asked.

'August 2001,' Drew said. 'Our family holiday near Málaga.'

The screen showed a village square, surrounded by old whitewashed houses and shaded from the sun. The square was bustling with people, who seemed to be crowding to watch some spectacle taking place, many of them craning their necks to see. Whatever it was, it was generating an excited buzz of chatter.

As Ben watched, the camera panned smoothly across to reveal what the crowd were so interested in. Sitting opposite one another at a café table were two chess players. On one side, playing black with a look of intense concentration, was a swarthy middle-aged man with the deep tan of a native of southern Spain; on the other side, playing white, was a younger, smaller Carl in shorts and a T-shirt. However long the game had been going on for, there were only a few pieces remaining on the board. After a few more moments' careful deliberation, the Spaniard picked up his surviving bishop and cut diagonally across the board to threaten a white rook. The move caused a murmur among the crowd.

'That's Ángelo Martín,' Drew said. 'He was the Spanish chess champion eight years running.'

With hardly a pause, Carl reached for his threatened rook and slid it across to capture the second black knight. It took a couple of moments for the spectators to realise why Ángelo Martín was now gaping at the chessboard in disbelief. Gasps broke out.

'Checkmate,' Carl said calmly.

Cameras began to flash. 'He's done it again!' said an offscreen voice in Spanish. 'It's impossible,' said another. 'Nobody beats Ángelo Martín just like that. He's the champion, for Christ's sake!'

Drew paused the video, the frozen image of the humiliated champ's dark expression filling the screen. 'He hadn't been playing long. Had you, Carl?'

''Bout four months,' the boy replied casually, trying not to look too proud of himself.

Ben stared at them both. 'Explain what this is about.'

'It was just a fluke, how it happened,' Drew told him. 'We'd rented a place in this little village, and that afternoon the three of us were having a drink in the square. I'd bought Carl his chess computer not long before, and he was sitting quietly playing when this friendly local guy at a nearby table took an interest in what he was doing. He spoke English and seemed pretty impressed with Carl's moves, giving him tips and advice. Before Jessica and I knew it, a proper chessboard had been brought out and the two of them were playing a real game.

'It was only then that we realised the man was Ángelo Martín. He started out playing gently, letting Carl take a few pawns. But then things started getting more serious. Carl was wiping the board with him. He seemed to be able to anticipate every move in the champion's mind, foil every strategy before it even had a chance to develop. Carl had always shown some odd abilities, but this was the first time I began to realise how strong his gift was.'

'Don't exaggerate, Dad,' Carl said shyly.

'I'm not, son. It was incredible,' Drew went on telling Ben. 'Soon there were whole crowds gathering. By the time Carl had already won two games in a row, I ran back to the house for my video camera and started filming. I had to get this on tape. Some people thought it was fixed, or that Carl was cheating somehow. But he wasn't. After three straight defeats, Ángelo Martín lost his rag and went storming off.'

Carl couldn't help smiling at the memory.

'Word spread during the couple more weeks we were there,' Drew went on. 'A local journalist called Isabella Saura got wind of it and asked for an interview. I've got that on tape too. Hold on.' Drew fast-forwarded the video. At high speed, Ben saw the disgruntled chess champion throw over his king and stomp angrily away. The picture dissolved into static for a second, then cut to the interview.

'I hate watching myself,' Carl muttered.

Drew let it play. Indoors now, a slightly younger Jessica was sitting proudly smiling with her arm around Carl. 'Mrs

Hunter,' said the interviewer, Isabella Saura in lightly accented English, 'what would you say to the sceptics who don't believe your son is a newcomer to the game of chess?'

'Carl's got a special talent,' Jessica said. 'That's all there is to it. Anyone who saw him play knows that he didn't cheat. He wouldn't have.'

Turning to Carl, the interviewer said, 'So now, Carl, when you return home after your holiday, you will be able to tell your friends at school that you beat the Spanish chess champion. Were you nervous?'

'Not really,' he said, blushing and looking down at his feet. 'It wasn't that hard for me to win.'

'Ugh,' the real-life Carl snorted, watching himself in disapproval. 'Talk about snotty.'

'Shush, Carl,' Drew said.

'You certainly made it look easy,' the interviewer chuckled. 'What is the secret of your amazing ability?'

'I sort of knew what he was going to do, before he did it,' replied the on-screen Carl. 'That's how I could beat him so fast.'

'You mean you could predict what the champion's every move would be? Surely this must take years of study and practice? But you have only been playing a short time?'

'I could read his thoughts,' the boy said nonchalantly.

'In Spanish?' the interviewer replied, making a joke of it.

'Doesn't matter what language,' the boy told her. 'I can just read people's minds. Anybody's.' He added, 'Yours too.'

Drew turned off the tape. 'It's the truth,' he said to Ben. 'Carl has an incredible gift. That's what I meant when I said he couldn't get into Mike's head. Because normally, he knows what people are thinking.'

'Come on,' Ben said.

'You think it's all bullshit, do you? You're wrong. Telepathy, ESP, whatever you want to call it, is recognised as a reality. The Russians have been researching it for decades. The Americans too. They take it seriously enough to spend millions. It's not a joke.'

'Is it true, Carl?' Ben said. 'You can read minds?'

Carl shrugged. 'Not all of the time. Depends.'

'Okay, then what's on my mind?' Ben asked him.

'You don't believe us. You think we're making it up.'

Ben smiled. 'You don't have to be a mind reader to figure that one out.'

Carl hesitated for a moment. A defiant look coming into his eye, he said; 'What you were thinking. Before you brought us back here. You were wrong. And you know you were wrong.'

'Thinking?'

'That Dad killed the detective man,' Carl said. 'It's not true. Dad wouldn't hurt anybody. And he never sent those men to get you, either.'

Ben was stunned. How could the boy have known about those suspicions that had been in his mind at the time?

'How many men, Carl?' he asked.

Carl thought for a moment. 'Three.'

'How do you know that?'

'I can see them,' Carl said.

'Inside my head? What else can you see?'

'There was a lion,' Carl said.

'A lion?'

'Just its head. Shiny. Like gold.'

Ben remembered the polished brass knocker on the door of the Finley & Reynolds detective agency.

'Black door,' Carl said. 'There was a railing.'

Ben stared at Carl, then at Drew. It wasn't possible. There had to be a trick. 'He's been to Dover. He's just describing what he's seen with his own eyes.'

'How could he have been there?' Drew replied. 'I wasn't allowed to see him, remember? Let alone take him with me. I went to see Paul Finley in Dover by myself.'

'Then you told him about it.'

'About my secret visit to the detective agency?' Drew said. 'You don't think I'd have kept that to myself, in case he let something slip? He's just a boy.'

'Then how's he doing this?' Ben asked. He remembered how Carl had appeared to know he was following them earlier that day in the street. The way he'd turned to stare, picking Ben out of the crowd as if some unseen finger had just pointed down out of the sky to give him away. It had baffled him then. It baffled him even more now.

'You tell me,' Drew said. 'There *is* no explanation. He just can. He's special. And Mike Greerson knows it. Don't you get it yet? That's what this is all about.'

Chapter 16

'Tell me about Mike, Carl,' Ben said.

The boy shrugged. 'He bought me stuff and he was always acting nice. Wanting to be my friend. But I never liked him much. He was always hanging around me when Mum wasn't there. Setting me these sort of tests.'

'Tests?'

'Yeah. Like, he'd show me a photo of someone I'd never seen before and ask me to guess what their name was, where they lived, stuff like that. Or he'd bring out a pack of cards, pick one and ask me to tell him what it was without looking. Sometimes he'd hide something in the house somewhere, a key or a spoon, all kinds of stuff. Then he'd get me tell him where they were.'

'And could you?'

'Most of the time,' Carl said nonchalantly. 'It was sort of a fun thing at first. After a while I started pretending not to be able to know the answers. I didn't like the game any more.'

'Did your mum know that Mike was playing these games with you?' Ben asked.

Carl shook his head. 'It was always just the two of us alone.'

Ben lowered his voice and put his hand on the boy's shoulder. 'Carl, I need to ask you an important question. Don't be afraid to tell the truth, okay? Nobody will blame you. I need to know if there was any other part of these games that you haven't told anyone about. Did Mike ever do anything, or touch you in a way that made you feel uncomfortable?'

Carl flushed. 'There wasn't anything like . . . like that.'

'All right. I believe you,' Ben said, withdrawing his hand. 'I just needed to be sure, Carl.'

'Okay,' Carl said.

'How did Mike act when you pretended not to know the answers to his questions? Did he get angry?'

'No. He was always quiet. He never yelled at me or anything. He just seemed like he didn't believe me. He'd leave it alone, then after a while if Mum wasn't around he'd start trying again.'

'Tell him about the newspaper cutting, Carl,' Drew said.

Carl nodded. 'It was in the summer house.'

'It used to be my studio,' Drew explained. 'Now it's Mike's office.'

'What newspaper?' Ben asked.

'The chess game episode in Spain didn't exactly make national headlines,' Drew told Ben. 'But Isabella Saura's interview with Carl did make it to the local media. Carl found a clipping of the article in Mike's briefcase. So what the hell was *that* doing there, eh? And since when did *he* understand Spanish?'

'How did you know Mike had it?' Ben asked the boy.

'Just had a feeling,' Carl said. 'Like there was something about me in the briefcase.'

'Is that how it works, you just get feelings?' Ben asked, and the boy nodded. Ben pondered this for a moment, then turned to Drew. 'So what are we saying here?'

'We're saying that this Mike Greerson, though I seriously doubt that's his real name, doesn't work for some optics company, or whatever he claims. He works for someone with some kind of special interest in my boy,' Drew said fiercely. 'I'm not talking about a benevolent interest. And they're not getting anywhere near him. Not while I'm alive.' Drew wrapped a protective arm around his son. The boy didn't respond. He was gazing into space, as if lost in his own thoughts.

Ben thought for a moment, but he still wasn't buying Drew's argument. 'And your ex-wife just happened to meet this guy who just happened to be interested in Carl?'

'No, I don't think she "just happened" to meet him,' Drew replied. 'I mean, how do people meet? I first met Jessica at a party. Something like that's easily arranged.'

'You mean he was planted,' Ben said.

Carl's face had turned paler. He bit his lip. 'Dad—' he murmured, plucking at his father's sleeve.

'That's exactly what I mean,' Drew said firmly.

'Dad—'

'Please, Carl. Dad's talking. Yeah, he was put there, all right. The whole thing was planned, right from the start.'

'Taking a bit for granted, weren't they?' Ben said. 'It takes two to tango, and Jessica's her own person.'

'Oh, you can bet they'll have had a whole profile on her,' Drew replied in a tone of barely contained anger. 'She was lonely. She was on the rebound from a marriage gone to pot. She had a kid to support. And let's face it, there's one thing about Jessica. She loves money and nice things. Along comes golden boy, right on cue. Good looks, plenty of cash, solid career. Not a loser like me. If she hadn't taken the bait, they'd just have kept trying until they managed to get someone else in. Taking over my place. Free to observe Carl every day. Test him. Assess him.'

'But *why?*' Ben insisted.

'Because a gift like that makes him incredibly valuable to certain people who might want to exploit it,' Drew said. 'Think about it.'

Carl was looking increasingly agitated, still plucking at his father's sleeve and trying to get his attention.

'I am,' Ben said. 'I'm thinking this would have to be a very highly organised conspiracy. As for who on earth would take such an interest in something like this—'

'They're a team of some kind,' Drew said. 'That's who Mike was meeting up with, reporting to them, keeping them updated on his observation of Carl. They're his colleagues. His fellow agents, or something. I'm well aware of how crazy it sounds, but I've never been more certain of anything in my life. I know it's the truth, and I'm damn sure that Paul Finley uncovered something about it before they got to him.'

'They?' Ben said, raising an eyebrow.

'Yes, *they,*' Drew said forcefully. 'This is their mission. They'll do whatever it takes. They want Carl.'

'For what?' Ben asked, still deeply unconvinced. 'Drew, for what?'

But Drew didn't reply. He'd broken off from the conversation and was gaping at his son in sudden alarm.

The boy had turned white with fear. He was trembling violently and staring fixedly into empty space with a look of dread, as if at some terrifying apparition that only he could see.

'They're coming,' he said in a hollow voice. 'They're here.'

Chapter 17

Nobody spoke for a moment. Carl's face was set in a look of terror.

And in the silence, the door chimes sounded melodiously in the hallway. Carl flinched as if struck.

'Carl, what are you sensing?' Drew asked him urgently, shaking him. But Carl just shook his head, apparently speechless with fear.

The chimes sounded a second time, more insistently.

'You two get in there,' Ben said, motioning at the door to the next room. He stood, taking Barberini's .25 from his pocket. Drew's eyes widened at the sight of the gun.

His jaw tight, Ben walked out into the hallway. He trod stealthily up to the door and put his eye to the security peephole.

Two men were standing outside the door, dressed in matching light blue overalls and caps. One was clutching a toolbox.

Ben silently cursed himself for the stupidity of the anticlimactic relief that flooded through him. It was nothing, after all that. Why had he let himself be lulled by the kid? He slipped the pistol back into his pocket. Undid the security chain, slid open the deadlocks and opened the door. 'What do you want?' he asked the men in French.

'Maintenance,' said one. The other, clutching the toolbox, just smiled.

'Now's not a good time,' Ben told them.

The maintenance man shook his head. 'Gotta come in. We've had a report of a leaky pipe in this apartment. You the proprietor?'

'Leaky pipe?' Ben said.

'Yup, leaking pretty bad. It's coming through the ceiling below. If we don't fix it right away it's gonna cause a lot of damage.' The guy held up a key. 'We're authorised to enter whether anyone's at home or not.'

'Hold on,' Ben said. Leaving the door ajar, he turned and walked back down the hallway. Drew and Carl had emerged tentatively from their hiding place. Carl looked even more terrified than before.

'False alarm,' Ben said. 'Building maintenance. Come to fix your leaky pipe. Time we were out of here anyway.'

Drew stared at him. 'But there's no leaky p—' he began.

Ben heard no more.

The silenced gunshot sounded like a muffled clap in the hallway behind him. A magnesium-flare flash filled his head, and suddenly the floor was racing up to smash him in the face as his knees crumpled and he fell forwards.

He couldn't move. A black tide of mist swelled up to obliterate his vision. All he could hear was the high-pitched whine in his ears that drowned out the sound of Carl's screams. He was only dimly aware of the blue-clad men stepping over his prone body and striding into the room . . . Drew and Carl backing away . . . Drew with his hands raised, yelling soundlessly . . . The inaudible pistol shot hitting him in the chest and slamming him into the wall as the other man in blue grabbed Carl and dragged him screaming away from his fallen father . . .

*

A long time after – or perhaps not? – Ben resurfaced from the dark lagoon of unconsciousness. One eye fluttered open, then the other. Gazing unfocusedly at close range into a pool of blood. This wasn't what the afterlife should look like, he thought.

Then maybe he wasn't dead. But when he tried to push himself up to his knees, the searing agony in his back and shoulder made him think he should be. The spasm of awful pain made him cry out. Instantly, his heart was thudding. Every movement, every breath, was a torment.

Now he could see that there was blood everywhere, all around him, spreading thickly on the marble floor, soaking into the rug. But not all of it was his. Drew's body was a few feet away, sitting half-propped against the wall, staring at him lifelessly. A trickle of blood from his mouth was quietly dripping down to add to the pool between his legs. Two bullet holes were punched into his chest.

Ben gritted his teeth and staggered to his feet, only for extreme nausea and agony to double him up and almost make him collapse again. He leaned against the wall for support, leaving a jagged smear of blood along it as he tried to fight his way towards the door. He had to . . . get out . . . of here. Had to . . . *find Carl.*

Ben's last memory was of the men taking him. The boy had been right. They'd come for him.

And Ben had let them do it.

A wave of crippling weakness made him stop, leaning heavily against the wall, his chest heaving as he fought to breathe. The air was thick and foul. What was that he could smell? His nostrils twitched. He tried to focus. His half-conscious mind telling him it was something important.

Gas. That was what it was. The reek of it filled the room.

Ben slowly turned. Blinked as he registered the sight of the heating timer control on the wall. The plastic cover had been removed. Exposed wiring.

And like the thudding of his heart, he heard the ticking of the countdown.

Move! shrieked a voice inside his head. He turned and staggered for the glass doors leading out onto the balcony. Crashed through the doors and swayed on his feet, blinking in the bright sun, fighting the rising blackness that threatened to overcome him at any moment.

He grasped the rail of the spiral iron staircase that led upwards. Marshalling all his strength he dragged himself up it like an injured spider. Now he found himself on a rooftop garden. He ran, stumbled, almost fell flat, somehow kept on running, then was tumbling into space—

And the whole penthouse apartment erupted in a fire-storm behind him.

Chapter 18

Jersey
Three weeks later

It was morning. Jessica Hunter sat alone in her empty kitchen. She blinked, feeling that she wanted to cry. But she'd cried so much already, and for so long, that now the well was dry. There was nothing left but the aching, desolate rawness she felt inside.

With an unsteady hand, she picked up the glass of vodka from beside the half-empty bottle on the breakfast bar surface in front of her. Closed her eyes and knocked back a stinging mouthful, then let the glass slip out of her hand back onto the surface. Beside the bottle was a small framed picture of Carl. She picked it up, gazed at it – and that was when the flooding tears finally came again.

Suddenly aware of a presence, she turned. She gasped when she saw the lean, silent figure in the doorway. How long had he been standing there, watching her?

'You,' she breathed.

He said nothing.

'I thought you were . . .' her voice trailed off and she just looked at him. She'd never seen him look this way. So still, so quiet, with a fire in his eyes that made her almost afraid.

Ben took a step closer. He stooped and picked up the crumpled three-week-old edition of *Le Monde* from the floor, to glance at the headline and the photo of the devastated apartment building belching smoke into the sky over Monte Carlo. The movement made him wince as a sharp jolt of fresh pain shot through him; and for an instant his memory drifted back, reliving the suffering of the last weeks like a nightmare daydream. The escape over the rooftops and through the chaos of Monte Carlo in the wake of the explosion. Stealing the car. The interminable fevered agony of the drive across the Italian border and northwards into Switzerland, to the tiny mountain village near Mont Blanc and the home of his old comrade, retired ex-SAS medic Frankie Gallagher.

Frankie might be every bit as crazy as they said he was, but he still knew how to get a bullet out. The nine-millimetre full metal jacket had clipped Ben's left shoulder blade on entry and bounced diagonally to plough a channel deep into his shoulder, stopping just a whisker from the collarbone. The surgery hadn't been easy. He'd refused to let himself pass out until he'd seen Frankie drop the flattened one-hundred-and-forty-seven-grain FMJ and six bone fragments from his bloody forceps into a surgical dish. An experience Ben wouldn't forget in a hurry – but still preferable to facing the kinds of questions he'd have been asked in any hospital.

And sometimes it was better to let them all think you were a goner.

For a while, at least.

'Heard that one myself,' he said to Jessica. 'But now I'm back.'

'My boy is dead,' she quavered, barely audible. 'Why would you show your face around here? Why can't you leave me alone? You failed. You said you'd bring him back and now he's—' her words dissolved into a spasm of tears. She buried her head in her arms, shoulders quaking.

'Where's Mike?' Ben said softly.

She slowly raised her head, pointed a trembling finger towards the French windows and the sweep of lawn beyond. 'Hiding down there in his office,' she sniffed bitterly. 'He can't even be near me now. Says he can't handle it. Says he's leaving me. My whole world . . . gone . . .'

Ben touched her arm as he walked past her. There was nothing more to say, not yet. He swung open the French windows and walked down the garden.

Mike was at his desk in Drew Hunter's old summerhouse studio, wearing a tweed jacket and getting ready to leave. All the desk drawers were open and empty, and he was busily packing the last of his papers into his briefcase when the door crashed in. Gaping up in speechless alarm, he was half out of his chair by the time Ben grabbed him by the neck and slammed his head twice, three times, against the desk.

'Going somewhere, Mike?' Ben rasped in his ear, then hurled him backwards into his chair so hard that it fell over backwards, spilling him to the floor. Mike could have done very little to fight back, even if he'd been conscious at that point.

Ben walked calmly around the desk. He closed the briefcase and tucked it under his arm. Then he seized a fistful of Mike's jacket collar and dragged him out of the summerhouse; dragged him all the way up the garden and along the pebbled path around the front of the house to the car. He didn't give a damn if Jessica saw him from the window. Didn't give a damn if she called the cops.

The car engine was running, and the boot lid and driver's door were open. Ben hauled Mike upright and bundled him into the boot. Slammed the lid. Walked around to the driver's door, threw the briefcase inside the car and then got in and took off in a spray of gravel.

Chapter 19

Mike's eyelids peeped open slowly at first, then snapped wide in panic as he realised he couldn't move. 'Where am I?' he yelled, straining against the bonds that held him to the chair and twisting his head wildly this way and that in the murky shadows. His glasses were badly twisted and cracked, and he couldn't see properly. Just a little light filtered through the drawn curtains. There was a smell of damp and mouldy carpet. He tried rocking the chair, but it was stuck fast to the floor.

Ben was lounging in another chair a few feet away, where he'd been patiently waiting for the man to wake up. 'Welcome back,' he said.

'Where am I?' Mike repeated shrilly.

'Somewhere nobody can hear you calling for help,' Ben said. He swung open the caravan door with his foot. 'See?' he said, motioning out at the empty field. 'Drew picked the spot pretty well, I'd say. So go ahead and make all the noise you want. It won't help you.'

Mike's eyes bulged. 'What the hell do you want with me?' he raged. 'Are you mad?'

'Mad, bad and dangerous to know,' Ben said. 'Very dangerous for you, Mike, if you don't co-operate.'

'Fuck you! You'll get nothing out of me!'

Ben sighed, standing up. 'Thought you might say that. That's why I brought some truth serum with me.' He walked across to the far side of the static caravan, picked up a plastic five-litre fuel can and walked back towards Mike's chair. Taking his time, he unscrewed the top of the can, then set it on the floor and slid it under the chair with a nudge of his boot. The tang of petrol rose sharply upwards as liquid sloshed out of the can's open nozzle.

'You wouldn't *dare*,' Mike sputtered, coughing in the petrol fumes.

Ben drew his own chair closer to the draught of fresh air from the doorway. 'Peaceful here, isn't it?' he said, taking out his Gauloises and Zippo. 'Nippy sea breeze, though. They say it might warm up quite a bit later. Smoke?' He flicked open the lighter and tutted. 'This damn thing's run empty on me again. Looks like I'm down to matches.'

'No,' Mike said, turning white. 'Please.'

Ben replaced the lighter in his pocket and came out with a matchbox. He struck one and flicked it into Mike's lap, where it fizzled out in a tiny puff of smoke. 'Whoops. Sorry.'

'No! Oh, Jesus! Don't do that!'

Ben paused, about to strike another match. 'You're right, Mike,' he said, putting the cigarettes away. 'These things'll kill you.'

'What do you want?' Mike asked, panting hard.

'Just a few simple answers,' Ben said. 'You tell me who you really are, who you work for and where they've taken Carl, and you stand a chance of seeing tomorrow. If not . . . and by the way, there are three more open cans of fuel under the caravan, right below where I nailed your chair to the floor. You're in the hot seat, Mike. How about we start with your real name and go from there?'

'Simonsen. Dr Mark Simonsen.'

'Nice to meet you, Dr Simonsen. You won't mind if I go on calling you Mike, though, will you? So tell me, Mike. You're not really a "development consultant" for an optics firm. What are you?'

Mike's head hung down to his chest. 'I'm a clinical psychologist,' he admitted.

'And not just any old one, either, not with a fancy PhD and such an important job to do. They must have been queuing up to move in with a nice-looking woman like Jessica Hunter, get paid to sleep in her bed every night with nothing else to do except send reports back about her son's, shall we say, *unusual* abilities? Where were you about to sneak off to, now that the job was finished? Your next assignment?'

After a long pause, Mike gave a reluctant nod. 'Germany first. Then onto North Carolina.'

'Quite the globetrotter, aren't you, Mike? I'm sure your accent would go down well over there in the States, with whatever divorcée or single mother whose life you were planning on worming your way into. Does she have a psychic kid too?'

Mike sighed heavily. 'So you know everything.'

'No, but I soon will. Who's paying you?'

'Linden Global. They're . . . they're a provider of technology solutions.'

'When I hear vague euphemisms like that, I get stressed out,' Ben said. 'When I get stressed out, I get this overwhelming urge to light a cigarette.'

'All right, all right,' Mike said. 'They're a private military contractor, okay? One of the biggest. Urban population control technologies. Surveillance and counter-surveillance. Defence systems. They're into everything. Recruit from all sectors. Ex-military, intelligence, science. I . . . I'm just a low level operative. I barely know anything that goes on—'

'Then I'm wasting my time talking to you, correct?' Ben said, taking out the matches again.

'Remote viewing,' Mike spat out in a hurry. 'ESP. The Indigo Project. That's what it's all about, okay? Please don't burn me. I can tell you everything.'

'Then you'd better get on with it. Starting with this remote viewing.'

'It was researchers at the Stanford Research Institute who came up with the term decades ago,' Mike explained, nervously eyeing the box of matches in Ben's hand. 'Basically, it's the practice of seeking impressions about an unseen or distant target using extra-sensory perception. When the Americans launched their Stargate Project in the seventies, the goal was to determine the potential military or domestic application of psychic phenomena. They funded a series of rigorously controlled trials at a think tank called The Science Applications International Corporation.'

'Go on,' Ben said.

'The results were classified at the top level, because they were so incredible that even the project leaders could hardly believe them. The first successful remote viewer who came out of the program was Joseph McMoneagle, codenamed Psychic 001, who went on to work for thirteen years with the Cognitive Sciences Laboratory in California. During his time with Stargate, he provided intelligence data that no regular spy could have fed back. Months before a top-secret new Soviet submarine was even completed, he predicted accurate launch data and in-depth design details that were so revolutionary at the time that nobody but a handful of Russian engineers could have guessed at them. All his predictions turned out to be correct, down to the last detail. Later, when a US army general was kidnapped by the Red Brigade, he was able to pinpoint the exact location where they were holding him captive.'

Mike swallowed anxiously, then went on: 'McMoneagle wasn't the only remote viewer who showed extraordinary abilities. Another predicted the release of a hostage in the Middle East three weeks before the kidnappers let him go, with a description of the medical problem that had brought about his release. Yet another, Pat Price, made detailed sketches of Russian weapons manufacturing plants that conformed to US intelligence photographs he'd never been shown. Stargate was declassified in the 1990s to give the impression that nobody took the research seriously any more. The Americans claimed it was history, axed, discredited as never anything more than a joke. The truth is, that was just a disinformation exercise, to make it look as if they were cleaning house while in reality they had no such intention.

'And it's not just the Yanks,' Mike continued. 'Russia. China. The big players in Europe, as well as emerging powers like North Korea. They're all at it. Now the floodgates are wide open for private corporations vying to secure billion-dollar contracts from any nation with deep enough pockets. The public has no idea this is happening. But it's a serious part of classified military intelligence R&D programmes worldwide, and competition is intense. In the days of

Stargate, an effective remote viewer could be expected to make contact with a target with about 65 percent reliability. Nowadays the expectations are far higher.'

'What's the Indigo Project?' Ben demanded.

'A secret initiative founded in 1999 by Linden Global, with the long-term aim of cornering the market in ESP research for defence and espionage,' Mike replied nervously. 'Its purpose is to locate and research children with extra-sensory potential, as studies have repeatedly shown a higher incidence of extraordinary psychic perception among the young. It often seems to fade with the onset of adulthood. A global network of scouts are employed to find these gifted children, by infiltrating schools, scouring local media reports and other sources, sometimes just from hearsay.'

Ben stared at him, appalled, as the pieces fell into place. The Spanish chess incident that had drawn public attention to Carl's abilities; the newspaper clipping hidden in Mike's briefcase. Everything Drew had said was true. Carl had been deliberately targeted by these people. 'And that's where you came in.'

Mike nodded miserably. 'Where possible, field agents with psychology training are inserted to gain further evidence. There's a 99-plus per cent elimination rate due to all the false claims and new-age bullshit that's out there. Early assessments strongly indicated that Carl was one of the genuine ones.'

'So what happens to the genuine ones?' Ben said through gritted teeth.

'The extent of the research needed isn't possible within the home environment. The subjects are removed to a secure location with the necessary facilities.'

'You mean kidnapped. What facilities?'

‘It’s a specialised laboratory unit in the Black Forest,’ Mike said. ‘Extremely secret, very well hidden in the mountains. Armed guards patrol twenty-four-seven.’

‘Germany. That’s where you said you were going next.’

‘I travel up to the lab from time to time,’ Mike admitted. ‘It’s part of my work.’

Ben glared at him. ‘To do what, help train your kidnap victims into little psychic spies for whichever government agency bids the highest?’

Mike shook his head. ‘It doesn’t work like that. It’s been tried, and it’s a waste of time. The subjects failed to perform under the duress of being separated from their families and placed in an unfamiliar environment. Coercion didn’t work, and the incentive of financial gain was meaningless to them. They were children. Simply too frightened and confused by what was happening to them, with fatal results for whatever ESP aptitude they might have shown under normal relaxed conditions. We had to come up with alternatives. It’s now essentially a neuroscience-based approach.’

Ben could feel the cold fury slowly spreading through him. Loose matches sprinkled the caravan floor as he crushed the box flat in his fist without even knowing it. ‘Neuroscience-based – what does that mean? That you pull their brains apart into pieces to see how they work? Is that the idea?’

‘No!’ Mike protested, blanching at the look on Ben’s face. ‘I mean, surgical procedures are strictly considered an extreme measure.’

‘An extreme measure. But not out of the question.’

‘Where at all possible, other analytic methods are used. CT scans, imaging techniques . . .’

'Carl had better be alive,' Ben warned. 'Or you're going to wish you never had been.'

'Look, I'm fond of that boy. I mean it. I've spent a lot of time with him. You think I'd want him to suffer?'

'What happened to the children who failed to perform under duress?'

Mike looked down at his chest and made no reply.

Ben stood up, fists clenched. 'Answer me, Mike. What happened to them? They couldn't be returned to their families, could they? Not after what they'd been through. Not in the state they were in. Did they just disappear?'

'Look, that's not my area,' Mike blurted. 'I'm just a field assessor.'

Ben stood over him, wanting to tear his head off. 'How many other children like Carl are they holding now?'

Mike's reply was almost a sob. 'Carl makes seven.'

'Boys and girls? How old?'

'Both. Gender makes no difference. The youngest is Franck. He's nearly eight. Satoko's the eldest now, with Kristina g—' Mike checked himself and shut his mouth.

'You were about to say "gone", weren't you?' Ben asked harshly. 'What happened to Kristina?'

'She . . . escaped. There was . . . an accident. She fell.'

'Fell?'

'Down a ravine. The mountains are full of them. They found the body at the bottom . . . but you have to believe me. I wasn't responsible for what happened, I swear. I wasn't even there.'

'Oh, you're not that involved,' Ben said, his fists clenched in anger. 'Then I suppose you didn't have anything to do with what happened to Paul Finley, either.'

‘He was asking too many questions,’ Mike jabbered. ‘By the time we realised he was following me and taking pictures of my meetings, he’d already identified one of my contacts from an old army connection. He was getting too close.’

‘So you had him killed. Just like your three goons for hire tried to do to me in Dover. Did they actually believe Drew Hunter had sent them, or is that just what they were told to say?’

‘We really didn’t want you to be hurt!’

‘No, you didn’t want to have to replace me,’ Ben said. ‘Not with your precious asset on the run, and the clock ticking. But you couldn’t let me get too close to Finley’s discoveries, either, could you? My purpose was just to recover your lost property, and you bastards were watching me the whole time to make sure I did my job. Dover. Monaco. Every step of the way. I know when I’m being followed. I wasn’t. How did you do it?’

‘You don’t even begin to understand what you’re dealing with here, do you?’ Mike yelled with a flash of defiance. ‘Linden Global is one of the biggest private defence corporations in Europe. Big enough to have their own satellite division. They see everything. And they’re watching us right now. They can pinpoint our location to within a metre.’

‘I doubt that very much, Mike. Nobody knew I was coming back to Jersey. I’ve been presumed dead for three weeks, remember? Burned up in the fire. And you know what they say about presumption.’

‘I’ll be missed, don’t you see?’ Mike threatened. ‘I’m due to report to the lab. If I don’t turn up at the pick-up-point, the pilot will report back immediately and they'll know something happened. It won't be long before they figure it out. They'll hunt you down. You'll be a walking dead man.'

Ben smiled. 'Then we'll have to make sure you don't miss that flight, won't we?'

Chapter 20

The small airfield was out in the countryside, twenty minutes from the ferry port of Saint-Malo. The corporate brains behind the Indigo Project were clearly hot on secrecy, as Ben could tell from the disused state of the rendezvous point. Buildings and hangars stood empty amid patches of yellowed and weed-strewn grass that waved in the breeze. There wasn't a soul about to witness the mysterious comings and goings of Dr Mark Simonsen, a.k.a Mike Greerson, and that was exactly how his employers wanted things to be.

Mike peered closely at his watch. 'Any time now,' he muttered, and squinted myopically up at the sky, shielding his eyes from the afternoon sun. He walked a few steps from the car towards the airstrip. He was still moving stiffly from his undignified confinement in the boot during the ferry crossing from Jersey. 'I hear it,' he said, scanning the sky.

So could Ben. The distant buzz of an approaching plane, growing steadily louder. Moments later, he saw the incoming aircraft's tiny white speck against the blue.

Ben grabbed Mike's briefcase from the car. He'd already examined its contents on the ferry. There was no incriminating paperwork inside, only a set of disks containing information that he was certain would be inaccessible to him even if he'd had a computer. The case also contained a laminated ID pass card and a clip-on name badge, both with the company header 'Drexler Optik GmbH'. In a zippered compartment was a spare pair of glasses, a comb and some pens.

'You do realise this isn't going to work,' Mike said, turning round with a scowl. 'The pilot's going to take one look at you and sound the alert. I'm supposed to be the only passenger.'

Ben nodded. 'You're right. It won't work. In fact, I was meaning to talk to you about that.'

Mike stared at him in blank incomprehension. 'But you said—'

'I know what I said,' Ben replied, laying the briefcase down on the bonnet of the car. 'That I didn't want you to miss this flight. Fact is, Mike, I lied. Which I have no problem doing to vermin like you. This is as far as you go.'

Mike's jaw hung open as he realised what Ben was saying. 'No,' he mumbled, staggering back a step, then another. 'Wait. Let's be reas—'

Ben made it quick, for the sake of economy if not merciful compassion. The blow to the neck was sharp, swift and instantly lethal, and he caught Mike's falling body before it hit the ground.

The approaching plane was beginning to drop in altitude as the pilot prepared to land. It would be here in ninety seconds. Ben had work to do, and he needed to move fast. Cupping his hands under the dead man's arms, he dragged the corpse a few yards and let it flop to the concrete next to the car while he transferred his own wallet from his leather jacket to his jeans. It contained only cash, no cards, no ID. Taking off his jacket, he bundled it into the back of the car alongside his bag. Next came off the dead man's tweed jacket, which Ben laid across the car bonnet beside the briefcase. He locked the car up, pocketed the key and then bent down to grab the dead body by the wrists and haul it hurriedly out of sight into the thick bushes at the edge of the airstrip.

It only took a moment to dump the corpse where nobody would find it for a good while. Ben ran back to the car. The plane was coming in to land. He slipped on the tweed jacket; not a bad fit. Opening up the briefcase, he took out Mike's spare glasses: chunky designer plastic, different from the thin wire frames Ben had always seen him in. Ben put them on. They made everything look too small, and threatened to start his eyes watering if he wore them too long. Next he took out the dead man's comb, and used the wing mirror to quickly smooth and part his hair in a rough imitation of the way Mike had worn his.

By this time, the plane had touched down and was taxiing along the strip towards him. A red and white Cessna 400. Single pilot, capacity for three passengers and a fuel range of over twelve hundred miles. Ben smiled and waved casually as he walked up to meet it, briefcase in hand.

The aircraft halted and its gullwing cockpit hatches popped open. The pilot climbed out to greet Ben. He was in his early to mid-forties, casually dressed in jeans and a check shirt. 'Dr Simonsen?' he called over the noise of the idling engine.

It was a worrying moment. If the pilot knew Mike well from previous trips, Ben couldn't be sure that the masquerade would fool him. That was where Plan B came in, involving two dead bodies in the bushes instead of one. Ben could fly the plane all right; he'd just have to hope that he could figure out his exact destination. The Black Forest was a big area.

But as the pilot broke into a smile, Ben's anxiety melted away.

'We haven't met,' the pilot said, extending his hand. 'I'm Tommy. Standing in for Jürgen today.' His accent was European tinged with American.

They shook hands. 'How is Jürgen?' Ben asked amiably, doing a passable imitation of Mike's voice.

'Lying on a beach somewhere for the next two weeks, the lucky fuck.'

'Nice for some, eh?' Ben said as Tommy ushered him on board. The plane's interior was like a small car's. Ben strapped himself into a passenger seat. The pilot climbed in after him, settled behind the controls and clapped on his headset. Moments later, the plane began to taxi round in a circle for takeoff.

Ben settled back in his seat, gratefully removed the eye-watering glasses and watched as the ground fell away below. For the next couple of hours of so, he'd have little to do but try to relax, clear his mind and prepare mentally for what lay ahead of him.

Chapter 21

Urban sprawl alternated with open country as the aircraft tracked in an eastward curve over France towards southern Germany; bridges and railway lines and industrial zones tiny down below. Ben took little notice, letting himself be lulled into a deep thoughtful state by the monotone of the engine. It was only much later, as he sensed they must be nearing their destination, that he looked out of the window and saw a completely altered landscape of rolling hills, lakes and alpine forest. The afternoon was slowly moving into evening, the sinking sun turning redder as it sank towards the misty mountain skyline.

Tommy brought the plane steadily down over a thickly wooded cleft between the hills, banked tightly around the base of a steep rise, and then Ben caught sight of the complex of white buildings perched high up above the valley, at the end of a single twisting road he could barely see through the trees. A little distance away, an area of woodland had been cleared to make way for a small airstrip. Tommy expertly brought the Cessna round, lining up their course and dropping the landing gear. 'Here we go,' he called cheerfully over his shoulder. 'Welcome to sunny Schwarzwald. Bet you're glad to be back.'

'No rest for the wicked,' Ben called back, and Tommy grinned.

Soon afterwards, the plane was rolling to a stop on the landing strip. Tommy shut down the prop, opened up the hatches and the two of them disembarked. 'Be seeing you,' Tommy said as he jumped down from the wing, and headed at a trot towards some buildings. He seemed like a decent kind of guy, with probably no idea of what really went on in this place.

Ben hoped he wouldn't have to kill him.

Now what? he thought, looking around him. The white buildings were just visible through the trees, and appeared to be connected to the airstrip by a little curving road. He stood and waited, the late Dr Simonsen's briefcase dangling from his hand. Moments later, a black Mercedes four-wheel-drive came speeding up the little road.

This must be the taxi, Ben thought as it halted near the parked aircraft. He slipped on the glasses, smoothed his hair and adopted the body language of the expert consultant on just another routine visit. The driver barely glanced at him as he got into the back with the briefcase across his knees. The Mercedes U-turned and sped off towards the buildings.

It was a short journey. A set of tall gates stood in front of the complex, which Ben now saw was screened off behind a high wire fence. The entrance was manned by a guard, who strode up to the Mercedes and rapped on the back window to check Ben's ID pass before returning to his little gatehouse. The gates glided open and Ben's driver, who hadn't said a word, proceeded on. The Mercedes crossed a concrete forecourt and turned in between two buildings. Left at a junction; then right at another. The place was a labyrinth. Here and there was a parked vehicle. No obvious sign of industrial activity going on; no sign of anything in particular.

Fifty yards further, the driver stopped outside what appeared to be the main building, stepped briskly out of the car and opened the back door for his passenger to get out. As he did, Ben was very much aware of the unseen eyes that could be watching him from behind any number of windows. He nodded casually to the driver and gazed around him as if he'd seen the place a thousand times before. The main building's entrance was glassy and modernistic, above which gleamed the name DREXLER OPTIK.

How charming, Ben thought. Secluded, picture-postcard alpine environment. Clean, unpolluted mountain air. Just the spot for a phoney optics manufacturing plant. And a little child abduction and torture on the side.

The facility might indeed have looked totally innocuous from the exterior, if it hadn't been for the armed guards. Two of them, flanking the doors. The privacy of the setting allowed them to carry their weapons openly; Ben instantly recognised the ubiquitous M4 automatic carbines that he'd been so familiar with in 22 SAS and used himself on three continents. As the Mercedes drove away and he walked towards the entrance, the guards maintained a steely eyes-front demeanour. Ben could tell at a glance that they were ex-services. The kind who took orders and asked no questions. That had always been the part he'd had trouble with.

He was on the steps leading to the entrance when the glass doors swung open and a third guard emerged to meet him. In a black cap and boots and with a holstered Glock on his hip, he looked almost like a military officer and was obviously in charge of security. He was in his fifties but trim and fit, his black uniform hugging his lean torso. 'Dr Simonsen?' The German accent was crisp. The grey eyes unblinking.

'Here at last,' Ben said jovially. 'Traffic was terrible.'

The man didn't smile back. His cold gaze scanned up and down Ben's features. 'You look different, Doctor.'

'Hardly recognise myself, even,' Ben said, pointing at his own face. 'New glasses. I'm still getting used to them.'

The head of security scrutinised the laminated ID card that Ben showed him. Ben watched the grey eyes flick from the photo on the card and up to his face; down, up. Then the man handed the card back to Ben and appeared to relax. 'My wife got new spectacles last month,' he said with a sudden smile that was incongruous on that reptilian face. 'She looks like another woman in them. Just what I needed, no?'

Ben laughed.

'Come inside, Dr Simonsen. Dr Rascher has been waiting for you.'

'He has?' Ben said, following the head of security through the glass doors.

'I believe he wants to discuss matters relating to our latest addition, Test Subject 16-M.'

A tremor of volcanic rage shot through every vein in Ben's body. Outwardly, he was completely calm as he nodded and said nonchalantly, 'The Hunter boy?' They might have been teachers talking about a child's progress in maths class.

They were walking down a bare white corridor with a gleaming tiled floor and doors on each side with small wire-reinforced windows. The head of security nodded. 'There have been problems. Resistance, aggression, unwillingness to co-operate. TS-16M has had to be kept heavily sedated and in isolation. Dr Rascher has expressed concerns about his suitability for the program.'

The head of security pushed through a fire door and led Ben down a short flight of steps to another bare white corridor. A pair of patrolling guards passed by in the opposite direction, pausing to nod deferentially at their superior, who barely acknowledged them.

'I see,' Ben said. 'That's very regrettable. The subject showed such promise. Did Dr Rascher say any more?'

'You can ask him yourself,' the head of security said, pointing at an office door up ahead, which bore a plaque reading DIREKTOR. He stopped and knocked three times. A voice from inside called 'Hereinkommen', and the head of security opened the door.

Rascher was a large, broad man with a shiny bald crown and a thick grey-black beard. He was wearing a white lab coat and holding a computer printout covered in graphs and figures. He turned to greet his visitor as the head of security ushered Ben into the office. 'Ah, Dr Simonsen, there you are,' he said in English, in a voice as big as he was.

This is it, Ben thought.

Rascher's brow creased in sudden consternation. He took a step closer and peered at Ben, then turned to face the head of security. 'What's the meaning of this, Aumeier?' he demanded. 'This man isn't Mark Simonsen.'

'I'm afraid Dr Simonsen isn't on top form,' Ben said, dropping the briefcase, taking off the glasses and flinging them away. 'So I'm here in his place.'

'This is an outrage!' Rascher shouted, his face darkening. 'Aumeier!'

Chapter 22

Aumeier reacted, but not quickly enough. Before he could draw his Glock clear of its holster, Ben's elbow caught him square in the throat and crushed his windpipe. The head of security fell to the floor, turning purple and choking for air that would never come. Ben pinned the arm holding the gun to the floor with his foot. In one fluid move, he scooped up the weapon and pointed it at Rascher's head.

'Here's the deal, Doctor,' he said. 'Show me where you're keeping Carl Hunter and *maybe* I won't perform a radical brainectomy on you with this thing.'

'Wh-who are you?' Rascher boomed.

'Just think of me as the end of your Indigo Project,' Ben said.

'You'll never succeed. They'll kill you.'

'Yeah, maybe,' Ben said. 'But not in time to help you.' He battered Rascher across the face with the butt of the gun. The man fell stunned to the carpet.

'Fuck it,' Ben said to himself. If he was going to die, he wasn't going to die wearing a tweed jacket. He stripped it off and tossed it over Aumeier's body. Then he bent down, heaved Rascher to his feet and spun him towards the open door. Rascher staggered out into the corridor, blood trickling from his face.

'You take me to him,' Ben said, shoving him along with the gun pressed hard up against the back of his head. 'You take me to Carl. Or should I say, TS-16M? You've got seven children captive here. Another had an 'accident'. If Carl's the sixteenth to be forced into the program, what happened to the remaining eight? What did you do to them, Rascher? Put them to sleep like dogs? Did you stick the needle in yourself or get one of your ghouls to do it for you?'

'Please,' Rascher moaned. 'Please don't shoot me.'

'No? Maybe I should just strap you inside a CT scanner and let you get fried with radiation for a few hours,' Ben said, shoving him along. 'Or how'd you like a pound or two of Valium pills to munch on? Stop your bleating and lead the way.'

'Isolation room four,' Rascher panted, sweating heavily and motioning up another flight of steps. 'This way.'

Ben shoved and wrestled the big man up the steps. At the top, the corridor went left and right. Rascher led him to the right. 'Along here,' he groaned, pointing to a bend ahead. 'Then we take the elevator to the isolation block on the top floor.'

As they rounded the corner, before Ben could stop him Rascher suddenly burst out yelling for help at the top of his voice.

Ben clubbed him over the head with the gun, but it was too late. A door burst open and three guards emerged into the corridor, looking startled. The one on the left was still clutching the mug of coffee he'd just been drinking.

It had been a trap. Ben realised that Rascher had led him right to a security personnel staff room.

As if in slow motion, the guards reached for their guns. The coffee drinker let his mug drop and spill on the floor as he made a grab for the M4 automatic carbine slung behind his back. The one in the middle was the first to squeeze the trigger. The weapon was set to burst-fire. Ben ducked. A window behind him shattered. He grabbed the struggling Rascher by the collar of his lab coat and yanked him backwards, nearly off his feet, using him as a human shield as another burst of gunfire erupted in the corridor. Ben felt the impacts of the bullets slamming into the doctor's chest. He ripped the Glock pistol from his belt, aimed it past Rascher's shoulder and fired twice, taking down the coffee drinker and the middle guard. The one on the right was still getting to grips with his weapon, wild-eyed with panic.

Rascher's dead body collapsed in Ben's grip, catching him off balance and making him stumble back a step. It was at that instant that the remaining guard brought his weapon to bear and fired. But in his haste to shoot, the gun jerked off-aim at the last moment and the shots went wide.

Ben had seen it happen before with men who were experiencing real combat for the first time. Training was one thing, but not even the best simulation could fully prepare you for the terror and intensity of the real deal. The extra pressure made some people slower. They fumbled. They lost their focus. This guy was one of those.

Ben wasn't. Before the guard could touch off another burst, two shots from the Glock snapped out in such quick succession that they sounded like one ragged explosion. The guard tumbled over backwards with a hole between his eyes and another in his chest.

Then, silence. Just the ringing in Ben's ears and the muffled tinkle of a cartridge case rolling across the tiles. Four dead men in the corridor. Their blood rapidly mingling into a spreading pool.

Ben knew his element of surprise was spent now. The sound of gunfire would have resonated through the whole building, sparking off a red alert. How many more guards were there? Could be five; could be twenty.

Ben stepped over Rascher's body. 'Never trust a doctor,' he muttered under his breath as he thrust the pistol back in his belt, behind the hip. Avoiding the blood so as not to leave a trail of red footprints, he bent over one of the dead guards and picked up his M4. Releasing the magazines from the two other automatic carbines, he slipped one mag in each of his trouser pockets.

'That's more like it,' he said to himself.

Already, he could hear raised voices and racing footsteps echoing through the corridors and getting rapidly closer. It was time to get moving.

As Ben broke into a run, four more guards appeared in the bend of the corridor behind him. Their shouts were drowned in gunfire. Bullets raked the wall inches from him. He reached another bend ahead and kept running.

He crashed through what he thought was another set of fire doors, and skidded to a halt, cursing. Too late to turn back, he realised he was trapped inside a room with no other exits. The guards were close behind.

He glanced about him. The room was huge and white, looking and smelling like a chemistry lab. Long tables stretched across the middle of the tiled floor, and its edges were lined with benches and racks covered with equipment. Wires and tubes, blinking lights, dials and readouts, screens, jars and beakers, and trays of implements. Mounted around the walls above were glass cabinets filled with rows of large specimen jars containing what appeared to be chunks of some kind of matter floating in a clear, viscous liquid. It looked like pickled cauliflower.

Footsteps outside. The doors crashed open and the four guards burst into the lab firing their weapons on full automatic and spraying bullets everywhere. Ben barely had time to return fire before he had to dive under cover of one of the long tables. Splinters flew from the tabletop; plaster dust exploded from the walls and showers of sparks from the electrical equipment as dials and readouts shattered. The cabinets on the wall burst into cascading fragments of glass, the jars inside them blown apart, liquid pouring over the benches and the floor.

Crouching under the table, Ben glimpsed the slippery white specimens that had been inside the jars, now sliding over the floor in puddles of strong-smelling surgical preservative – and he realised with a jolt of horror what they were. Not chunks of picked cauliflower, but dissected pieces of human brain.

And in that brief moment, he knew.

Knew he was looking at all that remained of those unaccounted-for eight children.

Knew that this was what the architects of the Indigo Project would ultimately do to Carl, and to all the others, if nobody stopped them.

More sparks spat and fizzed from the damaged electrical equipment; an instant later, there was a *whoosh* as the spilled preservative burst alight. A sheet of fire covered the bench along its whole length, quickly spreading to the floor. Flames shot up, suddenly filling half the room, hot, aggressive, leaping high. Ben had to scramble away as they licked the underside of the table. Spotting him, one of the guards shouldered his weapon with a cry and let off a string of bullets. Ben dived and rolled for cover under another table. From the floor, he saw the running feet of two of the guards moving round to flank him. He fired. A cry of pain. One of the men went down, writhing. Another burst into the man's body, and the cries of pain were silenced. Ben rolled again, emerging from under the table.

The fire was spreading alarmingly fast, gaining a purchase on the whole room now and threatening to block the only exit. Firing blind into the thick, black smoke that filled the lab, Ben ran for the door and burst out into the corridor, coughing. A glance through the billowing smoke told him that more guards were coming. Too damn many. This place was even better protected than he'd feared.

Smoke and flame were spreading out of the lab door now. He could hear the screams of the men still trapped inside, but he had little sympathy for them. He ran, keeping low. There was a shout; he'd been spotted again. More shots rang out.

No time to stop and shoot back. He sprinted hard up the corridor, skidded around a corner and came to a junction. He went left. Bounded down a short flight of steps. He was totally without bearings now, just trying to lose his pursuers in the labyrinth.

The fire in the lab could only spread to other rooms, and it would. Fast. He needed to make his way to the isolation block on the upper floor before the whole building started to burn.

Ben ran on. Another set of doors, another upward flight of stairs. Now he really was lost, in a part of the building that looked different from the clinical hospital environment of bright neons, sparkling white corridors and gleaming tiles. Here the floor was bare concrete, the lights dim, the walls unpainted. Where the hell was he going?

He was about to turn back and try another way when he saw the door. It was iron. Heavy deadlocks top and bottom. It looked like the door to a dungeon.

There's no time for this. You've got to find Carl.

But he couldn't leave without knowing what was on the other side of that door. He stepped closer to it and saw with amazement that the locks were undone.

Ben pushed open the door. Stepped through, and stopped in his tracks.

In front of him was another door with tall steel bars, like the entrance to a giant cage. Beyond it was what looked like a high-security prison cell, only much larger. Bunk beds lined the bare block walls, three high.

It was a dormitory.

And it was full of children.

Chapter 23

There were six of them in there, aged between about seven to early teens, all barefoot and wearing plain white garments resembling pyjamas. Three girls, three boys. Their hair was cropped. They looked like prisoners – which, Ben realised, was exactly what they were. The youngest was the little boy lying curled on one of the bottom bunks with his eyes closed. He was either in a dead sleep, or else he'd been drugged. The eldest was a Japanese girl of fifteen or less, who was sitting on a wooden chair watching Ben. There was no trace of fear in her eyes. One by one except for the sleeping boy, the children all turned to gaze at him.

They weren't alone. Two medical personnel in white coats, one male in his late thirties and one female about ten years younger, were in the cell with them. Neither adult had noticed Ben's presence. The man held a ring of keys. The woman was clutching the handle of a wheelchair: Ben sensed that they'd just brought the little boy back to the cell. That was why he'd been drugged.

'What were you doing with him?' Ben demanded.

The two doctors wheeled around in alarm at the sound of his voice. 'Wha—?' the man began, then fell silent as he saw the gun in Ben's hands.

Ben kicked against the cage door. 'Open it,' he said savagely. 'Open it, or I'll shoot you through the bars.'

The man hesitated, but not for long. He hurried to the door, unlocked it, and it creaked open. He retreated anxiously as Ben strode inside the cell.

For a few seconds, nobody spoke. Ben looked at the doctors in furious disgust. He ran his eye over the barefoot children, and at the little boy lying half-comatose on the bed. He thought of what he'd seen in the lab. Then glared back at the man and woman in the white coats, and his finger twitched against the M4's trigger.

'I ought to gun you down where you stand,' he said to them.

The woman just went on gaping at him in terror. The man fell to his knees. 'Do not shoot,' he pleaded in a German accent.

'Where's Carl Hunter?' Ben demanded. 'Isolation room four. Is he there? Answer me!'

'He's there,' the Japanese girl said quietly.

Ben turned to her. She was gazing at him with the same calm, unfrightened expression. 'Are you sure?' he asked her. 'You've seen him there?'

'I've never seen him,' she replied. 'But I know he's there. We all do.'

Ben could see she was being completely earnest. He nodded, then turned back to the cringing doctors. They were too pathetic to kill. 'Out,' he commanded them, jerking his thumb in the direction of the door. 'Go, move it. Before I change my mind.'

The man and the woman stared at one another, then bolted past Ben and scrambled out of the cell. He watched as they went running off down the dark passage.

'I'm Ben,' he said to the children. 'I'm here to get you out. Carl as well.'

The Japanese girl nodded sagely, as if she'd known that too. A younger girl managed a weak smile. A boy a few years younger than Carl began to sob.

'What's your name?' Ben asked the Japanese girl.

'Satoko,' she replied. She pointed at the younger girl, who was still smiling at Ben. 'That's Nicole. She doesn't speak English. That's Sylvie. That's Luca. That's Peter. And that's Franck,' he finished, pointing at the sleeping boy on the bunk.

Ben gazed at their faces, and his heart went out to them. How had they ended up here? How had Linden Global's agent network found them? Each child's story would have to be told, but not today.

'Listen, Satoko,' he said, 'we have to get out of here quickly. Bad men might try to stop us. Things might happen. You're the oldest, so I need you to be really brave, and I need your help to look after the younger children. Can you do that?'

She nodded again, then shot an anxious glance at Franck. 'He won't wake up. They gave him the medicine.'

'Does it wear off soon?' Ben asked.

'An hour, sometimes less,' she said. 'But it gives you a headache.'

'You'll never have to take it again,' Ben promised her. 'None of you.' He went over to the bunk and picked up the drugged boy, thinking that maybe he should have shot those doctors after all.

The boy murmured in his sleep as Ben slung him carefully over his shoulder. 'Come on,' he said to the group. 'We're leaving this place.'

Back in the main part of the building, alarms were shrilling and the sprinkler system had activated. But from the spread of smoke, the stifling heat and the strong stench of burning that filled the air, it was clear that the fire was raging out of control and Ben worried that the sprinklers would be overwhelmed. As he carried Franck and led the rest of the children through the waterlogged corridors, the walls shook violently to an explosion, then another. The place was full of chemicals and surgical supplies, gas and oxygen tanks and God knew what other volatile materials. How long before the whole place went up in flames?

'It's all right, children,' he said. 'Stay close to me.'

Every step of the way, he expected to meet more guards and was ready to shoot first lest a stray bullet come anywhere near the kids. But they saw nobody. Ben glanced left, glanced right, memorising the layout of the building as best he could for when he'd have to come back for Carl.

And there it was, the blessed sight he'd been praying for: an exit. Ben kicked open the doors and a rush of fresh air cooled the sweat on his brow. Dusk was falling, the first stars beginning to twinkle over the dark forest. The compound was deserted. All that stood between them and the trees was the perimeter fence. 'Come on,' he urged the children.

They ran from the main building, reached the next and skirted along the wall. From its corner, it was only a short dash across the concrete to the fence. Ben's heart was thudding ferociously. Almost there.

Eighty yards along the length of the wire fence, they came to a padlocked gate. 'Stand behind me,' he told the children. Holding the carbine one-handed and well away from Franck's little ears, he aimed at the lock and fired. The deafening shot echoed off the buildings. One round from a high-velocity 5.56mm rifle was enough to mangle the padlock. Ben tossed the twisted metal away, unbolted the gate and it swung open.

He glanced back, half-expecting to see the place's remaining guards come swarming out in pursuit, drawn by the noise of the gunshot. All he saw was the smoke pouring from the windows of the main building, rising up in a column into the darkening sky.

They ran for the trees. In the deep shadow of the pines, Ben gently took Franck down from his shoulder and laid him on the ground. He gathered the rest of the children together in a small circle. 'Satoko, all of you, listen to me carefully. This is nearly over. But I have to go back for Carl.' He took off his watch and gave it to Satoko, showing her the luminous dial. 'Satoko, remember what I said. You're in charge. If I'm not back here in fifteen minutes, I want you to take the children somewhere safe. You'll have to carry Franck. Can you manage that?'

Satoko nodded.

'Good. There'll be a farm, or a house, somewhere not too far away. Get there and call the police, all right? ' He stood. 'I'm going now. Fifteen minutes.'

'Be careful, Ben,' Satoko said.

Chapter 24

Ben ran back towards the fence, clutching his carbine. Time was ticking by much, much too fast. He could only hope that the fire hadn't yet reached the top floor.

Through the gate in the fence; across the open ground towards the main building. Two guards came out of a doorway to his left, saw him and froze. Ben didn't even hesitate. He levelled the M4 and shot them both before they'd had a chance to go for their weapons.

He sprinted for the main building, retracing his steps. Inside, the smoke was thicker and even more acrid than before. The floor was swirling inch deep in filthy black water, but just as he'd feared, the sprinkler system had been ineffective at stopping the spread of the blaze. Almost every way he tried, fire and smoke blocked his way and forced him to hunt for an alternative route. The power hadn't shut down yet, but it could at any moment and he didn't dare risk using the lift to the upper floor, for fear of being trapped inside.

Every moment counted. Each second, the fire was blocking another path. He held onto the rifle, even though he didn't think he'd need it any more. The remaining guards had all fled the building, as well as the rest of the staff. It was just him and Carl in here now.

As he searched desperately through the smoke for a staircase, he stumbled into a medical theatre. The operating table was on fire. Soon, any gruesome traces of the things that had gone on here would be burnt out of existence. He ran on, battling against the smoke. The heat was scorching. Just as it seemed hopeless, he crashed though another door and his heart jumped at the sight of a stairway leading upwards. He bounded up it, two and three steps at a time.

It was as he reached the top floor that the power system finally melted down, plunging him into darkness. He groped his way along, kicking doors open. One, two, three . . . 'Carl!' he yelled. 'Carl!'

The fourth door was locked, and he instantly knew this was it. He took two steps back and then ran at it with all his might, smashing it open with his shoulder.

The isolation room was barely less like a cell than the cage down below. In the gloom Ben could make out a sink unit, a toilet, a chair pulled up to a bare table. And the iron-framed bed on which Carl was lying completely still.

Ben threw back the thin sheet. He shook the boy by the arm. 'Carl, can you hear me? Wake up. We have to go.'

Carl stirred. He faintly murmured something, then fell back into his drug-induced unconsciousness. At that moment, Ben hated the men who'd done this to him more than ever. He ripped a strip from the bed sheet, dampened it at the sink and then returned to the bed to prop the limp boy against him and wrap the wet cloth loosely over his nose and mouth to help reduce smoke inhalation. He quickly did the same for himself, tying the torn material behind his neck like a bandana. Then lifted the child from the bed and carried him to the door.

The flames hadn't yet reached the stairs, but they very soon would. It wouldn't be long now before the building would either blow up completely or start to collapse in on itself. Ben reached the bottom. The route he'd taken before was blocked by fire, so he took another. The boy was a dead weight in his arms, the carbine slapping against his back as he staggered and stumbled through the building with only the flickering fiery glow to light the way.

Now Ben was lost again, and for an instant he truly believed that they'd never get out. Then he suddenly recognised the dark corridor as the one he'd walked along with Aumeier earlier. That meant the main entrance was just ahead!

He was right. But he hadn't reckoned on the two guards who were making for the doorway from another direction. He saw them at the same instant they saw him. They all stopped. Ben stared at them, and they stared back. Their faces were blackened from the smoke. Their weapons within quick and easy reach.

One of the guards shook his head. He let his gun slip to the floor and raised his hands as if to say, 'No more trouble, okay? We only work here'. His colleague did the same. Then they were gone, running outside into the darkness.

Ben emerged from the building and gasped cool air into his raw, aching lungs. They were out. They'd made it.

He was pushing through the side gate in the perimeter fence when the building blew. The rumbling blast split the night with a fireball that rolled high up into the sky and lit the forest for miles around. The explosion's hot breath scorched Ben's back as he turned his body round to shield Carl.

Ignoring the pain, he hurried towards the trees. The shadows of the forest seemed to leap and dance in the firelight. He could see no sign of the other children.

Then he spotted them, all except the sleeping Franck, standing in a huddled group at the foot of a huge pine.

Someone was with them.

Someone who had his arm wrapped tightly across Satoko's throat and a pistol to her temple. The rest of the children looked even more terrified than she did.

'Hello again,' the man said, and Ben saw that it was Tommy, the pilot. 'Stop right where you are. Not another step.'

'Let her go,' Ben said. 'This isn't your fight.'

'You don't think?' the pilot replied.

'Everyone else is gone,' Ben told him. 'Rascher, the director, is dead. It's over.'

Tommy smiled, and the fire made his teeth red. 'Rascher wasn't the director,' he said. 'I just let him use my office now and then. I never did like to be deskbound. More of a high flyer, you might say. Truth is, I'd rather be in the air than do much else.'

'You—?'

'That's right,' Tommy said, and his smile turned into a grin. 'I didn't introduce myself properly. Thomas Holzmann, Senior Executive Vice President of Linden Global. *I'm* the big cheese around here. Free to come and go, free to stand in for Jürgen if I so choose, or whatever I want. That's why I never met the real Simonsen – Doc Rascher was in charge of the everyday running of the place, and personnel was his department. But the Indigo Project is my baby, and it always will be.' He took the pistol muzzle from Satoko's head and pointed it towards Ben. 'And I'm afraid I can't let you take my assets away. They're unique. Buildings we have plenty more of. Now put the boy down, please.'

Slowly, carefully, Ben crouched and laid Carl on the ground.

'Step away from him and toss the rifle,' Holzmann said.

Ben unslung the M4 and threw it away with a clatter.

Holzmann chuckled. 'I don't know who the fuck you really are, man, but you came pretty close to pulling it off. Tripped up at the very last hurdle. I almost feel sorry for you.'

'I'm nobody,' Ben said.

'Suits me,' Holzmann said. 'I'll have the engraver put it on your headstone.' He raised his pistol, took deliberate aim at Ben. His finger tightened on the trigger.

Ben reached behind his hip. He pulled the Glock that Holzmann hadn't seen tucked into his belt.

The screams of the children were swallowed by the double report of both handguns going off at once.

Ben felt a burning pain in his side. He swayed on his feet. Dropped his gun, put his hand to his shirt and looked at his bloody fingers.

Holzmann smiled.

And his eyes rolled back, his knees buckled under him and he fell dead.

Ben staggered, then righted himself as the children came running and crowded around him. He picked Carl up in his arms. The boy opened his eyes and looked up at him in drowsy recognition.

'Now you're going home,' Ben said.

DON'T MISS BEN HOPE'S RETURN IN *THE JERICHO ROAD*

Ex-SAS soldier Ben Hope has tried to leave his past behind him – both in the forces and the dangerous choices he's made since. But for some people, a quiet life is no life at all.

Ben has long felt the moment was coming that would propel him back down that fabled Jericho Road, the only road he's ever known. It's not just the path of the Good Samaritan, helping the weak, the needy, the victims of evil. It's his calling, the road he can never turn away from. The question is: will that calling also lead him to his death?

Multi-million bestselling author Scott Mariani brings his best-loved hero back in his unmissable new novel.